SPECIAL MESSAGE TO READERS

This book is published under the auspices of

THE ULVERSCROFT FOUNDATION

(registered charity No. 264873 UK)

Established in 1972 to provide funds for research, diagnosis and treatment of eye diseases. Examples of contributions made are: —

A Children's Assessment Unit at Moorfield's Hospital, London.

•

Twin operating theatres at the Western Ophthalmic Hospital, London.

•

A Chair of Ophthalmology at the Royal Australian College of Ophthalmologists.

•

The Ulverscroft Children's Eye Unit at the Great Ormond Street Hospital For Sick Children, London.

You can help further the work of the Foundation by making a donation or leaving a legacy. Every contribution, no matter how small, is received with gratitude. Please write for details to:

THE ULVERSCROFT FOUNDATION,
The Green, Bradgate Road, Anstey,
Leicester LE7 7FU, England.
Telephone: (0116) 236 4325

In Australia write to:
THE ULVERSCROFT FOUNDATION,
c/o The Royal Australian College of Ophthalmologists,
27, Commonwealth Street, Sydney,
N.S.W. 2010.

Otto Penzler is the owner of The Mysterious Bookshops in New York and Los Angeles. An authority on crime fiction, he is the founder of The Mysterious Press and Otto Penzler Books. He has received an Edgar Award, and was honoured by the Mystery Writers of America in 1994 with the Ellery Queen Award for his contributions in the publishing field. He lives in New York City.

MURDER & OBSESSION VOL II

In this star-studded collection of previously unpublished short mysteries, award-winning editor Otto Penzler has gathered the best of the best — bestselling authors who dare to explore a deliciously chilling subject: obsession at its most insidious . . . What happens when a hard-nosed insurance investigator lights up a joint and sniffs out a case of arson? It's a tale only Elmore Leonard can tell in SPARKS. In SLOW BURN, Eric Van Lustbader describes a beautiful detective haunted by a past injustice, a consuming passion, and a savage crime that links them both. In BARKING AT BUTTERFLIES, Ed McBain tells of a man who goes barking mad when a Maltese terrier takes over his life . . .

Books Edited by Otto Penzler
Published by The House of Ulverscroft:

MURDER FOR LOVE
MURDER & OBSESSION VOL I

Edited By
OTTO PENZLER

MURDER & OBSESSION
Vol II.

Complete and Unabridged

ULVERSCROFT
Leicester

First published in Great Britain in 2000 by
Orion
London

First Large Print Edition
published 2002
by arrangement with
The Orion Publishing Group Limited
London

British Library CIP Data

Murder & obsession.—Large print ed.—
Vol II. edited by Otto Penzler
Ulverscroft large print series: mystery
1. Detective and mystery stories, American
2. Compulsive behavior—Fiction
3. Large type books
I. Penzler, Otto
813′.0872′08′054 [FS]

ISBN 0–7089–4682–8

Published by
F. A. Thorpe (Publishing) Ltd.
Anstey, Leicestershire

Set by Words & Graphics Ltd.
Anstey, Leicestershire
Printed and bound in Great Britain by
T. J. International Ltd., Padstow, Cornwall

This book is printed on acid-free paper

FOR MICHELE SLUNG,
my indispensable friend,
my indispensable colleague

Contents

Introduction

More than twenty years ago, a man I know met the woman who he knew, instantly, was perfect for him. He fell in love on the spot and, after waiting a reasonable period of time (about twenty-four hours), he asked her to marry him. She said yes and so the deed was done. After fifteen years, she left him, and he wept every day for a year or more. He spoke of her constantly until only his best friends could bear to hear another word. To this day, he thinks of her a hundred times a day and recognizes that there is a hole in his heart that can never be filled by anyone or anything else.

More than thirty years ago, a man I know enjoyed reading mystery fiction and decided that, since his means were extremely limited and there was little competition, this would be a nice area in which to collect books. It started with Sherlock Holmes and moved on to other favorites. As he read more, he discovered more and more writers to admire. And to collect. Today, his collection numbers about fifty thousand first editions, after he decided some years ago that he ought to collect it *all* — a first edition of every book in the history of crime, mystery, suspense, espionage, and detective fiction.

More than forty years ago, a man I know (he was a boy then) saw some picture, or some movie, or read about a house that spoke to him. It was a big stone pile, vaguely Tudor in style, and he loved it. He knew that, no matter what, someday he'd live in a house like that. Every time a magazine crossed his desk with a picture of such a house, or some lavish costume drama was set in such a house, he was filled with longing. As the years passed and he had some success in his career, he decided to build that house of his dreams. And he did.

Would it be a surprise to know that all three of these obsessions dominated the life of a single person? He built the house for the wife of his dreams and his great book collection. The irony, as if you couldn't see it coming, is that she left him before the house could be completed, and to this day he hasn't found quite enough money to finish off one room in the mansion. The library.

To him, of course, none of this smacks of obsession. If you want something, you go after it and, with enough hard work, a little patience, and some luck, it will happen.

So where is the line, that narrow border

crossing that separates the areas of normal drive, or desire, and obsession? My best answer is that it is impossible to know. What seems entirely normal, planned, and reasonable to one person seems obsessive to another. Missing someone you love, collecting a lot of books, and living in a nice house seem perfectly normal to, well, me, for one. It is the perception of others that moves it into the murky twilight zone of obsession.

Perhaps another good way to spot it (since I don't think it's possible to define it satisfactorily, the best we can do is compare it to art, or pornography — you may not be able to define it, but you know it when you see it) is when it is in violation of universal standards of behavior by such a wide margin that laws have been written to prevent it.

There are no laws to prohibit mourning a lost love, or to stop someone from assembling a library that some might regard as excessive, or to prevent one from living in a manor more suited to an aristocrat than to a guy who grew up in the Bronx.

There are, however, laws that are designed to inhibit the commission of a form of behavior that most of us would concede had stepped out of the arena of enthusiasm, even passion, into the zone of obsession. That is the subject, more or less, of the stories in this book.

In spite of its title, not all the stories are about murder. One is about a cop obsessed with catching burglars, another about a woman who simply cannot stand for one more instant the sight of her husband's collection of Chinese art, yet another about a man who cannot stop staring at the painting of a woman long dead.

Perhaps the story that best captures the notion of obsession is James W. Hall's 'Crack,' a double entendre only for those with filthy minds.

Obsession is rarely harmless. It may appear to give great pleasure to the obsessed (else why would they continue with the obsession? Because they can't help it, to answer the question), but there is usually a price to be paid. Sometimes, the price is affordable. Sometimes, as witness the following tales, the price cannot be paid by anyone.

— Otto Penzler

Elmore Leonard

Can there be any doubt that the voice of American crime fiction over the past quarter century has belonged to 'Dutch' Leonard? He speaks to his contemporaries but, astonishingly, he also speaks to people who are the same age as his grandchildren.

He was recently booked into one of New York City's hippest clubs, down in the East Village, where hipness is next to godliness. He was booked with one of the hippest rock bands in America, The Stone Coyotes. And you knew the crowd was hip, because they were all in their twenties, all wore black, and body piercing was as common in that room as long-necked beer bottles. The band played and sang, and Leonard read from his latest Chili Palmer adventure. And what was extraordinary (at least to a stodgy old guy like me) is that it soon was apparent that the crowd had come to hear Leonard — not the band. And they got it. Every joke, however subtle, caused ripples of laughter. And Leonard loved every minute of it — including the very loud band.

When Leonard wrote a story for Murder for Love *a few years ago, he liked the character so much that he put her in a book. The book was so good that it was filmed.* Out of Sight, *if you haven't followed the movements of Karen Sisco. He likes the characters in this story, too, he says, so let's see if they show up again.*

Sparks

By Elmore Leonard

They sat close to each other on the sofa, Canavan aware of Mrs. Harris's scent and her dark hair, parted to one side, she would hold away from her face to look at the map spread open on the coffee table.

Canavan was showing her the areas destroyed by fire, explaining how the hot Santa Ana wind swept the flames through these canyons and on down toward the Pacific Coast Highway. Close to four thousand acres destroyed but only nine homes this time, including Mrs. Harris's Mediterranean villa, here, at the top of Arroyo Verde. Nothing like five years ago when over two hundred homes were lost. He showed her photographs, too, fires raging against the night sky.

Robin Harris said, 'Yeah . . . ?' looking at the photos but not showing any real interest.

Canavan kept glancing at her, Robin a slim turn-on in a trendy kind of way: pale skin and heavy eyeliner, silver rings, designer-ripped jeans, barefoot, a black sleeveless top that showed the chain, tattooed blue steel, around her upper left arm, the one close to Canavan.

The profile he had in his case file described her as the former Robin Marino: sang with a rock band that played L.A. clubs, produced one album, gave it up five years ago to marry Sid Harris: the legendary Sid Harris, lawyer to platinum-selling recording artists. Now a widow at thirty-seven, Robin was estimated to be worth around ten million. She had lost Sid to a coronary thrombosis, at home, only three months ago, Sid sixty-three when he died. And had lost the house in the Malibu hills three weeks ago, close to a million dollars' worth of furniture and contents destroyed. But she had bought the Wilshire apartment, where she was living now, right after Sid's death. Why? It was on Canavan's checklist, one of the things he'd ask her about.

She said, 'What's the point?' Meaning the map and the pictures. 'I saw the fire, Joe. I was there.'

Arriving, he had introduced himself and handed Robin his business card that said *Joseph Canavan Associates, Insurance Investigations*. She had looked at it and said, 'Are you a Joe or a Joseph?' He told her either, but usually Joe. She said, 'Well, come in and sit down, Joe, anywhere you like,' picking up on his name in a way that sounded natural and gave him a glimpse of her personality. She looked at his business card again and said, 'You're not with the insurance company, like the ones before.' He told her they called him in when they red-flagged a claim, had questions about it. All it meant, certain conditions existed the company felt should be investigated. Canavan said they wanted to know in their hearts the fire was either accidental or providential before paying the claim. Robin said, 'Well, I can tell you the same thing I told the fire department, sheriff's deputies, the state fire marshal's office, the California Forestry Department, and a guy from Alcohol, Tobacco, and Firearms. The fire marshal's guy brought a dog that sniffed around. He said when the dog was working it ate seventy kibbles a day. What would you like to know?'

This was when Canavan first arrived.

Now he turned from the map to look at Robin sitting back in the sofa. She resembled a girl in the movies he liked a lot, Linda . . . very sexy, had an Italian name. He said, 'I wanted to show you the path of the main fire, where it came down west of your place, on the other side of the ridge.'

'So how did my house catch fire,' Robin said. 'Is that the question? How about sparks,

Joe? The wind blows sparks over the ridge from the brush fires in Boca Chica and they land by my house. You buy that? Or a rabbit or a coyote caught fire and ran like hell right through my yard. They said on the news, look out for animals that catch fire and spread it around. Otherwise, I have no idea. Joe, I watched my house go up in flames. I might've stayed till it burned down, I don't know, maybe not. A deputy came up the road and made me leave.'

Linda Fiorentino.

That was who Robin looked like, in that movie — he couldn't remember the name of it — where she goes in a bar called Ray's, remembering that because of the sign, the Y in RAY'S shaped like a martini glass. Linda goes in and asks for a Manhattan. The bartender ignores her and she asks him who you have to blow to get a drink around here. Those weren't the exact words, but that was the idea. Robin had that same effortless way about her, confident, with the New York sound like Linda's, a cool chick, tough. Watch your step with her.

'So you weren't living in the house at the time.'

'I was here. I happened to see it on TV — fire trucks, people loading their cars, coming out of the house with their insurance policies, running around looking for pets. One guy had all their good china in a basket and was lowering it into the swimming pool. I thought, I better get up there, quick.'

'Load your car,' Canavan said, 'with anything of value, huh? But I understand the house was already on fire. I think that's in the statement you made.'

'By the time I got there, yeah.' Linda waved her hand in the air. 'The back of the house, by a brush thicket. Sid was supposed to have it cut back but never got around to it. The sky by that time was thick with smoke.'

'See, what the company wonders about, why your house was the only one on Arroyo that caught fire.'

'I guess 'cause there aren't any close by. I'm at the very top of the road. Have you been up there?'

'I had a look at your place,' Canavan said, 'the chimney and some of the walls. What's hard to tell is where the fire started.'

'I told you, in the brush thicket.'

'Maybe, except it looks like the direction of the fire in the thicket was away from the house. I'm told the wind shifted that afternoon and came off the ocean.'

'I don't know,' Robin said, 'it's always windy up there.'

Canavan gathered the map from the coffee

table. 'You bought this place a few months ago?'

An easy question, but she paused before telling him, 'Not long after Sid died. But I haven't bought it. I'm leasing it furnished, nine grand a month with an option to buy.'

Canavan looked around the formal living room, white and cream, touches of color, landscapes framed in gold tint, a garden terrace through the French doors, poppies and ficus trees fifteen stories above Wilshire Boulevard. A nine-thousand-a-month penthouse she might or might not buy. He said, 'This place is worth as much as your house?'

'They'd go for about the same price,' Robin said, 'two and a half million. Sidney said the house was underinsured. That's why, just before he died, he had the value of the policy increased.'

'And when that happened,' Canavan said, 'and the house burns down soon after, the claim gets a red flag.'

Looking right at him Robin said, 'Well, you know Sid didn't do it. And I'd have nothing to gain, would I? I'd already made up my mind to sell the house.'

'That's why you moved out?'

'It's too lonely up there. Just me and the coyotes. Once they ate my cats, both of them, Puddin and Mr. Piper. I bought a shotgun, see if I could even the score, a 20-gauge Remington. But then a couple of deputies came by to tell me I had to stop shooting. A neighbor had complained. Some woman said I was shooting toward her house. I go, 'What neighbor? I don't have any neighbors. She might've heard shots, but how does she know I'm the one shooting?' They said she saw me.'

'Mrs. Montaigne,' Canavan said. 'She uses binoculars.'

It caused Robin to pause, and he felt her looking at him with new interest.

'How do you know that?'

'I spoke to her. Mrs. Montaigne's a self-appointed fire warden. Twice a day she drives to a spot up on Piuma Road, near Rambla Pacífico, and looks for smoke. She lost a house in '93 and had it rebuilt.'

'She actually saw me shooting coyotes? I'm a good mile below Piuma Road.'

'Not as the crow flies. I went to see her, talk to her about spotting fires, and she surprised me. Said she saw you the day your house burned down.'

'Saw me where?'

'At the house. She spotted the main fire and called the county fire camp. They were already on it. Still, eight houses burned to the ground.'

'Nine,' Robin said.

'She saw your car, too, the Mercedes convertible?'

'Yeah, as soon as it came on the news I got dressed, jumped in the car — '

'But why the convertible?'

'Why not?'

'If you were going there to save some more of your stuff, and it might be your only chance . . . Don't you have a Range Rover?'

'I was thinking about the *house*,' Robin said. 'I wanted to find out if it was still there. I'd already picked up my jewelry, moved out most of my clothes.'

'There wasn't anything else of value?'

'You have a list, don't you, on the claim?'

'In my file. I haven't really looked at it.'

'It's all Asian art, Chinese, some authentic, some copies. But even if I'd brought the Rover there wouldn't have been room for the big pieces.'

'So for about three months the house was locked up, nobody there?'

'I'd spend a weekend.'

'Alone?'

She smiled, just a little. 'Where're you going with that, Joe?' And said, 'No, I wasn't always alone.'

He smiled the same way she did, just barely. He said, 'You got up there and the house is on fire.'

'Yeah, but I didn't see the flames right away. I told you, the fire started on the other side of the house, away from the road.'

'You say in that thicket.'

'Yeah. You have a problem with that?'

'I might,' Canavan said. 'According to Mrs. Montaigne, you were there a good twenty minutes to a half hour before there was smoke or any sign of a fire. And she had a pretty good view of the back side of the property.'

There was a silence.

'In fact, she said she saw you go in the house.'

Robin took her time getting up from the sofa. She said, 'Joseph,' walking across the room to a bar with a rose-tinted mirror behind it, 'what would you like to drink?'

'Whatever you're having,' Canavan said.

* * *

Straight-up martinis. He sipped his watching Robin roll a perfect joint, tips of her fingers working but not looking at it, Robin asking in her Linda Fiorentino voice why he would want to be an insurance-company stooge, Jesus, or why anyone would — Canavan letting it happen, giving Robin time to make her play. She said, 'No, first let me guess where you're from. The Midwest, right?' He saw this could take time, so he told her he was from Detroit, born and raised. Came out to sunny California six years ago. She wanted to know what he did in Detroit and Canavan said:

'I was a police officer.'

She said, 'Jesus, really? What kind?'

Radio cars and then ten years on the bomb squad. Offered a job out here with an insurance company, investigating claims, before setting up his own company. He said he'd learned to recognize arson from working on the bomb squad. See what Robin thought of that.

She was cool. Handing him the joint she said, 'You left out your wife.'

'I don't have one,' Canavan said, hoping this was a variety of weed that inspired wit and not the kind that put you to sleep. He took a pretty good hit and passed the joint back to Robin.

She said, 'You don't have to tell me if you don't want to, but I'll bet anything you had a wife at one time.'

He told her yeah, he got married while he was a cop. They came out here, he happened to get involved with a girl at the insurance company, and his wife found out about it.

'She divorced you for *that*?'

'You'd have to know her,' Canavan said.

'So it wasn't the first time.'

He told her it was, as a matter of fact, the first and only time he ever fooled around.

She didn't believe him. Lying back among little pastel pillows on the white sofa, Robin raised her eyebrows. She said, 'Really? You look to me, Joe, like the kind of guy, if it's there you don't pass it up. You still see her?'

'Who?'

'The girlfriend.'

'That was over before it went anywhere. I see my ex-wife now and then, we go out to dinner. Sometimes she does jobs for me. Chris's a photographer.' He picked up the raging-fire shots from the coffee table. 'She took these. Chris takes long-lens shots of people walking around who claim they can't walk. A guy shooting hoops in the backyard who's supposed to be in a wheelchair. Insurance-fraud situations, all kinds, including arson,' Canavan said, bringing it back to Robin.

No reaction. Ducked that one like she didn't even hear it, saying, 'You go to bed with her?'

'What's between Chris and me,' Canavan said, 'stays between us. Okay?'

'That means you do,' Robin said. 'You keep Chris for backup, right? Call her when you haven't scored in a while.' Robin pushed up from the sofa with her empty glass. 'You ready? One more — I have to go out tonight.'

* * *

Her husband dies and three months later fire destroys the house. Canavan wondered if there was a connection. He had no reason to believe there was; still, he didn't rule it out. He watched Robin sipping her martini. The only apparent effect the gin had on her, she spoke in a quieter voice and stared at him. Canavan could feel a buzz; combined with the weed it allowed him to stare back at Robin, time suspended, and ask her whatever he felt like asking.

'When you got married, did you have to sign a prenuptial agreement?'

She said, 'Don't worry about it.'

So he tried another tack. 'How'd you and Sid meet?'

'He saw me perform and we talked after. He asked me out. He knew who I was. But basically, Joe, we got together the way people usually do, and fall in love.'

'He was a lot older than you.'

'What you're asking now, did I marry him for his money. Sure, that had a lot to do with it, but I liked him. Sid was full of energy, played tennis — he'd sit down and cross his legs you'd see his foot going a mile a minute. You want to know how he was in bed? Not bad, though we had to get almost perpendicular — you know what I mean? — to do it.'

'Wasn't he kind of heavy?'

'That's what I'm talking about. But then toward the end he lost a lot of weight, like thirty pounds. No, Sid was tender, very gentle, till Viagra came along and he turned into Attila the fucking Hun. If you can picture that.'

'I thought he had a heart condition.'

'It wasn't serious. He took something for it. His blood pressure was a little high.'

'And his doctor let him have Viagra?'

'Sid got it over the Internet.'

'But he must've known the combination was dangerous, Viagra and heart medication?'

She said, 'Joe, Sid was a shooter. He didn't get where he was being cautious. It helped he was a genius.'

'You were happily married.'

'Yeah, very.'

'But you fooled around a little.'

'Once in a while I'd find myself in a situation. You know, but it was never serious. Like you and the chick from the insurance company.' She sipped her drink and then finished it. 'I'll tell you the truth, Joe, I miss him. Sid was good to me.' She got up with her empty glass, saying, 'You're ready, aren't you?'

'I thought you were going out.'

'I changed my mind.'

Watching her cross to the bar he said, 'Tell me something,' and watched her looking in the mirror, staring at her image, her pale skin tan in the tinted glass.

'What do you want to know?'

'Why you burned your house down.'

* * *

Robin didn't answer until she was coming back with the martinis, her raccoon eyes in the dark liner holding on Canavan.

'Why would I?'

'That's what I'd like to know.'

She gave him his drink and placed a hand on his shoulder as she edged past the coffee table and sat down again.

'You tell me,' Canavan said, 'you'd have nothing to gain, you were gonna sell the house. Now you don't have it to sell, but you get two and a half million when they pay the claim, plus the value of the contents.'

'I could've sold the house for more, easy.' Robin sipped her drink and said, 'But what if . . . This is hypothetical, okay? What if a person does actually burn down her house? She owns the property, she can rebuild if she wants. She might even tell the insurance company to forget the claim.'

'They'd want to know why.'

'Because they piss her off acting so suspicious, dragging their feet, sending out adjusters and investigators instead of paying the claim. She's above dealing with people with small minds.'

This was one Canavan hadn't heard before. He said, 'Tell me how she starts the fire.'

'She rolls up the *Wall Street Journal* and lights it with a match. The point I'm making, Joe — '

'She starts the fire inside the house or outside?'

'Inside. The point I'm making, they can pay the claim or not. If they choose to, fine. If they don't, who's out anything?'

'She's already out the Mediterranean villa.'

'And doesn't care.'

'What makes it Mediterranean, looking down at the Pacific Ocean?'

'Tile roof, big oval windows and doors. The outside wasn't bad, even though pink's not one of her favorite colors. It's the inside of the house she can't stand. The decor throughout, the furniture, the art, floor to ceiling everything's Chinese. And she doesn't even like Chinese food. Listen, I can roll us another one if you want.'

'Not for me.'

'It's local, Malibu Gold, but pretty good, huh?'

Canavan said, 'Yeah, great,' and asked Robin, 'Why didn't this hypothetical woman change the decor?'

'Her husband loved it. He knew what everything was and where it came from. It was like a culture thing with him. He becomes an expert on something besides picking hits. Incidentally, not one of the artists he represented ever made a record that stiffed.'

'He bought all the Chinese stuff?'

'His previous wife, the second one. They redecorated completely after a trip to China.'

Canavan said, 'You couldn't — ' caught himself and said, 'She couldn't get used to it?'

'Joe, it was like living in a fucking pagoda. Jade figurines, Tang horses and tomb figures, that honey-colored *huanghali* furniture, blue and white Ming garnitures — they're vases — Ming *kesi* panels on the walls, ink paintings, opium beds, snuff bottles, ivory carvings, coromandel screens, Quing dynasty court rugs . . . '

'She could've sold it.'

'Cloisonné enamel incense burners, Sung dynasty Buddhas. Five years,' Robin said, 'she lives with all this Chinese shit cluttering up the house. Big, heavy pieces, the tomb figures almost life-size. Five years, Joe. She begs her husband, 'Please, can't we try something else?' No. 'A Mediterranean house, why don't we do it Mediterranean?' No. Not, 'No, and I don't want to hear any more about it.' Her husband was a cool guy for his age, never raised his voice. But, really, it was all she thought about. She'd smoke a jay and scheme. Like hire a burglar; he takes it out a piece at a time. Or have it done all at once while they're in Cabo, or Maui.'

'Once her husband's gone,' Canavan said, 'why didn't she get an auction house in and sell it?'

'She felt it would be disloyal to his memory and it would be on her conscience.'

Canavan thought that was interesting. 'But it's okay if something happens to it.'

'Yeah, like an act of God.'

'Or a fire, in an area known for its fires. You know who you remind me of?'

'Linda Fiorentino?'

'You look just like her.'

'I know.'

'That movie where she goes in the bar . . . ?'

'*The Last Seduction*. She wants a Manhattan and the bartender won't look at her. So she goes, 'Who does a girl have to suck around here to get a drink?' '

That was it. Not who do you have to blow.

'But as I was saying, when you come right down to it, Joe, who's out? Who's hurt? Who gives a shit outside of this person who owns the house?'

'I'll tell you who,' Canavan said, 'if you really want to know. The law. Arson's a second-degree felony. A conviction can get you two to twenty years. There's a death as a result, it goes up to five to ninety-nine.'

Her reaction: 'For Christ sake, Joe, come on. You want to put me in *jail*?'

'I'm not the law. All I'm supposed to do is let 'em know when I see a crime's been committed.'

She said, 'Joe, come on, you're not a snitch. I can tell you're a very practical guy. How much you want?'

Like that, ready to pay him off.

He said, 'What's your best offer? So we don't waste time.'

'How about fifty grand?'

'You can do better'n that.'

'A hundred?'

He said, 'Mrs. Harris,' and paused. 'You mind if I call you Robin?'

Sounding formal now and he could see she didn't know what to expect, hesitating before she said, 'Sure, why not,' in a kind of vague tone of voice, her mind looking ahead.

He said, 'Robin, you've talked to a lot of people. Fire, law enforcement, insurance company stooges . . . One of 'em even brought a dog out to sniff around. But no one's accused you of burning your house down, have they?'

She shook her head and brushed that soft, dark hair away from her face.

'You drive up to the house, the sky's full of smoke. You've already seen houses burning on the TV news, and they're right over in the next canyon, not half a mile away. You're thinking, Damn it, why can't my house catch on fire?'

She was nodding, staring at him with a thoughtful expression, following every word.

'You go inside and stand there surrounded by all this oriental stuff you hate.'

'You don't say oriental, you say Asian.'

'Either way, you hate it. You stand there looking at all that lacquered stuff, Buddhas and dragons, and you light a joint.'

He watched her raise her eyebrows.

'The joint is to take the edge off, calm you down. But now you look at the match in your hand. It goes out and you light another match and look at the flame.'

She was nodding again, staying with him.

'All that smoke, and remembering what you saw on the news, you're convinced sooner or later your house will catch fire.'

'I was, I was sure of it.'

'You're about to lose part of your life, and there's nothing you can do but stand back and watch. Five years up in smoke.'

Robin waited.

'What you do then is part acceptance and part a farewell gesture to the years you spent here with Sid.'

'Yeah . . . ?'

'You light the *Wall Street Journal*.'

He watched her nodding her head, thoughtful now. She looked up at him and said, 'You're not putting that in your report, are you?'

Canavan shook his head. 'I have no evidence to prove it, or disprove what you said. The house was burning when you got there.'

'What about the lady fire warden?'

'Mrs. Montaigne? She must've been mistaken.'

Robin paused and said, 'How do I pay you the hundred thousand?'

'You don't,' Canavan said, getting up from the sofa. 'I was playing with you, that's all.

Seeing what I could score if I did that sort of thing. You should hear some of the offers I get, I come across a fraud situation and I can prove it. Some bozo in a neck brace looking for a million bucks, says he'll split it with me.'

'You turn them in?'

'If they're pros, like the ones that stage car accidents and people are injured. Or if they get ugly about it. Otherwise I tell 'em, forget the claim and don't try it again.'

'You're not turning me in?'

'I told you, I believe your story.'

'So what should I do?'

'If I were you?' Canavan said. 'I'd keep after the insurance company. Make 'em pay.' He turned to leave, saying, 'It was nice talking to you, Robin.'

And saw her raccoon eyes staring at him.

'You can't stay awhile, Joe?'

Seeing what I could score if I did that sort of thing. You should hear some of the others I get. I come across a fraud situation and I can prove it. Some bozo in a neck brace looking for a million bucks, says he'll split it with me."

"You turn them in?"

"If they're pros, like the ones that set up accidents and people are injured. Or if they get ugly about it. Otherwise, I tell 'em, forget the claim and don't try it again."

"You're not turning me in?"

"I told you, I believe your story."

"So what should I do?"

"If I was you," Gannon said, "I'd keep after the insurance company to make 'em pay." He turned to leave, saying, "I was just talking to your Robert."

And saw her raccoon eyes staring at him.

"You can't stay awhile, Joe?"

Eric Van Lustbader

Versatility in authors is even less common than it is among actors. One would be surprised at (and wary of the results of) Chuck Norris playing in a light romantic comedy, or Tom Hanks playing a bloodthirsty macho villain, or Madonna playing any role for which Donna Reed might have been appropriate. Equally unsettling would be to see the new Harlequin romance come from the pen of Norman Mailer, or to have Mary Higgins Clark walk the mean streets of drug dealers in the ghetto.

While it would be preposterous to suggest that Eric Van Lustbader's range equals Laurence Olivier's, it is, nonetheless, remarkable. The early books were martial-arts thrillers, then he moved on to tales of oriental intrigue that have become highly successful bestsellers. His short stories, including the one that follows, have nothing to do with those huge canvases, but they are no less compelling. Had you read the entire collection of Van Lustbader's twenty novels, you would be unprepared for this very human story set in a small town.

Slow Burn

By Eric Van Lustbader

Evil is in the details, my uncle Ben used to say to me. And he ought to know. He was a priest — a fine one, a man people looked up to in this community, a kind of principled hero they came to with their problems with the certain knowledge that he would help them — until he crossed the thin white line, did the unthinkable, and the Church turned its back on him. Even though that was seven years ago, a biblical interval, his advice has never left me. That was because he more or less raised me after my parents died. In fact, in many ways I thought of him as my father.

'Pris, looka how small Kent is with his jammies all crumpled up,' Mickey Brunt said, pointing his powerful flashlight down at the small blue-white body. At 2:00 A.M. of a dripping August night alive with tumbling, ominous clouds and the patio screened by huge Australian pines, it was inky dark out here, even with all the house lights on.

'Deceased,' Don Murtry said, giving up on the CPR. He was the town doctor, also its coroner and funeral director, as well as our forensics expert. In response to the emergency call, he'd arrived just before us, in the company of the paramedics from St. Francis. 'God rest his soul.'

From the other side of the teak pool fence, where two sweating patrolmen under Mickey's direction were keeping them away from the scene, Kent's parents reacted. Kitty Seams shrieked and tore at her hair; her husband, Morgan, pulled her to him with one hand and, with the other, clamped a cell phone to his ear.

'How pale the little tyke seems, jes like he's been drained of blood.' Mickey was my partner in the Placide sheriff's office. We'd been together five years. He'd hated being partnered with a woman and had made no bones about it. To be honest, I don't think a whole helluva lot had changed since then. Still, we managed to function okay as a team — see, down deep where it mattered we trusted each other, which is a damn sight more than you could say for most married couples of our acquaintance.

I saw Morgan Seams, the six-year-old's father, break away from the officers and stride toward us. 'I'm sorry for your loss, Morgan,' I murmured, but he didn't even give me so much as a look. He was a moose of a man, with craggy features below close-cut iron-and-steel hair. For the four years Don Murtry and I had been there he'd played linebacker at FSU — Florida State University — in a bruising style that some admired and others criticized as brutal intimidation. He'd ripped up his knee pretty good his first year in the pros in some kind of Old Testament retribution, I had thought. But, unfazed, he'd cleverly used his signing bonus to buy an auto dealership. Now he had a dozen throughout the state, as well as a couple of other even more lucrative businesses. He still walked with a slight limp, and it seemed to me he'd never lost his flair for brutal intimidation, save perhaps during the eight months he'd been wooing the former Kitty Winn, a striking deb from St. Augustine with all the right assets who over the years had blossomed into a real fine lady.

'Mr. Seams,' Mickey began, 'could you tell us what happened?'

Morgan stared at him. 'You already spoke to the boy's nanny — '

'Maria Escondido,' Mickey said, consulting his notepad. 'That's right. She found your son.'

'Then you know what happened.'

'We'd like to hear it in your own words,' I said.

'Maybe the nanny forgot something.' Mickey shrugged. 'Miz Escondido was very upset.'

'And I'm not?' Morgan shook his head. 'Gordon Lett is on his way over.'

I knew Gordon Lett only professionally. He was an eely attorney with a practice in Jacksonville who wouldn't let me or Mickey get away with a thing.

'I'm just asking for the facts as you know them, Mr. Seams.' I could see Mickey's patience was already wearing thin.

'Shit,' Morgan said under his breath. He still hadn't looked at me directly, even when I'd spoken to him. He told us how the nanny's scream had awoken him and his wife. It was approximately 2:40, he told us. They raced downstairs. Maria was crying, incoherent, but she was pointing outside toward the pool. Together, Morgan and Kitty ran outside. Once they broke through the stand of pines, he saw Kent floating face down in the pool. He had Kitty call 911 while he dove in and pulled his son out. He spent the remaining time until we got there trying to pump the water out of Kent's lungs. 'I got him to vomit some of it up,' he concluded, 'but then . . . ' He shook his head.

'So he was alive when you got him out of the pool?' I asked.

Now his eyes met mine. They held in their depths a glittering coldness I knew was just for me. 'I don't know,' he said. 'Maybe the water came up by reflex. I tried to get a pulse . . . '

'Any idea how your son got through the gate and into the pool?'

'Ask the nanny,' he snapped. 'Kent was her job.' He stalked back to his wife before we had a chance to question him further.

'Charming as ever,' I said.

'Cold fucking bastard, ain't he?'

By the time we got back to Kent, Don had finished his prelim.

'You got anything for us?' Mickey said when we huddled down with him.

'Look here.' Don pushed Kent's left ear forward, revealing the tender flesh just behind. Training his pencil flash on the spot, he said, 'See it?'

Mickey nodded. 'Seems like an imprint of some kind.'

'That was my take.' Don turned to me. 'What do you think, Pris?'

All of a sudden, with Kent lying there and us talking about him as if we'd never known him, I began to cry a little bit, and Mickey turned away because this was one of the things he didn't like me doing. 'Officers of the law don't have no room for cryin',' he'd told me more than once.

'Anyone who's got a heart's got room for tears,' I'd tell him.

'Ain't it jes my luck I got you,' he'd shoot back.

'Take your time, Pris,' I heard Don saying now. 'I know it must be kind of weird you coming back here under these circumstances.' He meant about my uncle Ben, because it was here on this huge, moneyed estate Uncle Ben did the dirty deed that sent a knee-jerk spasm through the archdiocese and got him shit-canned. Weird wasn't all it was, not by half. But then there were a lot of weird things here in Placide. We were an honest-to-God backwater, a righteous rock sitting square in the stream of time, still heavily steeped in the nineteenth century, full of good old-fashioned values, friendly and neighborly but bigoted as all get-out and mighty suspicious of change. It was damn ironic us being right down the road from that postmodern experiment called Celebration, the Disney-made community that gets so much press.

I looked at Don gratefully. 'I'm okay.' He was handsome as sin: coffee-colored eyes that crinkled ever so nicely when he smiled, a shock of dirty-blond hair, the wide, muscular shoulders and long, narrow waist of a competition swimmer, which he had been when we'd been at FSU. I'd hoped the fact that I'd been on the varsity track team would have impressed him, but no dice. Cheerleaders were more his thing, the prettier and more pliant the better.

I forced myself to look at the oval welt behind Kent's left ear. 'It looks to me like the imprint a ring might make.'

Mickey snapped his fingers. 'A college ring, maybe.'

'Just the thing,' I said.

'That would mean pressure.'

'A lot of pressure,' Don agreed. He showed us the small bruise behind Kent's right ear.

'Someone held him under the water,' I said, 'while he fought.'

'With his left hand,' Mickey added, 'the mark of the ring being behind the left ear.'

'We're talking murder here,' Don said, 'aren't we?'

* * *

'You ain't never gonna get over him, are you?' Mickey growled as we walked back to our cruiser. Neither of us was yet prepared to talk about the horror we had just witnessed.

'What can I say?' I shrugged. 'I've been jonesing for Don ever since college.'

He made a rude sound. 'Why doncha go get him then?'

'Nah. I'm not that kind of girl.'

He paused. 'What kind of girl are you, Pris?'

The kind of girl who despite appearances drew lines in the sand. Take, for instance, last Friday night when we'd broke up that little fracas at the pool hall across the river. I call it that, but no doubt Mickey would have another name for it. He charged in and busted some heads, all black of course, and more blood would have been spilled if I hadn't taken a stand. Sometimes it just doesn't pay to deliberately take a backseat.

'You've got nothing more to prove here,' I'd said as I forcibly dragged him out of the pool hall.

Outside, he'd heaved a sigh as with his usual flourish he'd holstered his nightstick. You could still hear the juke merrily playing 'Blueberry Hill' just as if nobody had been hurt. As he climbed ponderously back into the cruiser, he'd said, 'Who you like on Sunday, Tampa Bay or the Jets?'

'Take the Bucs and the ten points,' I'd told him so he could win again and keep his life afloat. He had a witch of an ex who was just bleeding him dry.

‘Excuse me a sec,’ I said now. ‘I’ll be right back.’

The front door to the house was unlocked. In the living room, I found Kitty weeping on an oversize sofa that curved around her like an earth mother.

‘Kitty, I’m so sorry about Kent.’ I could hear her shuddered breaths, and I poured her a glass of water from the black marble wet bar and made her drink half of it.

‘Where’s Morgan?’ I asked, mainly to get her talking.

‘Upstairs,’ she said. ‘On the phone.’

Not much had changed inside this house in seven years. It was as thoroughly oppressive as ever. I saw the same sweeping vista of immaculate cream-colored satin upholstered furniture, polished walnut wainscoting, Old World antiques, lush, gleaming Italian tile. And the enormous matriarchal portrait of Morgan’s mother, Livia, peering hatefully at us from her position of dominance above the outsize stone fireplace. The place had the magnificent, musty air of a museum, with not one trace of the inevitable chaos with which, like a tyrant’s edict, a six-year-old indelibly stamps a household. Instead, around every corner there was the same evil memory, ready to pop up and drag me back into the shadows that glimmered even when all the lights were blazing. That memory, God help me, had a life of its own.

'Kitty, when was the last time you saw Kent alive?' I asked softly.

She shook her head and, without facing me, said rather mechanically, 'Morgan told me not to say anything until Gordon gets here.'

'Can you think of why he would do that?' I kept my voice low and even and nonjudgmental. People in shock often revert to their younger, helpless selves. The thing is to guide them back, kindly but firmly, until they can again stand on their own emotional feet.

She looked at me just like I'd wanted her to, but she remained mute. That was okay; I just wanted her to begin thinking about it. Of course, it served no useful purpose to linger on how I might be manipulating her. I had a job to do, and it only took a tenth of a second for me to think of Kent Seams, made mute and bound by death, and I knew I had to forge on, no matter the cost. Mickey and I were his only advocates now.

'Did he suffer, do you think?' She said this in a tiny voice, clotted with shock and rampant emotion.

What could I tell her, knowing the truth.

'Of course you don't know. No one knows.' Her tear-filled eyes searched mine. 'How did he get out there? I mean, the gate should have been . . . Oh, Jesus God . . . ' She buried her face in her hands, sobbing all over again.

'It's God's will,' I said, holding her. 'He will provide for you, no matter how shattered and despairing you feel at this moment.' But I knew that was my uncle talking, not me. How could a six-year-old's death be God's will? It couldn't; someone was to blame. This is why I had become a cop and not a priest.

'You're very kind, Priscilla.' Her head came up and for an instant her cornflower-blue eyes held mine. 'I never believed all the stories about your uncle. I know Morgan — ' She choked on her words, and I couldn't say I blamed her. Morgan Seams despised me simply because Ben was my uncle. After all, it was largely his doing that Uncle Ben got hounded out of Placide. With a self-righteous fervor, he had taken up the archdiocese's official complaint and made sure that even in a secular way there was no longer room in Placide for my uncle. From him, I learned an important lesson in how easily public opinion could be aroused, how quickly it could be turned, and how irrational a thing it could become. Sentiment finally got so bad that one night my uncle just up and disappeared. Too late, I caught up with him inside a dingy motel room off I-75. It looked like he'd blown his brains out with a cheap pistol bought in a pawnshop. After that, Morgan and those who followed his lead were never wanting for verification of their accusations.

'Morgan and I will never be friends,' I said with ironic understatement.

'No,' she said in genuine sadness. 'Morgan never forgets anything. And his own particular view of the world — ' She touched me then, just her fingertips against mine. 'I need to know — ' Her soft eyes looked up at me. She was, indeed, very beautiful in the full flower of her womanhood. 'I need to make some kind of sense of this. Otherwise, Priscilla, I'll just go out of my mind.'

'I know, I — '

'No,' she said quickly, emphatically, 'you don't.' Her words seemed to catch in her throat, as if they were a swarm of bees. 'You see, it was — '

'Kitty, that's enough now.' Gordon Lett swept into the room as if let loose by the gods of Olympus. He was a small man with a barrel chest, a halo of silver hair on his otherwise bald pate, and one mother of a Napoleonic complex. His voice was nothing short of stentorian, so much so that I wondered how he ever handled sidebars in court, let alone pillow talk with his wife.

He inserted himself between us as if we

were two boxers in the ring. 'I'll kindly ask you not to continue taking advantage of my client, detective. Even you should understand she's in a fragile emotional state.'

'Don't make a federal case out of it, counselor,' I said as I got up.

Lett's round, rosy-complexioned face was darkened by a scowl as he planted his feet. 'I assure you there's nothing minor about invading my client's privacy. I am truly appalled at your callous lack of common decency.'

'Oh, for God's sake, get down off the stump,' I said.

Always ready for a good fight, he was about to respond when Kitty interrupted: 'Gordy, it's all right. Priscilla did me a great kindness, that's all.' She gave me a wan smile, which was as much as she was capable of at the moment. 'She was just being a friend.'

'Rule Number One: Cops don't have any friends.' Lett shot me a look heavy with menace. 'I'm putting you on notice, detective. I will not tolerate this kind of unprofessional behavior.'

'Lighten up, counselor,' I said to him. 'For the record, I wasn't asking for an official statement. That can wait until tomorrow.'

Mexican standoff.

Lett put his arm around Kitty and said in a

deceptively offhand manner, 'It must have been a bitch coming back here.'

Not trusting myself to speak, I cursed him silently as I left.

* * *

'That sonuvabitch Lett.' Mickey blew smoke from his cigar out the cruiser's open window. That meant the air-conditioning was off and we were sitting in a pool of sweat. 'He loused up a couple of cases for me before you came along. He and I, we don't exactly see eye to eye.'

I laughed. 'That's because you both know how to massage the system.'

'That and the fact he's got a powerful hate on for cops.'

After my little go-round with Lett, I was in no position to argue. The blue smoke seemed to release through the cracks in this town all the old hatreds, racial and otherwise, drifting aimlessly like the rotten smell of the mangroves. That rolled leaf burning was to me the smell of rich men conniving, of those in power wanting more, and getting it. Mickey had made no move to start the engine, which meant for sure he had something on his mind. I longed for a swim, then thinking of Kent, was immediately ashamed. How long would it be, I wondered, before I could sink into cool water without seeing his little blue-white body?

'You know when we was in church the other day, watchin' my daughter get confirmed,' Mickey said through a halo of smoke. 'Well, I didn't say nothin' to you at the time, but I'm thinkin' to myself, What the hell am I doin' here? The priest is spoutin' this mumbo-jumbo means sumthin' to my wife, I guess, but it don't mean dick to me.' He hitched himself around on the well-worn seat. 'Anyways, I turn around an' look at you. An' I see that special light in your eyes an' I know you got your faith, an' all, from your uncle, who was about as devout a priest as I ever hope to meet. An' then I haul ass out here tonight to see this, an' I think, I wish I had your faith. I wish I could say a prayer an' know for a fact God was listenin', because I gotta tell ya, Pris, right now, seein' this here, I feel like dogshit.'

He seemed to listen to the high-pitched din of the tree frogs, then he picked a piece of tobacco off his lip and sighed deeply. 'Morgan's left-handed.'

'I know.'

'And he's got a college ring on the third finger of his left hand.'

'Plus, he lawyers up when he should be

mourning the loss of his son,' I said. 'So far we're on the same page.'

'The very same paragraph, I'm thinkin'.'

'Morgan did for his own son.'

'Makes me sick to my stomach.' He flicked his butt, making it pinwheel into the darkness. 'Let's get some sleep. Seven A.M. sharp we get all our ducks in a row. With Lett itchin' to earn his three hundred an hour, I don't wanna make no mistake when we charge the murderin' sonuvabitch.'

When I got home, I jumped into a cold shower, and while I was washing the night's filth off I had myself a good, long cry.

* * *

The phone woke me from a dream in which I had switched on my flashlight, only to discover that it was an upside-down cross, and felt dread clutch at me as it emitted a widening cone of purest pitch black. My eyes snapped open and, still half immersed in the dream, I snatched up the phone.

'Mickey?' I answered in reflex.

'No, it's Don. Don Murtry.' He waited a beat. 'Jesus, Pris, I didn't wake you, did I?'

'Uh-uh.' My heart pounded as I peered at the bedside clock. 6:03 A.M.

'Listen, Pris, I just finished my autopsy on Kent Seams.'

Wide awake now, I gripped the receiver more tightly. 'I'm listening.'

'Not over the phone,' he said in an odd, tight voice. 'How soon can you get over to my office?'

'Half an hour?'

'See you then.'

As I climbed into the shower I considered calling Mickey, then decided what the hell. To be honest, I suppose I should have, but I didn't often get a shot alone with Don Murtry, and even though the morgue had never been my idea of a romantic setting I was determined to make the most of it.

I don't know how it is in other towns, but in Placide the morgue is adjacent to Don's funeral parlor. The public building was a one-story brick-faced structure with a sober dark blue canopy out front to protect the mourners in inclement weather and a thoroughly depressing blacktop parking lot to one side. MURTRY'S FUNERAL HOME in simple stainless-steel letters was affixed to the concrete just to the left of one of the tasteful stained-glass sidelights that flanked the entrance.

The morgue was nothing more than a

cinder-block bunker painted an incongruously frothy turquoise. Inside, the thermostat was set all the way down to tundra level, and all the lights were kept dim except where they burned purple-white bright in the single autopsy room.

Don jerked like a startled deer when I walked in. His skin seemed drained of all color. I thought it was an unfortunate effect of the lights, until I got near enough to see the haunted look in his eyes. He was clearly shaken.

'What is it?' I asked. Despite the cold, the place stank of chemicals and intimate human gases you just never got used to. 'Are you all right?'

'No.' He shook his head in that peculiar, distracted manner people have after they've been in a serious accident, as if the deepest part of them had fled to some safe inner place. 'Not nearly.' He glanced quickly, almost furtively over to the slab where Kent was lying. Then his eyes met mine. 'I've made a disturbing discovery. It's horrendous . . . unthinkable.'

My eyes were drawn to the corpse as if it had become magnetic. The big raw T-incision seemed an abomination, an affront to God's handiwork, as Uncle Ben would have said. 'Don, what the hell is it?' It was so cold I could see my breath as I spoke.

He stared at me mutely for so long, I finally took him outside for a moment. We stood in the recessed doorway, watching the rain, hearing it hiss down like a thousand tiny swarming insects. The air was so heavy the clouds looked like they were going to crash down onto the rooftops. I shivered at the unnaturalness of his expression and, leaving him there a moment, ran across the slick street to Rosie's, where I bought us a couple of coffees.

He took his gratefully, sipping the rich, hot liquid from the Styrofoam container.

'Don, whatever it is you can tell me. I can deal with it, I promise.'

This little smile of his, so slight and shy, made him seem boyish, far younger than he had been in college when I'd first fallen for him. The dense, sopping air or the shot of caffeine seemed to give him courage. 'I'd better do this before I lose my nerve again.' Returning to the cold room, he snapped on a pair of disposable latex gloves. 'Cause of death looks to be drowning. No surprise there.' Gently, as if Kent were still alive, he turned the body over onto its stomach and pointed. 'But, Pris, this poor child was sodomized.'

I felt a profound shudder go through me. 'Before or after?'

'Before he died, I'm certain of that.' Don looked up at me and I saw again that awful haunted look in his eyes. 'But the fresh trauma hides an even more dreadful truth. This . . . behavior was chronic.' He took a breath. 'Over a period of a year, I'd say.'

'God in heaven.'

'So you see, Pris, it appears there's some kind of demon at work here.'

'Demon.' I stared at him for a moment, despite my best efforts my mind rushing back in time. 'Why would you use that word?'

He shrugged. 'Can you think of a better way to describe this monster?'

The fact was I couldn't. 'But demon or no, we have him,' I said. 'The semen. We can do DNA testing on it.'

Don shook his head. 'This is one clever demon. I found no traces of semen.'

'What?'

Don appeared at once helpless and angry. 'I imagine you've read the same pathology texts I have. The offender doesn't always simply use his phallus. He could have inserted a lead pipe, a broom handle, almost anything of the right circumference.' He looked at me darkly. 'This form of rape is often as much about punishment as it is about sex. And, more often than not, it's a repeated behavior handed down from parent to child.'

It was taking some effort for the entire situation to sink in. 'Unbelievable that this is happening here in Placide. My God, this isn't New York City.'

'Maybe it just proves it can happen anywhere.'

'Not on my watch.' I considered a moment. 'Don, would you be okay holding the autopsy report for a while?'

'Sure. I'm not finished with the toxicology tests, anyway. I had to send out for those; no facilities here. It'll take a week, sure. But when they come back . . . '

'Gotcha.'

'There is one stipulation to my cooperation,' he added.

'What's that?' I said, instantly on my guard.

He paused, cocking his head to one side. 'You've changed your hair. It's shorter, isn't it?' He nodded. 'I like it, Pris.'

'Thanks.' I hardly knew what else to say, my heart was beating so fast. I was astonished he'd noticed.

'Anyway, I want to thank you for helping me over that bad patch.'

I waved away his words. 'Forget it. Anyone

would have gotten unnerved by what you found.'

'I feel differently about it. And I'd take it kindly if you'd have dinner with me tonight.'

A hammer the size of the Everglades seemed to have landed on my throat. I made a pathetic little croak, which caused him to lean toward me. A clean, fresh scent — cologne mixed with fresh-washed clothes — wafted at me, and I felt a sudden thrilling wetness between my legs.

'Can I take that as a yes?'

I nodded, unable to utter a single word.

* * *

Because I was forty minutes late Mickey had already worked himself up into a lather.

'Well, shit,' he said. I thought he was going to spit right there on the scarred linoleum when I told him where I'd been. 'You know, skirt, you disappoint me sorely. Plenty people in the office say you're taking a job should be filled by a man with a family to support. They say you ain't got the expertise or the discipline to be a peace officer. Jeez, you sure know how t' make 'em look good.'

'Don't talk to me that way.'

'Brought it on yourself.' When he shrugged he looked like a woolly mammoth I'd seen once in a museum diorama. 'Dammit, Pris, this is the thanks I get. Just 'cause I don't ask you t' get me my coffee every morning doesn't mean you have leeway to go do whatever the hell it is you want.'

'Don called and asked me to get on down there.'

'What, you forgot my home number?' Mickey pursed his lips, which meant he was digging in his heels.

'He made it sound personal.'

'I'll just bet he did.'

I shook a waxed-paper bag in front of his face and he snatched it away from me. Peering inside, he said, 'Shit, what's this, the baby portion? Jeez, you think you can buy me off for one of Rosie's goddamn sticky buns?'

'Nah.' I handed him the box I'd been hiding behind my back and watched his face as he opened it.

'A dozen!' He looked up. 'Now, *that's* a he-man-size bribe.' He shoved half a sticky bun into his mouth. 'Okay, I forgive your cute little ass. Now, why did Mr. Donald Juan have his jock in a knot?'

He whistled when I told him, and of course he got right away why I wanted Don to keep the report secret for the time being. With the Seamses already lawyered up, the sensation caused by the autopsy findings would just make all the suspects clam up. Right now, I told him, it would be best to keep the Seamses unsuspecting and as compliant as Gordon Lett would allow.

He licked the caramelized sugar off his fingertips. 'Speak of the devil, Lett called two minutes 'fore you showed up. We have an audience with the king and queen at ten this morning. I want you to interview Kitty.'

'Maybe it would be better if I take Morgan.'

Mickey's eyes narrowed. 'No fuckin' way. Morgan's the perp. His ass is mine.'

'Listen, Kitty was about to tell me something last night when Lett walked in and stopped her cold. If I depose Morgan, there's no way either Morgan or Lett will have a clue she wants to talk with me. Otherwise, they'll make sure she never sees me.'

'What is this all of a sudden, a goddamn democracy?' But I could see he was chewing the idea over. 'Okay, let's give it a shot.' He looked at me gimlet-eyed. 'Hey, you ain't angling for my job, are ya?'

Knowing him, he was only half kidding. 'Mick, you have nothing to fear from me.' I clapped him on his meaty back. 'I could never hope to fill your shoes.'

'Don't think you could,' he said smugly as he reached for the other half of that sticky bun. 'By the way — ' I'd almost escaped. 'Mr. Juan didn't put any moves on you — I mean, you bein' alone with him an' all in the cold room.'

Vainly, I tried to keep the color out of my cheeks. 'As a matter of fact, he asked me out to dinner.'

I heard his derisive whoop all the way down the hall.

* * *

Sure as sugar Gordon Lett found a way to fuck us. He insisted that his clients make their statements together, and because as far as he knew this wasn't a criminal investigation, there was nothing we could do about it but grin and bear it. So in the end we did the best we could: I let Mickey do the talking while I sat back and observed everyone's reactions.

We convened back in the Seams's vast living room with Livia's forbidding countenance observing us like a presiding judge. It went something like this: Morgan went first. His story was in all respects identical to the one he'd given us last night, just here and there more detailed.

'Who normally got Kent ready for bed?' Mickey interrupted. The question, I knew, was meaningless for us, but it was Mickey's intention to break Morgan's rhythm. You always want to do that when you get the feeling statements have been carefully prepared. The more you do that, the better the chance the person will get rattled and say or do something that will be significant.

'Is this really necessary, detective?' Lett broke in rather testily.

'Just tryin' to get as complete a picture as we can, counselor,' Mickey replied in a voice like honey. He fixed Lett with a neutral stare. 'No harm in that, is there?'

'I don't want to prolong what is obviously a very painful procedure,' Lett said as if by rote. 'Mr. Seams needs to see to the final arrangements.'

This caused Kitty to expel a kind of moaning sob.

'Let's get on with it, then,' Mickey said directly to Morgan.

He nodded. 'The nanny had that particular chore,' he said with a curious edge. 'In fact, she has a lot to answer for, if I have anything to say about it.'

'That'll be enough,' Lett said warningly.

'Excuse me, Mr. Seams,' Mickey said, 'but I'm going to have to ask you to explain that statement.' I noticed that he had adopted the tactic of speaking directly, urgently, almost intimately to Morgan in order to try to cut

Lett out of the loop.

'It's my opinion that the nanny is directly responsible for my son's drowning.'

'Morgan! How could you . . . ' Kitty gasped. They were the first words she had uttered since we had entered their house. Her eyes were watery, sunken, and bruised-looking in that unmistakable way people get when they've been crying for hours on end.

'Someone's going to have to pay, Kitty, that's all there is to it. She left the pool gate open. That's negligence in my book.'

I felt immediately sorry for Maria Escondido, who had cared for Kent and had loved him when they were too busy.

'Morgan, this isn't the time or the place,' Lett admonished.

Morgan's face grew dark with rage. 'That's what you've been saying since you arrived. But I terminated her employment; what else could I do? So you tell me, when is the time or the place?'

'Excuse me, Mr. Seams,' I said, 'but was it among Maria's duties to make sure the pool gate was closed?'

'For Christ sake, it was her duty to make sure Kent was safe!'

'Even in the middle of the night?' I asked.

'*Especially* then!'

'My son — ' Kitty began, but it ended in a

deep-felt sob. She pulled herself together and began again. 'You see, Kent had a habit of sleepwalking.'

Morgan seemed even more incensed. 'Kitty, for God's sake — '

'He's dead, Morgan. My baby's dead.' Bowed, she put her head in her hands. 'What more harm can come to him now?'

In his extreme agitation, Morgan jumped up off the sofa. 'God-dammit, I will not have my son's disabilities paraded in public like a common — ' He looked around him bewilderedly, as if he had woken up to a madman's ranting only to discover that the madman was him. He sank back onto the sofa as quickly as he had risen.

'You'll have to excuse my client,' Lett said. 'Grief and stress take a terrible toll.'

'Understandable,' Mickey said kindly. 'No problem.'

'Under the circumstances,' Lett continued in his oily manner, 'I think we should call a brief recess.'

'As long as we're taking a break,' I jumped in before Mickey could object, 'I'm wondering if I could get a cup of coffee.'

Kitty's head came up as Lett interjected himself once again: 'I think that would be a capital idea.' By his triumphant expression I could tell he thought I was an idiot. 'Kitty, would you be so kind?'

Mickey gave me a look like he was going to murder me on the spot, but I cheerfully ignored him. Now that he had Morgan wound up the last thing he wanted was a recess, but I had something else on my mind. When Kitty was in the kitchen, I excused myself. I could see Morgan's eyes on me as I headed down the hallway to the bathroom. It was the one, I recalled, that had two doors, the other one leading into the library. From there, I made my way around the other side of the house to the kitchen without the men seeing me.

I stood watching Kitty carefully measuring out the coffee. She wore black silk slacks and a man-tailored shirt of the same material. Her long, light-brown hair, alive with artful highlights, was pulled back in a bun. Unlike poor Maria Escondido, she had the knack of making the aura of intense sadness work for her, her grief revealing other facets of her beauty.

'How you doing, Kitty?' I said as I came in.

She turned, one hand clutched between her breasts. Some ground coffee spilled onto the granite countertop and I smelled its pungent aroma. 'Oh, you startled me.'

'Did you get any sleep?'

'A little.' Her eyes slid away. 'No, not

much. I dreamed of Kent. He was laughing, running toward me, but when I woke up his death hit me all over again. So this is the nightmare — I'd like to sleep for a year and just dream him back to life.'

'It would be wonderful, wouldn't it.' I went over and stood behind her as she cleaned up the coffee. 'I know you want to talk to me.'

'It's not — ' She put the pot of water on the stove. 'I've been told it's not a good idea.'

'Did Lett forbid you to talk to me?'

She stared straight ahead. 'Gordy has been occupied with other matters.'

She meant Morgan had told her to keep her mouth shut. 'Listen, Kitty,' I said in a low tone, 'I'm going to tell you something confidential. No one else knows, except my partner. Someone violated Kent.'

She turned to face me. 'What do you mean?'

'The coroner discovered that Kent had been sodomized just before he drowned. Wounds in that area indicate there had been a pattern of abuse for quite some time.'

I wanted to go on, but she had pressed her fists against her ears. Her mouth was open in a soundless scream and all the color had drained from her face. Her mouth worked for a moment before she whispered, 'How could you . . . How can you say that?'

I saw her begin to shake and I held her for a moment. 'Kitty,' I said. 'I've taken a big risk telling you — and only you. But I feel you have a right to know — to try to make sense of — '

'Stop!' Her paper-thin voice went through me like a knife. 'Please stop! I can't take any more.'

'But there is more. Someone raped your son, then held him forcibly underwater until he drowned.'

She gave a tiny inarticulate cry and I held her silently, rocking her a little, until she stopped shaking. Her heart was still beating fast, and I thought of how I used to hold my little sister, Jenna, when she got scared at night of sounds outside or shadows moving. I felt now as protective of Kitty as I had then of Jenna. At the hospital where Jenna was dying of cancer five years ago, I had held her as the dark came down and reassured her that I had banished all the ghosts and goblins to a land far away.

'Kitty, I know you have something you need to tell me.' She bit her lip and turned away. The coffee began to perk, filling the kitchen with its rich, homey steam.

I was astonished how calmly and dispassionately she dispatched her statement. If it had been me, given what she'd just been told,

I couldn't have managed it. For his part, Lett just couldn't hide his smug pleasure at the way her statement coincided with Morgan's.

'Are you quite finished, detectives,' Lett said after her voice trailed off. It was not a question. 'My clients need time to themselves now.'

'Sure.' Mickey slapped shut his notepad and stood up. 'Long as it's understood that we may need a couple more questions answered at a later date.'

This got Lett's attention. His head came around like a dog at point. 'What questions?'

Mickey had an evil little grin lying in wait for him. 'Questions that may arise in the course of our investigation.'

'What investigation?' Lett said as we were leaving. 'This is an accidental death, pure and simple.'

* * *

'Pure and simple,' Mickey said to me outside. 'Far as I can see, that's exactly what this here is. Morgan did it. I can feel it in my bones.' He lighted a cigar. 'Why the fuck did you peel him off the ropes?' He was trying to be calm, but his fingers were trembling. 'He was getting woozy, carried away by his emotions. I was getting to him.'

'Wishful thinking. Lett wasn't going to allow you to go much further. Besides, it was a perfect excuse to corner Kitty without anyone seeing.'

His eyes had that red shift, and I knew he was nearing his boiling point. 'You are so fuckin' lucky I'm your partner, because sure as shit no one else would let you get away with this kinda crap.'

'Guess I'm just blessed.'

He gave me a wicked sidelong glance as he smoked in silence for a time. 'So was it worth it? What did she give up?'

'Nothing yet.' We headed for the cruiser. 'I told her about Don's findings.'

He pounded the top of the car with his fist. 'Christ on a crutch, Priscilla, you are some fuckin' piece of work.' He peered at me over the light bar. 'Why?'

'The faster she comes apart, the quicker she'll come to me,' I said. 'She's got a bone caught in her throat, and she needs to get it out. She only wants a helping hand.'

'I hope you're right,' he said, 'because it could be dangerous to give Lett too much — ' He broke off prematurely. 'Holy shit,' he said under his breath, 'Morgan Seams is heading our way.'

I looked back at the front door. Sure enough, Morgan, a light raincoat across his shoulders, was heading straight for me. 'Quick,' I hissed at Mickey, 'go off somewhere.'

'An' do what?'

'How should I know? Take a leak or something.'

Grumbling, he did as I asked so that I was alone by the cruiser by the time Morgan came up. 'I suppose you're surprised to see me here.' Not Hello, how are you? Not Sorry I nailed your uncle's ass to the wall. Not Let's let bygones be bygones. Jesus.

I gazed at him levelly. Just the sight of him made my stomach churn. His face, baby-pink, clean-shaven, expensively scented, was in such stark contrast to Kitty's sad, dark, sunken-eyed appearance I wanted to lash out at him or at the very least scream so loudly that everyone in Placide would at last know what a demon he was. 'Today, I don't believe anything would surprise me.'

'I suppose that's admirable in your profession,' he said rather vaguely. Was he kidding or what? 'The reason I wanted to speak to you . . . confidentially' — his eyes now locked on mine in that intense manner I'd seen before when self-interest caused his awareness to be fully engaged — 'is to find out your thoughts on this matter. Your plans, as it were.'

'For what?' I said.

He appeared genuinely surprised. 'For bringing Maria Escondido to justice, of course.' When I said nothing, he was forced onward. 'She's gone, you see. Packed up after I fired her. All but an admission of guilt, don't you think? But I found out where she is. I have my sources. I thought you should know. Unlawful flight and such.' He frowned. 'Shouldn't you be taking notes?'

'So far I can remember this conversation perfectly.'

'I see.' He paused for a moment, perhaps wondering if he detected sarcasm in my voice. 'In any event, she's at the bus terminal, preparing to flee like a common felon. You need to get over there as quickly as possible.'

'You can be sure we'll do our best.' I saw Mickey ambling back toward us. I went around the cruiser and got in. Mickey slid in behind the wheel and started it up.

'What was that all about?' he asked as he pulled out in a spray of gravel and a squeal of tires.

'Morgan dropped a dime on Maria. She's at the bus terminal with a ticket to wherever. Unlawful flight, in his eyes. As far as he's concerned, she's just confessed to the crime of negligent homicide.'

'Oh, boy,' Mickey said. He was about to go

on about that sonuvabitch Morgan, no doubt at length, when Lydia, our operator, patched through a call from Don.

'Hi, how you doing?' he said in my ear.

I would dearly have liked to have told him, but all I said was a neutral 'Tolerably well.'

'I've got a bit more news. First, I got a good impression of that oval. Get me the ring and I'll be able to tell you if it's a match.'

'Great.'

He sighed. 'Also, I went back in and pulled out a microscopic particle of wood. So we can rule out a pipe or something metal. You're looking for a broom or a baseball bat.'

I said nothing; my stomach was too busy trying to rebel against gravity.

'Pris?' Don said.

'Here.'

'I thought maybe I lost the connection. How's the investigation going?'

'Slow but sure.'

'There's progress, then. Good.' He paused. 'You know, Pris, being here with Kent, going over him so intimately, hours go by and I can't help thinking of the boy's pain and suffering. It's not just professional. I guess I've become an interested party.'

'That makes all of us.' The glorious warm spot in my heart for him was growing. As I turned the corner, I saw the bus depot come into view.

'I also seem to be thinking about your new hairstyle.' He laughed a little as if he was embarrassed. I found my cheeks were hot. 'So I'll see you tonight then. Seven at the Glades.'

'Looking forward to it,' I said as I hung up. Was I ever.

I told Mickey Don's latest forensic discoveries as we got out of the cruiser.

'That why you're flushed all over?'

'Stop it,' I snapped.

He made disgusting smooching sounds with his lips, but then immediately sobered up. 'A baseball bat.' He shook his woolly head. 'Jesus H. Christ, what kinda sick people in this world.'

We found Maria Escondido inside the terminal sitting on a slatted wooden bench smoothed to glass by ten thousand patient passengers. She sat with her full striped skirt and her woven cloth bags around her like surf lapping at her feet. She had a ticket to Miami clutched in one hand, which we took from her.

'Maria,' I said, 'do you remember me from last night?'

She nodded even while she gave Mickey a long fearful look; he held her ticket. Sorrow and fear and disillusion had done their insidious work. The face of the once-pretty señorita from Colombia now looked like so much crumpled up gum wrapper.

'That's my partner. Mickey Brunt.'

'I'm afraid you'll have to come with us, Miz Escondido,' Mickey said, half bending over her.

'I got fired,' she said. 'The señor, he let me go just like that, no money in my pocket, nothing.'

'We're sorry, Maria,' I said as we led her to the cruiser and put her inside. Already battered by a fate she could scarcely fathom, her face shut tight as a clam all the way over. We put her in a room with a wooden table and a couple of chairs. The one window had thick wire mesh over it. I gave her some iced tea while Mickey glowered at her.

'Why you want to talk to me again?' she finally blurted out. 'I told you what I told you last night.'

Mickey waved her ticket in her face. 'That was before you decided to run away.'

She turned her head away and fiercely bit her lip.

'Listen, lady,' Mickey told her, 'your ass is to the wall.'

Maria's eyes got big and round. 'For why does he talk to me that way?' she asked me.

I pushed the tea toward her. 'Maria, for

whatever reason, Mr. Seams has it in his head that you are the cause of Kent's death. He says he's going to sue you.'

She burst into tears. '*Ay de mí!* I loved that little one like I gave birth to him, but I no have eyes when I am asleep!' She looked at me. 'What am I to do? This is America, yes?'

'Yes, and we want to protect you,' I said.

'But unless you cooperate with us — tell us everything — our hands are tied,' Mickey continued. 'I'm afraid Mr. Seams will — ' He drew a forefinger horizontally across his throat.

I sat down opposite her. 'Maria, listen to me, your only hope is to help us here. If you do, if we solve the case, Mr. Seams won't be able to sue you.'

Maria pulled out a handkerchief, blew her nose, then looked from Mickey to me. 'All right.' She nodded. 'What is it you want to know?'

'See, here's the thing,' Mickey said. 'We don't think Kent's death was accidental.'

'*Ay, ay, ay!*' Maria cried. 'Who would do such a thing?'

'We were hoping you could tell us.'

'Me?' Her eyes opened wide.

'Well, you live with the Seamses, you're with Kent almost all the time,' I said. 'It stands to reason that maybe you saw something.'

Maria sat very still and erect, her hands folded in her lap. She had not touched the tea. Mickey leaned over her. 'C'mon, Maria, give us something — anything. Did the Seamses fight?'

'Fight? No, they never fight.' She eyed him suspiciously. 'Okay, so then maybe they don't agree about the *pobrecito*.'

'What about him?' I said.

'He goes into fits. They argued about how to fix it. Señora Kitty wanted to take him up to Atlanta, to a clinic, but the señor refused.'

'Why?' I asked.

'It is a secret. Now I tell you and they will be more angry with me.' Tears welled up in her eyes. 'So then the *pobrecito* wasn't perfect, but all the better to love him, no?'

'Excuse us a minute, Maria.' I grabbed Mickey and we went out of the room. 'Good Christ, this is like what happened to my uncle all over again,' I said to him.

'You mean Kent and his grandmother — '

'It's hereditary.' I nodded. 'They wouldn't acknowledge that Livia had it; they wouldn't acknowledge Kent had it, either.'

'Looks like we got our motive for murder, anyway.' I could almost see Mickey licking his chops just like the Big Bad Wolf. 'Oh, man,

Morgan, we are gonna take your ass down.'

We spent the next hour formally deposing Maria. When she had signed her statement and it had been duly witnessed, I took her over to the rooming house where we'd set her up for the time being. If everything went as planned, she was going to become a state's witness. She seemed grateful enough when I told her I'd keep her ticket personally and give it back to her after the trial.

We stood on either side of the bed, she unpacking her clothes and personal things, me thinking about what a frightening thing it must be to be a stranger held in a land for criminal proceedings.

'Is there anything I can get you?' I asked her.

She shook her head as she set out a small folding frame. Inside were a pair of photographs.

I held out my hand. 'May I?'

'My parents,' she said as she handed it over.

I saw a handsome woman with a lace shawl and a shy smile, an imposing man with a huge, curling mustache and beetling brows.

'My mother, she is still alive, but my father is dead.'

'Mine, too.'

'Was an *abogado*, a lawyer.' She cocked her

head. 'Do you speak Spanish?'

When I nodded, she switched to her native language. 'My father fought the drug cartels until they murdered him.'

'My uncle was murdered, too,' I said. 'By Morgan Seams.'

Nothing stirred in the room save the swampy air pressed down on us by the slowly circling ceiling fan. Something seemed to swim at last behind Maria's eyes. I could almost see it work its way to her mouth.

'When I was a child,' she said, 'I found in the forest near our house a horned beetle. It was bound by thin threads to the center of a large leaf the shape of a knife blade. Sometimes, I think that life is like that leaf, that secrets are like the horned beetle, bound to its fabric. My father died because of the secrets he had found out about the cartel. I am leaving here because of the secrets I know.'

'Like what?'

'Señora Kitty gave me money; she bought me the bus ticket. She wished me Godspeed.' She turned away from me and sat on the bed. I came around so that I could face her. I could see the renewed agony on her face.

'Maria, listen to me, no matter what, your loyalty right now must be to yourself. You understand that, don't you?'

'I understand that the choices in life are always hard. Always.' She squared her shoulders. 'So then I promised myself I would remain silent. But now, because of the child, because of how he died, I think I must tell you what I have seen. Secrets. I hate secrets.' She shuddered. 'It may mean nothing, but then . . . ' Her voice trailed off. Then she looked up at me. 'You see, the way it was . . . There was a change in the air. It seems to me that Mrs. Kitty became fed up with the little one. For the past several months she was short with him, saw him less.' Her gaze dropped to her restless hands. 'Her tongue was sharp even with Mr. Seams. And then she would not meet my eyes, as if there was much to hide, as if she was planning something difficult, dark, permanent.'

* * *

I went home at six and spent forty harrowing minutes after emerging from the shower trying on one outfit after another. Not that I had that many. When I realized I had my dark blue pleated skirt on for the third time, I groaned at my nervousness, decided to wear the skirt, and then discovered I was in such a sweat I needed another application of antiperspirant. Nothing has ruined a date more effectively than having those dark half-moons appear under my armpits.

I did not want to think about what Maria had told me, not yet. I needed to let it percolate through so I could get a sense of how it changed things — or even if it did at all. In any event, tomorrow morning would be soon enough to decide on a course of action.

In the restaurant parking lot, the normally friendly pink and pale-green neon sign of The Glades winked at me; even the alligator logo seemed to be leering, making fun of my expectations. I felt like fifteen again, going out on my first real date.

The restaurant was as dead as a used matchstick, just a couple of old barflies sucking down gin and one lonely-looking businessman no doubt on his way north to Jacksonville or Tallahassee. The Glades might be empty, but it was the only restaurant in town that wasn't a complete dump. Don was waiting for me at a corner table near the back. He stood as soon as he saw me.

'Hi,' he said, 'you look great.'

'Thanks,' I mumbled, my cheeks flaming again.

Marge, the waitress, saved me from further embarrassment. I ordered a vodka and tonic. 'Bloody Mary?' I asked him as I sat down.

'Virgin,' he said. 'Ever since I turned forty, my body doesn't react well to alcohol. Just like my father.'

When my drink had been set in front of me, Don offered a toast. 'Here's to getting reacquainted,' he said. I laughed a little as we drank.

'I guess we both had a hard day today,' he said with his dark eyes on me. I felt their weight as clearly as if his body was pressed against mine.

'It was nice what you said on the phone, about how involved you'd gotten.'

'How could I help it?'

It was wonderful how unself-conscious he was about his compassion. 'But you see death every day.'

'Not like this I don't.' He shook his head. 'Poor kid. I really feel for him.'

I found myself staring into his eyes and wanting with all my soul to get lost in there. But the more I thought about that the more tongue-tied I got, and the silence between us just got longer and more embarrassing. Finally, Don grabbed my hand and said, 'I'm not really hungry, are you?' When I shook my head, he grinned. 'I've got a better idea.'

He took me across the river to Neddy's Place, an old roadhouse, more or less off-limits to whites, filled with blacks, jazz, and abandoned dancing. The place was jumping. Don glided through this throng with the ease of a regular. People shook his hand or gave him the hi-sign or slapped him on the back. He led me to the crowded dance floor, took me in his arms, and said, 'Ready?'

Was I ever. For me, dancing is the great liberator. In its grip, I forget everything. The music flows around me, through me, energizing and elating.

'How did you know I love to dance?' I asked him an hour later. We were sitting at a small table. I was on my second vodka and tonic and he was nursing another Virgin Mary. My head was spinning and I felt more alive than I had in years.

'Took a chance.'

Which was just what I was going to do. With my heart in my throat, I said, 'You know, I used to dream about this moment.'

'How d'you mean?'

It seemed to me an odd smile was frozen on my lips and I thought, Oh God, Priscilla, you are a fool. But I'd crossed some kind of Rubicon and, despite the wild detonations of my pulse, I couldn't turn back. 'At FSU, I used to watch you practice when I was finished with my sprints. I remember watching your big shoulders glistening as they came out of the water and wishing with all my heart you'd ask me out.'

He appeared startled. 'I never knew.'

'Would it have mattered if you had?' I screwed up my mouth. 'I wasn't your type.'

His gaze dropped to his drink.

Stupidly, I felt ashamed. 'That was a cheap shot. Sorry.'

'A cheap shot?' His eyes found mine. 'No. I don't believe you're capable of a cheap shot, Pris. Sure, I saw lots of girls. But it wasn't what you imagine. Back then I could never keep a relationship going for more than a couple of months.'

'Really? That's the truth?'

'As far as it goes.' He held his hand out to me. When I took it, he said, 'The real truth is I watched all your races, too.'

My heart went *kuh-thump*! 'You did?' I could hardly believe it.

'Yeah, but I never — God, I'm embarrassed to admit this. You know, I could never get up the nerve to approach you.'

I was stunned. 'For heaven's sake, why not?'

'You were intimidating, that's why not. Dean's list student, champion track star, first contralto in chapel choir, campus fundraiser — Jesus, you were so damn accomplished in *everything*.'

I was astonished at how my own opinion of

myself could differ so radically from that of other people. Good lord, I thought, melting, I wish we'd had this conversation in college.

'And if that wasn't enough,' he went on, 'there was your uncle. He was famous — *infamous*. Everyone at FSU knew about him, even before he gave his legendary 'Hellfire and Brimstone' sermon the night before Easter recess of our junior year.'

'He wasn't as intimidating as all that,' I said, going into my all-too-familiar defensive mode. Even in death I was fiercely protective of him. But privately, at the center of my soul, what I could tell no one because it was so painful to admit even to myself was what a struggle it had been for me to hold everything right side up for him. 'He was a wonderful man — warm and sweet and forgiving . . . *especially* forgiving.'

'Maybe so,' Don said. 'But when he was in the pulpit he sure could put the fear of God — or the devil — into you.'

'That was his job,' I said. 'Or part of it, anyway. He was into saving souls, especially those he saw in torment.'

A waiter arrived with the gator popcorn Don had ordered — deep-fried chunks of alligator tail — and we both dug in. I don't know about you, but dancing makes me hungry as well as happy. We laughed a little over our mutual appetites.

When the band took a short break, Don said, 'Speaking of souls in torment, Pris, what happened that night out at the Seams estate?'

Something inside of me irised closed. 'You know what happened. Everyone does.'

'They *think* they know. But I've often wondered what *really* happened with your uncle and Morgan's mother. Did he perform an unsanctioned exorcism like the archdiocese claimed?'

'Yes,' I said. 'That much is true.'

'But the rest is all conjecture — and, I've always imagined, lies.'

'All right.' I took a breath. It had been a long time since I had spoken to anyone about it. Like battery acid, the facts of Uncle Ben's demise had been eating away at me. And now to be confessing them to Don Murtry of all people! This was truly, as my uncle would say, a night of revelations.

I asked him to order me coffee before I began. 'As you know, Morgan's mother, Livia, was a devout Catholic. My uncle had been her confessor for years. She was a strange, domineering woman who ruled the Seams household with absolute authority. Even Morgan's father deferred to her. It was her family's insurance business, after all, that supported him once they were married — and it was he who finally ran it into the ground.' I paused as the coffee came. I drank some to steady my nerves; caffeine has that effect on me. Like my mother, I often brewed myself a cup before I went to sleep. 'Anyway, Livia adored my uncle, attended all his sermons. One day, she came to him after services. She was very concerned, almost panic-stricken. She told my uncle that she had started having visions.'

Don frowned. 'You mean like Joan of Arc or Thomas Aquinas?'

'In a sense. It was clear by her descriptions that she was in an altered state.' I stopped suddenly. 'She'd had them once or twice when she was young, but now she firmly believed that she was being periodically invaded by a demon.'

Honestly, I thought Don was going to laugh at me, but instead he looked away for a moment, and I saw him staring through the smoke-filled room. Then he turned back to me and said, 'Go on. Please.'

'Before I do, you have to understand something. My uncle was a profoundly religious man, but he was in no way superstitious. He had never before performed an exorcism and he did not take the possibility lightly. In fact, he tried to explore every alternative avenue. He suggested bringing in a psychotherapist friend of his from Atlanta, other specialists to test her for a brain tumor or epilepsy. She refused, and Morgan became increasingly hostile to his interventions. By that time, my uncle had begun a habit of looking in on Livia three or four nights a week because she was having more and more visions.'

Feeling anew the weight of my agitation, I sucked down more coffee. 'Anyway, one night while my uncle was visiting, she was gripped by a vision so horrible, so relentless, he grew frightened for her. She begged him to help her in the way only he could. She wanted to be exorcised.'

'And he hadn't gotten his bishop's approval.'

'The archdiocese was firm on the issue. They'd never had an exorcism performed, and they weren't about to start now.' I shook my head. 'But even worse for my uncle, Morgan was against it. He'd been raised as Catholic, as Livia decreed, but in college — '

'He was as irreligious as could be. I remember.'

'Besides that, he had grown jealous of all the attention my uncle was paying Livia. He had become suspicious that some kind of hanky-panky was going on between them.'

There was a sour taste in my mouth just saying it.

'But your uncle ignored all that — '

'It simply wasn't true.'

' — just as he ignored the ruling of his archdiocese.'

'The archdiocese had made a political decision. It was far removed from the front line. All that aside, however, he would not abandon a parishioner in spiritual agony. He performed the exorcism.'

Don, who had been gripped by the events once again come so vividly to life, leaned forward. 'What happened?'

'Basically, he failed,' I said.

'The story was he raped Livia and she went mad.'

'Yes, that was Morgan's story,' I said. 'But it was a lie. As my uncle had come to suspect, Livia was suffering from an insidious form of dementia. He could see it happening as her 'visions' accelerated. She was a proud woman, from a proud and prominent family. The shame of premature dementia was intolerable for them.'

'Then why did your uncle put himself on the line to perform a meaningless exorcism?'

'But it wasn't meaningless, you see. He hoped that the ritual might arrest the progress of her affliction, or if that weren't possible at least ease her suffering.'

'But it did neither.'

'No. He had waited too long. Livia was too far gone.' I still had nightmares about it. 'Within six weeks she was dead.'

'So Morgan blamed your uncle.'

'With a vengeance.' I drained my cup.

'He killed himself, if I remember right. Put a gun in his mouth.'

A twist inside me, as if an old wound was alive, tearing open its sutures. 'That's what the county coroner ruled.'

'Who was that? Duke Peterson, right?'

I nodded. The band returned and broke into a heartfelt rendition of Thelma Houston's 'Don't Leave Me This Way.'

'Retired now,' Don said reflectively. 'I see him from time to time. Still plays golf with Morgan, doesn't he?'

'Uh-huh.' The coffee seemed to be turning to battery acid in my stomach. 'They were pals from way — '

We both looked up as a beautiful young woman with skin the color of coffee-and-cream and a skirt cut way too high brushed by the table. She was pulling behind her a tall man with very dark skin and wavy hair that looked like it had been polished. The way his eyes devoured her, you could see he was thrilled to be anywhere she wanted to take him. As she passed, her hip bumped provocatively against Don, and she turned to him, giving him a dazzling five-hundred-watt smile. Her eyes slid from his face to mine, where they emitted the chill, penetrating pall of an X ray. Then the two of them were twirling out on the dance floor. Don tried not to look, but the urge was apparently too powerful.

'Someone you know,' I said, appalled at the vicious surge of jealousy washing over me.

'Colette. We used to go out.' He turned back to me. 'It wasn't good for either of us, but you know how it is with forbidden things.'

'No,' I said snappishly. 'How is it?'

'Oh, c'mon, Pris,' he said immediately. 'Don't be like that. You already have enough anger on your plate.' He took my hand and pulled me out onto the dance floor. 'Let's have some fun tonight.'

The band was playing the Dreamlovers' 'If I Should Lose You,' a sad, nostalgic song for me. At FSU, I used to play it late at night, swaying dreamily to its beat while silent tears rolled down my cheeks. Thinking, as always in those small hours, of Don.

Now I was in his arms, he was holding me close, and I was nearly fainting with the sensation. I nestled my head against his shoulder, his hand went to the small of my back, drawing me a little closer, his right leg slipped between my thighs, and my mouth opened in a silent moan. Occasionally, I could see Colette staring at us as she and her partner whirled by on the dance floor, but I no longer cared. When, at three-thirty, Neddy's Place closed down, I let him take me back to my house. There was no point in either of us being coy; we both knew what we wanted and it was the same thing.

When I was a kid, I'd sometimes drift off during the day and dream of waking up in a bed of rose petals. That's what making love with Don felt like: soft and fragrant and heady and sensuous and oh, so delicious. I had one bad moment. It had been so long since I'd been with a man I was stupidly afraid I wouldn't remember what to do or how to do it, but as soon as I stopped thinking and used my body everything flowed from there. The weight of him on me was like a soothing balm. He seemed to melt into me, filling that dark and aching space I had reserved for him from the nights of my fantasies, fueled by the sight of his gorgeous body knifing at speed through the water. We fell asleep to the ticking of the alarm clock and the somnolent purring of Lama, my watchful Tibetan cat.

Sunlight stroking across the bed like a

swimmer woke me, and the insistent ring of the phone. I stretched across the bed, realized that Don wasn't there, and fumbled the receiver to my ear. I felt a small clutch at my stomach. It was Kitty Seams. I looked at the clock: It was just after eight. She sounded breathless, as if something very nasty was nipping at her heels. Morgan was out and she was able to escape the house — those were her words. We agreed to meet down by the river in forty minutes. Glancing around the bedroom, I came upon the note Don had left me telling me he had an early appointment, that he'd made grits and left enough for me, and that we'd catch up with one another later today. Which blissfully buried my fear that this had been a one-night stand.

⋆ ⋆ ⋆

She was waiting for me, a large-brimmed expensive sun hat and Chanel sunglasses all but obliterating her from view. I thought of Audrey Hepburn in *Charade*. Growing up, I'd skinny-dipped many times in this cool, tree-shaded place with just the bees and crickets droning obsessively. I'd often imagined being swept away on a sudden swift current, swirled like a leaf far from here, as if the river could take me all the way to Oz.

Kitty held on to the bole of a weeping willow as if for dear life. It was scarred with my initials, as well as those of so many other kids who were now grown up, with their own children and curious thoughts of the past.

She handed me a small package, hastily wrapped, as if it were burning her flesh. 'Here. I brought his ring, just as you asked.'

'Thank you,' I said.

Kitty looked out over the water. 'When we were courting, Morgan used to take me here.' She shook her head ruefully. 'It seems like a million years ago.'

I opened the package, making sure I didn't touch the ring. 'Maybe it *was* a million years ago, emotionally.' Rewrapping it, I put it carefully away.

'It's like this,' she whispered. 'Morgan never wanted this child. I forced the issue, more or less.'

I couldn't see her eyes. Those damn sunglasses. 'I didn't know anything could be forced on Morgan.'

'You're right, of course. Except in certain matters where females have the edge.' She gave me a knowing smile that had no humor in it at all. 'When we made love I lied to him about using the pill.'

'Why didn't he want a child?'

'You know,' Kitty said. 'You of all people.'

She took a breath. 'Because of Livia. Morgan was terrified his child would inherit her premature dementia.' The tip of her tongue circled her lips. 'Morgan doesn't have the disease, but Kent did. Apparently, this hereditary condition has a tendency to skip a generation.' She paused, as if lost within herself. 'Morgan was furious. Naturally, I was prepared for him to take it out on me. But no, he did something far, far worse. He punished his own child for being imperfect.'

'Kitty — ' My heart was in my throat. 'What do you mean, Morgan punished Kent?'

'You know.' She was not looking directly at me, and sunlight flared off the dark, convex lenses. All at once, she fell to her knees, clawing off her sunglasses. 'You know exactly what I mean!' she cried, and, burying her face in her hands, bowed down until her forehead touched the saw grass.

'My God, Kitty.' I knelt down beside her, but she violently brushed aside my attempt to throw my arms around her.

'No, no, leave me alone,' she moaned. 'I want to die.' And she collapsed, slipping quickly into the water.

'Kitty!' I reached down after her, and her sunglasses snapped beneath my weight. Hauling her back up the bank, I drew her, dripping and shaking and weeping, into my lap. The wide-brimmed hat, upended and filled with water, was whirling away to that lost place of my childhood imagination. So much for the Audrey Hepburn fantasy. Kitty looked now like what she was: a mother faced with the unthinkable — the mutilation and murder of her child.

'If you save me this will be on your head,' she whispered thinly. 'I deserve to die. For letting him . . . For saying nothing while he defiled my child.' Her eyes rolled upward. 'How could I be so weak. I'm vile, filth . . . '

'Hush, Kitty.' I stroked tendrils of hair off her face. 'Hush now. We're all locked inside ourselves. We all do what we have to do in order to survive.'

'How often I dreamed of leaving,' she cried. 'But with what? To go where? To live what kind of life? He'd drag me down in a settlement, and you know him, he'd hold a grudge for the rest of his life. He would find all the ways to make my life without him miserable.'

It all seemed so sad, so needlessly wretched. I felt her heart beating close to mine, felt the communal bond of our shared gender. It was clear that what Maria had told me had no bearing whatsoever on the case. It was cut and dried. Morgan was a monster and had to be put away for the rest of his life. 'As a child, when I swam here I had nothing but dreams,' I said. 'Now I find only complications, duties, responsibilities, and I wonder where all those sweet simple dreams went.' I was near to tears, thinking of her heartbreak, which chimed with intimacy in the sudden and unexpected flowering of my own life. This morning, waking up smeared with his scent, I could for the first time imagine myself a mother.

'Now you have a way out,' I told her. 'You have the ammunition to fight him, if you have the will.'

* * *

'Mrs. Seams wants to make a statement,' I told Mickey when I brought her back to the office. 'She's implicated Morgan.'

'I'm gonna kill that stinking rat bastard myself.' Mickey's eyes bulged in their sockets and it was all I could do to restrain him. 'A child, a helpless *child*.'

'Everyone was helpless in that household,' I said, sneaking a glance at Kitty. 'He made damn sure of that.'

We took her into a back room, gave her a yellow legal pad and a pen. Mickey made her a fresh pot of coffee; it was good therapy for him. He stared out the window, glowering at the live oaks hung with Spanish moss, while her pen scratched like a huge beetle over the paper. A vein in his temple throbbed with terrible menace. Once, I approached him, but his rage seemed to repel me like the wrong end of a magnet, and I stepped back, returning my attention to Kitty, who was weeping as she wrote. I placed a box of tissues at her left hand and gripped one shoulder in an effort to keep her from coming apart.

When she was finished, Mickey and I read the statement. It was all there, everything she had told me.

Mickey's hands trembled as he stalked in a frightening stiff-legged manner around the room. 'Take her out of here,' he whispered hoarsely to me. 'Now.' I did as he asked and, as soon as I shut the door behind him, I heard the sharp crack of a chair being hurled against a wall. Kitty, startled, tried to turn around, but I led her to my desk, where I put my hand on the phone. 'If I remember right you had a sister in St. Augustine. She still there?'

Kitty nodded almost numbly as I gave her the phone.

'Why don't you stay with her for a while.'

Mickey emerged from his den of pain while

Kitty was speaking with her sister. I left her in the care of one of the other officers while he and I went to round up Morgan.

'What? Are the two of you insane?' he said when we snapped the cuffs on him at his dealership. 'I want to speak with my attorney.'

Mickey read him his rights as we herded him into our cruiser. 'You've got the wrong person,' he said. 'Christ, the two of you are completely incompetent.'

'Shut up, you.' Mickey boxed him on the side of the head. 'You ain't even shed one tear for your son.'

Morgan gathered himself in the backseat like a fulminating volcano. 'My private life isn't on display for the likes of you.' To my surprise, he turned and spoke directly to me: 'What shocks me gravely is the accusatory statement my wife has written. It's all a pack of disgusting lies.'

Lett wasted no time getting Morgan out on bail. You can guess how he did it: son of Livia Seams, family roots in Placide, pillar of the community, yadda yadda. 'Don't worry,' I heard him tell Morgan, 'their case is so ludicrous it won't even make probable cause.'

Three days later, at the hearing before Judge Kronos, we trotted out for the assistant district attorney the county had assigned to the case the baseball bat Morgan had bought for Kent for his last birthday.

'My partner and I found this in Kent Seams's room,' I testified, 'and it's covered with Morgan Seams's fingerprints.'

'Is this some kind of joke?' Morgan looked incredulous as he jumped up. 'I live in that house; I gave the bat to Kent; I spent time showing him how to hit a ball. Of course my prints are all over it.'

The judge instructed him to keep quiet, and the assistant D.A. called Don to the stand, who identified the bat as being the instrument used to sodomize Kent.

This news took the wind out of Morgan's sails. He slumped in his chair beside Gordon Lett, his face drained of blood. 'There must be some mistake,' I heard him say to no one in particular.

That was the moment the assistant D.A. chose to introduce the ring into evidence. The judge asked Morgan to identify it. 'It's my college ring,' Morgan said. He appeared confused. He turned to Lett. 'Where did they get it?' But Lett was too busy hyperventilating to answer.

'See the face of it?' Don turned it around. 'It matches the imprint found behind Kent Seams's left ear.'

'And in your expert opinion, Mr. Murtry, that would be indicative of what?' the assistant D.A. asked as Judge Kronos compared the ring with the close-up photo of the side of Kent's head.

'That imprint, along with the bruise mark behind the deceased's right ear, would be consistent with someone pressing down with some force.'

'As in pushing Kent Seams's head underwater.'

Don nodded. 'Yes.'

'Against the child's will.'

'Of course. Yes.'

Lett jumped to his feet. 'Objection!'

But the damage was done. The case was bound over for trial.

* * *

That night, I made love to Don with a passion I scarcely knew I had inside me. Its intensity brought about an elation as well as a fright I had not felt since I was six years old. That was the moment I discovered that I wasn't an extension of my parents, that there was inside me a force wholly independent of either of them. I learned, in other words, that I possessed the power of deception. Up until then, it had been my perception that the scope of my life — private, unalterable, complete — had been written in my uncle's hand. I was to be the vessel from which he would sip the heady liquor of immortality. Into me he would pour all that he had learned, all that he had been, so that when the time came for the Last Rites to be murmured over him in an officious cloud of incense, he could take with him into the endless night the certain knowledge that he would live on through me.

Climbing atop Don, taking control of his organ as well as my own, I was feverish, avid to do all the lascivious things I had dreamed of but had never done before. Hours afterward, when he had left, I sat drinking iced coffee, staring with blind eyes out onto the street. I had turned off all the lights, had even in the face of the unrelenting humidity thrown open all the windows. Listening to the tree frogs, the crickets, the gentle patter of the rain that had rolled through sometime when Don and I had been insensate, I considered the matter of Morgan Seams. After all this time, all the rage and bitterness, it was a distinct letdown to see him in jail. What did his incarceration mean, after all, but a temporary blow to his sense of propriety? He had Gordon Lett and pretty much anyone else he cared to hire. Looking ahead, I imagined how he would assemble a crack team of lawyers: forensics, technical, and psychological experts who would use their high-priced razzle-dazzle to convince a jury that he was innocent because there was more than a shadow of a doubt as to his guilt or — failing that — that the abuse he himself had, no doubt, suffered at the hands of his father when a child would absolve him of any willful volition or culpability in atrocities visited upon his son. This future was an abomination, utterly contemptible.

I padded into the kitchen, refilled my mug, and returned to where I had been sitting. This time, I looked out into the night. A dog ran down the center of the street, its tongue lolling, its nails making rhythmic skittering sounds like sand draining through an hourglass. Far away, I could hear the soft susurrus of the interstate. Nothing else moved, save the dripping from the eaves in the aftermath of the rain, like someone from long ago inconsolably weeping. There was an old Ford Mustang parked outside my house that had seen better days — it had been repainted by hand in an ugly matte finish. Here and there, it had been eaten away by rust as if with the pointed teeth of tiny gremlins, and its antenna was bent into the shape of a pretzel. The odd thing was that it had been there when I'd let Don in hours ago.

As I watched, someone opened the driver's side door and got out — a woman, slim and sinuous as she walked up the path to my front door. I heard the soft rapping of her knuckles reverberate through the darkened house like an evil omen, and I almost did nothing. For a moment longer I sat still, the sweat popping out on me in the sluggish darkness. I could hear the rushing of my pulse in my ears. Then the rapping came again, more insistent this time, and I put aside my mug. I imagined I heard again the skittering sound, not of time passing, but of it draining away.

'Do you remembah me?' she said when I opened the door.

Even in the mean yellow porch light I recognized her from the night Don and I had spent dancing at Neddy's.

'Colette, isn't it?'

She nodded and, despite the heat, drew her long shiny raincoat more tightly about her. 'May Ah come in? Ah'm not comfortable here'bouts at night.' She meant the white section.

How beautiful she was. I stepped back, too late remembering the malignant look with which she had meant to paralyze me.

'Coffee?' I asked automatically, heading for the kitchen.

'No.'

That one word brought me up short, the resonance in the syllable making the hair stir at the nape of my neck. We stood facing each other in the darkness of my living room. Don's scent was still in my nostrils and no doubt on my skin like some exotic moisturizer, and I was at once triumphant and chagrined.

'Ah have sumthin' t' say t'yo.'

I was close enough to her to see the small pulse at the corner of one eye.

'Don told me all about the relationship you and he had,' I said as much in defense as to cut her off at the knees, because I was dead certain this was what she had come to tell me. She'd had poison in her eyes that night at Neddy's, and it was surely on her tongue now.

'That's as may be,' she said simply, 'but did he tell yo 'bout his relationship wid Kitty Seams?'

'Excuse me?' It was all I could say with my heart suspended like a cold stone in my chest.

A slow smile spread across her face, making her, incongruously, even more beautiful. 'Of course he hasn't.' When I turned away, she went on. 'Ah guess yo think Ah came here crazy wid jealousy, but yo'd be wrong. Ah got over Don fast when Ah found out he was ballin' Kitty Seams same as he was me. Ah ain't that kinda girl.' She said this in such a straightforward, unself-conscious manner it had the unmistakable ring of truth.

'How long?' I knew it was my voice, but I wondered where it was coming from. Some tiny part of me concerned solely with my survival had taken over and was directing me with a general's icy control.

'Kitty Seams, Ah s'pose yo mean, 'cause you sure as shoot wouldn't concern yo'self wid how long him 'n' me were hittin' the sheets. Lessee now, it mus' be goin' on a year now, an' Ah like t' say that's the least o' it.'

'Did you ask him to break it off with her?'

'Did Ah? Shee-it, course Ah did, sugah. We got some mighty fine mojo kickin'. But he refused. Said he wanted us both.'

'Does she — ' I swallowed. 'Does she have some kind of hold over him?'

'Seem like it's the other way round. Took all I had t' walk away, tha's the truth. T' this day, I can feel his hands on me. But no, it be a evil thang. They had plans.'

That was really the first inkling I got that Kitty had been lying to me all along. My scalp began to crawl. 'What kind of plans?'

'Wouldn't know nuthin' 'bout that. Don never said specifics, why would he? But Ah knows it.' She bared her fine teeth. 'Ah knows when a married woman won't leave a man they's got be a pow'ful reason.'

I sat down on the arm of an oversize upholstered chair. My head was spinning. Don was Kitty's lover? I was too numb to yet feel the depth of his betrayal. As I said, this hyperefficient little part of me was too busy keeping my head above water. No time for recriminations, my little general ordered. No time for self-pity. I stood up. 'I'm very much obliged to you for coming here tonight.'

She nodded gravely and gazed deep into my eyes. As with everything she did or said, these small, passing gestures were imbued with the weight of inner conviction. Perhaps we'd never be friends, exactly, but we wouldn't be enemies, either. 'Ah do believe Ah'll take that cup o'coffee now.'

⋆ ⋆ ⋆

Don opened the door to my knock. 'Pris.' He grinned. 'Here for more?'

'More.' I nodded as I came in, backing him up. 'I want everything.'

'Well, now.' His grin widened. 'I think that can be arranged.'

I stared at him. 'Do you always answer the door naked?'

'I saw you coming up the walk.'

Vigilant little fuck, I thought. I kicked the

door closed behind me. As he took me in his arms, I could feel my skin break out into goose bumps. Then I unwound myself from him and started to walk around the place. I'd never been here before. It was paneled in cypress, furnished in pieces from the fifties that must have come from the odd lawn sale. A couple of oval rag rugs hugged the floor between stacks of books on anatomy, forensics procedure, and criminal psychology. The pictures on the wall, of flowers and hillsides, looked as if they had been left behind by the previous owner.

'What is it?' he asked in a bantering tone. 'Looking for ghosts?'

'No,' I said. 'I'm looking for Kitty.'

Revealed in the swell of lamplight, his face had become ridged, like the stone facade of a well-defended fortress. In this same illumination, his long, lean swimmer's muscles had taken on a bristling menace. 'Kitty Seams?' His laugh was brittle, false. 'What in the world would she be doing here?'

'That would be what I was wondering.'

'I mean, I barely know the woman.'

I stood in front of him and smiled. My hand reached out and took hold of his penis. 'You barely know me, and just look at us.' I began a rough pulling, just as he liked, and he got hard.

He began to unbutton my blouse. 'Pris — ' His hands cupped my breasts.

'No, really, I mean it.' I squeezed him so hard his eyes fairly popped. 'How long have you and Kitty been getting it on?'

'Who told you that?' he gasped.

'Colette.'

'Ah, that explains it.' Sweat had broken out across his upper lip. 'Colette hates my guts. She'd say anything to — '

He gave a little yelp as I applied more pressure. 'Don't treat me like a moron, Don.'

'I don't — ' He gasped again in pain. 'I don't think that of you. I know you're different from all the others.'

'Even Kitty Seams?'

His nostrils were flared, and now his eyes closed. 'Even her.'

'No, it's Kitty you love, Don. That's clear enough.' I leaned forward and whispered in his ear: 'Still, you're right about one thing. I *am* different. Because I'm the one who can keep you and Kitty apart.'

His eyes opened like windows into a dark and mysterious world I had never suspected. 'Why on earth would you do that?' he said. 'You hate Morgan as much as she does. Maybe more.'

Who was being more devious, Don or

Kitty? 'So we all want to see Morgan fry, is that it?'

'Yes.' He said this as if the wish were the most natural thing in the world. 'We're all in this together, Pris.' His smile was gentle, sensuous. 'And as far as I'm concerned, whatever I have going with Kitty has absolutely nothing to do with you and me.' He kissed me once. 'Different animal.' He kissed me twice. 'Different ride.' I felt his tongue. 'Colette couldn't handle it, but I know you can. You're better, you're stronger. I know you and Kitty can become good friends. I don't want to lose either of you.'

'So — what? — we'll all become Mormons and live happily ever after?'

He laughed, certain now we'd turned a corner. 'Those Mo-mos certainly have the right idea, don't they?'

I could hear Colette's soft drawl in my head: *They had plans*.

'With your cock dangling between us?'

He was so hard he was throbbing. He put his hands on my thighs. 'You know, Pris, your skin is as smooth as candy.'

'And where do I fit in?'

'What d'you mean?' His fingers had slipped higher and, despite myself, I felt a small thrill like a flame flickering in the night. The danger was palpable, his lure intoxicating.

I pressed my thumb against the moist tip of him. 'You know what I mean. You need me, don't you?'

'That's right.' His eyes fluttered closed and he swayed a little in rising ecstasy. 'I was right when I told Kitty we'd never be able to fool you. You're too smart, Pris. Too smart by half.'

He hit me, then, the heel of his hand smashing into my nose. My head flew backward, and he kicked me so that I lost my balance. He took my gun while I slid down the wall. Tears of pain inflated his image, so that he seemed to tower over me like an ancient god in a thunderous rage.

'Too smart to live, maybe.'

He hauled me to my feet and dragged me into his bedroom. That's when I saw them: the photos of Kent Seams covering the walls like an obscene wound. Impossible to hold the horrific images in the mind's eye for long, let alone to describe. The boy was naked in all of them, and the positions . . .

'It was you, not Morgan!'

He shrugged. 'We all have our hobby.'

'Is that what you call it?'

'Among other things.' He considered a minute. 'The irony is, I could empathize with Kent, really I could. He'd inherited his disability from his grandmother; I inherited mine from my father.' He reared back, a dangerous look transfiguring his face. 'Oh, how he exulted in punishing me. I never did anything right, and the consequences of my fucking up was . . . a good fuck!'

I felt chilled to the marrow of my bones. 'But how could Kitty — '

'She doesn't know. As far as she's concerned, Morgan's the villain of this piece, just like he was in the death of your uncle. In her case, it bound her to me ever so tightly.' He slapped me down. 'Why do you fight me, Pris? I'm doing you a favor — the biggest goddamn favor of your life, if I can be so immodest. Morgan Seams will never be tried for murdering your uncle, but he sure as hell will go upriver for this.' His face twisted. 'Isn't that revenge?'

'No,' I said. 'It's obsession.'

'In the book of my life a sweet, sweet word.' He put his face between my breasts and licked me while he flipped off the gun's safety and pressed the muzzle between my thighs. He arched away without warning, his face a mask of rage. 'I don't want to pull the trigger, Pris. I like you, honest to God I do. You make love like a fucking priestess, like you're tuned in to some holy channel. You take possession of me in a way even my hot little Kitty can't.' He jammed the muzzle inward. 'But so help me if you don't stop fighting me you'll be nothing but a goddamn mess all over my bed.'

I lay back and listened to the jangling of my nerves. My heart beat painfully in my chest, and the adrenaline was rushing in my ears like a summer torrent.

'There's still a way to save this,' he said. 'You were right, we needed you to back up my autopsy report, which I must say is here and there fudged in favor of implicating Morgan. See, people around here trust you — even the blacks on the other side of the river. You think I could have brought Mickey into Neddy's like I did you? Mickey's got a temper like a wasp, he's as bigoted as shit, and nobody thinks he's straight.'

'He is straight.'

'Doesn't mean squat. Didn't you learn anything by your uncle's death, Pris? The truth doesn't matter. All that matters is what people think.' He grinned. 'Everybody trusts me, everybody likes me.'

'Colette doesn't.' Now, there was a dumb thing to say.

His expression darkened. 'I'll take care of Colette in time.' He wiggled the gun barrel. 'But right now I've got to concern myself with you. What the hell am I going to do with you?'

'Shoot me,' I said. 'Go ahead. It's what you want to do.'

'But I don't want to do it, Pris. I told you — '

I slapped him so hard I could feel it all the way up my arm.

'Bitch!' he cried, and, putting the gun under my chin, pulled the trigger.

As soon as I heard the dry snap of the hammer hitting home I moved fast. I had deliberately left the first chamber empty, but if I gave him the chance to pull the trigger a second time . . .

I didn't. I jammed my knee into his groin and, at the same time, slapped the gun to one side. He cursed again, but I was already inside his defense and, locking his elbow against mine and, with a quick, fierce release of energy, I broke his left arm. But even maimed, he came after me. He almost dislocated my jaw, swinging the gun barrel into my face, and then he dropped it and his hands were around my throat and I had no air to breathe.

My world was turning red. I could hear the tiny gasps sawing out of my mouth, and there was a frantic beating in my temples as of a caged beast fighting to be set free. In short bursts, I glimpsed the gun, already half off the edge of the bed. My hand scrabbled over the covers for it, I felt its cool, reassuring surface against my fingers. I reached for it and it dropped to the floor. I moaned in despair. Don bore down on me. A moment more and my life would wink out. Just like that.

Never.

I reared up, pushing him, if not off me, then over so that we both tumbled off the bed. We landed hard on the cypress floorboards. I felt the gun against my right hip and I closed my hand around it, brought it up, tilted the barrel toward him.

I pulled the trigger.

⋆ ⋆ ⋆

I sat next to Kitty all during the trial. I had a lot of time to savor the story of Don's death because there were no loopholes. The first thing I had done was to call Colette. I did this from a phone booth so there would be no record of a call coming from Don's house. She was only too happy to back up my story of rape, by coming forward to say he'd tried the same thing with her. Then I went back to Don's and stripped the place of all the photos of Kent and the other children I found stuffed in his drawers. I set fire to them out back, stamping on the ashes until they melted like mud into the ground. Then I called

Mickey. My voice was shaky and frightened enough to bring him at the run. That excellent actress Kitty Seams would have been proud of my performance. The rest laid itself out like the Yellow Brick Road. There was a very brief inquest, but all the forensics evidence — my bruises and scratches, the state of Don's apartment as well as his own wounds — was entirely consistent with the forcible rape story.

During the trial I looked for Colette, but she never appeared. Mickey took me out to dinner on the nights when Kitty and I didn't get together, and I asked to spend more time with his kids. Their shouts of laughter acted as an annealing balm to my fractured psyche. When I was with Kitty, she preferred to listen to me talk about my uncle and the days before she had been married to Morgan. As a consequence of this, I think, she started attending Sunday services. I could see her always as I sang in the choir, and knew she was watching me as her sweet alto lifted and fell, the hymnal open before her. I thought often of Maria Escondido and her theory of secrets. I recalled her brave, handsome father and his bitter, premature death.

Don was the enigma. Why had he revealed himself to me — first through the autopsy, which he could so easily have suppressed, then showing me his bedroom? He could have gone to Mickey, who, wearing his hatred of Morgan on his chest like a medal of honor, wouldn't have questioned a thing Don had told him. In the end, I suppose there had been a part of Don that had wanted to be stopped — finally, irrevocably.

When, at the end of the second week, the foreman of the jury pronounced the verdict, I was watching Morgan Seams's face just as Kitty was. Guilty, on all counts. Of course, at that moment, we must have been consumed by completely different thoughts.

Then again, maybe not. We had both been possessed by a demon, and now he was gone. For me — as well as for her, I think, despite her deep and lasting pain — it was a blessing that the Seams house had been exorcised.

After it was all over and Morgan had been moved to the state penitentiary, I took myself to Neddy's. Colette and I sat together, drinking ice-cold beers, listening to the band play 'Time Is Tight' and 'I'm Walkin',' songs I'd adored in college, when I'd had nothing more on my mind than Uncle Ben's impending guest sermon. I wondered what he thought of me, of what I'd done deliberately and calculatedly. *I make it a point never to judge anyone*, he often told me. *I leave that particular bit of nasty business to the*

Heavenly Father. The band was so hot that Colette and I danced together until two lithe, dark-skinned guys joined us. It was molten in there, abandoned and sweaty, with the smoke rising in arabesques just like in the movies, and the music was like liquor in my veins. I was conscious of the river of life, filled with a boundless energy, flowing through me, and my heart was as light as the notes streaming out of the tenor sax.

Angel or devil, how would Uncle Ben see me? Maybe, tonight as on that night out at the Seams estate when he'd performed the exorcism, there was very little difference between the two.

Michael Malone

A few years ago, Michael Malone wrote his first short story in more than a decade. 'Red Clay' went on to win an Edgar Allan Poe Award from the Mystery Writers of America, a nomination for an Agatha, and was selected for Best American Mystery Stories, 1997.

The following is his first mystery story since then, and it is a worthy successor. The northern milieu of 'Invitation to the Ball' is very different from the southern locale of 'Red Clay,' and the sophisticated young socialites of this story are very different from the simple small-town folks of the previous one, but the style is as pure and rich in one as in the other. It is recognizably a Michael Malone story, than which there can be no greater compliment.

The author has recently completed his long-awaited third novel in the Justin

Savile and Cuddy Mangun detective series, following the impeccable Uncivil Seasons *and* Time's Witness.

Invitation to the Ball

By Michael Malone

'A dinner invitation once accepted is a sacred obligation. If you die before the dinner takes place, your executor must attend.'

— Ward McAllister,
the man who made up
'the Four Hundred'

Mark told Tugger Whitelaw, who was Chanler's best friend, that something had to be done, and that he'd found a girl, the perfect girl. Mark had been telling their whole group for months that Chanler was in a bad way, that he was getting weird about this woman in the picture. Now Mark brought Tugger along to witness what he meant. Later, when Tugger testified for the prosecution in what the tabloids called the 'Honeymoon Murder,' he would refer to this meeting as 'the day it all started.' But that was from his perspective. According to the prosecutor, the original plan had been set up for over a year when it was replaced by a daring improvisation. He said that's the thing about the most successful con artists. They have qualities not often combined in the same personality — both a ruthless patience and an imperturbable spontaneity.

At the Parnassus Club, in the high-ceilinged, oak-paneled dining room, they found Chanler seated in front of the painting again. The Parnassus was a private arts club in the Forties just off Fifth Avenue, though very few members were in the arts anymore. It was an easy walk from everyone's office, and the young group to which these friends belonged had all joined, but only Chanler appeared to feel at home there.

Mark gave Tugger a nudge, pointed at the painting, and asked Chanler if they could talk. Ruffling his sandy hair, straightening his expensive thin glasses, Chanler was happy to see them. Had something happened to Mark? As he ordered Parnassus cups for them all, Tugger affably noted that it was true, they were usually talking about Mark — whether Mark was in trouble again at the brokerage firm where he and Chanler worked, or whether he was broke again (Mark had an impulsive way of playing around with stocks that no one had ever heard of — usually for good reason). They'd been talking about Mark's problems since the three had been in prep school together.

Mark interrupted; this time *he* was fine.

'Channie,' Mark began, squinting over the disk of his silver cup. 'It's you. We're all getting worried about you. Aren't we, Tug?'

'Sure are.' Tugger smiled to show that his concern for his best friend was benign.

Turning his face back to the painting he'd been looking at, Chanler asked, 'Worried about what?'

Mark pointed at the picture of the woman over the mantelpiece. 'This. You're like Dana Andrews in *Laura*. Isn't he, Tug?'

Chanler was surprised. 'I'm like *Laura*? The old movie?' (This was an easy guess for Chanler, as so many of Mark's analogies came from the classic Hollywood films he'd spent most of his Yale years watching.)

'Yeah. Dana Andrews fell in love with Laura's portrait, remember? Laura.' Mark sang a line of the song.

Popping cashews in his mouth, Tugger tried to help. 'Kim Novak played her.'

Impatiently Mark grabbed the silver bowl of nuts away from Tugger. 'Not *Vertigo*, jerk.' He glowered at such ignorance. 'Gene Tierney, Laura. They thought she was murdered but she wasn't. This cop had a fixation on her portrait. That's the point, Channie, okay. You're spending way too much time with old Mrs. DeWitt Rawlings here.'

Chanler considered the life-size portrait of Mrs. Rawlings in front of him. 'I thought *not* having a fixation on a woman was my problem.'

It was true that friends of Chanler Swaine's, and he was famous for having the most friends of anyone in his young group, were always telling him he didn't want things enough. Of course, they'd also agreed that the same equanimity was what made him so pleasant to be around. Born into a fashionable family and an enviable trust fund, blessed with reasonable looks and brains, he appeared to be entirely satisfied with his life — a state of mind that was, if not unnatural, certainly unusual. Didn't even the rich always want more money, the successful more success, didn't the beautiful labor to make themselves more beautiful? Mark, with his black hair and startling blue eyes, so handsome that women stared at him in public places, certainly wanted a great many things he didn't have.

Chanler, on the other hand, had seemed able, in a lackadaisical way that charmed and frustrated his friends, to win or lose without much caring which happened. It was the way he played his little old-fashioned tunes on the piano, his long fingers wandering softly over the keys. But if he tended to drift, he did so in a fairly steady direction, steered by virtues that his friends had come to rely on. He'd been a good boy; he was a good man. He just wasn't a passionate one, although he'd always admired the passions in others.

Yet, as Mark was trying to get everyone to see, Chanler had changed. He had begun to develop a bizarre infatuation with Mrs. DeWitt Rawlings. He gave every indication of having fallen in love with the woman, or rather with her portrait, which hung in the dining room of the Parnassus Club, above a green marble mantelpiece ripped a century earlier from some hapless Veronese palazzo. In this painting, the 'ravishing' Mrs. Rawlings (as the nineteenth-century social arbiter Ward McAllister had christened her) stood in a gold gown on a curved stairway, half turned, but looking back as if she had just whispered the viewer's name in an intimate way.

The portrait had made the reputation of a struggling young artist and it was one of the prizes of the Parnassus Club's famous collection. The Rawlings family had sold it years ago to the club, where the artist himself, Jacob Zanski, had once applied for membership and been blackballed. Chanler had discovered in the records of the membership committee this instance of a time when prejudices were so sure of themselves that they kept records. Though some of the old ways were still sequestered behind the varnished doors, it was a far more diverse group of young Parnassus members who met there monthly to plan the BGC — Ball for a Good Cause — that Chanler hosted every Christmas at his mother's town house on East Fifty-fifth. (Chanler was chair of the Invitations Committee, and invitations were avidly sought by New Yorkers of twenty- and thirty- something.)

Lately at these meetings, as Mark pointed out to their friends, Chanler had made certain to sit facing the portrait of Mrs. Rawlings, even if he had to ask someone to change places with him, so that her strange low-lidded seductive green eyes stared straight into his. Even Tugger, who'd resisted Mark's alarm, was growing concerned about the way Chanler had started dropping in at the club every night, pulling up a chair, ordering a champagne Diana, and staring at Mrs. Rawlings for an hour or more. He couldn't seem to keep his eyes off a woman a hundred years older than he was.

'This wasn't,' said Mark, 'what we meant when we told you to really go after somebody.'

Tugger nodded. 'We meant find somebody

you love and get married.'

Chanler said he hoped Mark wasn't about to matchmake again. Apart from Tugger (who'd been recovering for years from the heartache of a broken engagement), Chanler was the only bachelor left in their group. Thanks to Mark, he'd once been briefly on the verge of proposing to a bond trader named Belinda, but the moment had passed. Asked why, he admitted that when he wasn't with Belinda, he couldn't remember what she looked like. But Chanler now spent so much time gathering information on Mrs. Rawlings's life in the Gilded Age (for example, that the drink 'the Diana,' brut champagne with a dash of Cointreau, had been named for her) and so much time staring at her portrait here at the club that he could have picked Diana Rawlings out of a large crowd in a fog, from the lobe of her ear alone, from the nail on her little finger.

'Which is why we're just all getting a little worried about you, aren't we, Tug?'

'A little. I mean, Mark here likes old movies and stuff, but there's such a thing as too much of the past, Channie. I don't even know why we joined this place. The old farts here just snooze around and complain about their prostates.'

Now, Chanler's friends, many of them

raised on the Upper East Side, had nothing against the past; in fact they thought of themselves as stylistic reconstructionists, social neo-classicists. After all, they put on fancy dress balls for charity, just as their great-grandparents had. Like their grandparents, they knew how to dress and how to foxtrot. Tugger enjoyed his Broadway shows and porterhouse steaks; Mark, his film noir, braces and Borsolino hats, martinis and cigars. But Channie's falling in love with a woman in a fin de siècle painting was taking the traditional too far.

'Here's the point,' Tugger admitted. 'She's dead.'

'That's the whole point,' Mark agreed. 'He finally picks somebody and she's been dead a hundred years. You see the problem, Channie?'

'She's only been dead since 1951.' Chanler smiled.

'In 1999, that's still a problem.' Mark stroked his new mustache with a tan, well-manicured hand. 'Not that you should have married Belinda.' (Mark's former wife had been Belinda's best friend, and Chanler's breakup with her had caused some awkwardness in the group until Mark had left his wife.) 'I mean, Belinda and my wife both turned out to be real class-A bitches.'

That night Mark called Tugger for his views on Chanler's fixation. Everyone in their group relied on Tugger's dogged literalism as a 'reality check,' trusting him despite (or because of) his inability to play the social games at which Mark was far more skilled. 'So, okay, Tug? Am I right, Channie's got a problem, and we need to fix it?'

Tugger admitted that Chanler appeared to be determined to fall in love, and therefore it might be better if a real woman could be substituted for the one on canvas.

The next week, Mark had Tugger bring Chanler to the club. He found them sitting in front of the portrait. He told Chanler, 'I want you to meet somebody tonight. You're gonna thank me.'

Chanler gestured that Mark should step backward. 'Don't try to fix me up again, Mark, please. Fix Tugger up.'

'Not me,' said Tugger. 'Let me finish my diet.' But Mark was hurrying away down the wide stairs, presumably to bring back the perfect female for Chanler, who asked, 'Has he got some girl hidden down in the coatroom? Do you know who she is?'

'He thinks you'll like her.' Tugger was looking at the painting of Mrs. Rawlings. 'So what is it about this picture?'

Chanler confessed that he'd never seen a

contemporary woman in the same class as Mrs. Rawlings.

Tugger gave a closer look. 'Are those real, painted on her dress?'

Chanler drew Tugger even closer to examine the jewels sewn all over the gold gown. 'They're real.' (Mrs. DeWitt Rawlings's husband had inherited a rather large copper mine at a time when there was no income tax.) 'But,' he added, 'you should have seen Alice Vanderbilt that night. Alva's sister-in-law. She came to the party as 'The Electric Light.' Her whole head was covered with diamonds.'

'What night, what party?' Tugger asked. Chanler pointed at the portrait's title. *Mrs. Rawlings as Dido. Mrs. Vanderbilt's Ball, 1883.* It had been a fancy dress affair, which was why Mrs. Rawlings was costumed in this jeweled outfit: She'd come as the Queen of Carthage — or at least the fashionable tailor Lanouette's bizarre notion of what that ancient queen might have looked like. Chanler explained to Tugger how this picture, painted a year afterward, commemorated Diana Rawlings's great triumph at the most famous ball ever given in New York City, when Alva Vanderbilt had spent $250,000 on a dance and dinner in order to break into Society. Chanler told Tugger $250,000 then would be about four and half million today.

'For a party?! Four and a half million?'

Chanler agreed, it was no small change, even for a Vanderbilt. But it was worth every cent to the social-climbing Alva because it had done what it was meant to do. It had forced Mrs. Astor to pay a visit to her home, and where Mrs. Astor went (and she went wherever a man named Ward McAllister advised her to go), the Four Hundred followed.

'But what exactly is it about Mrs. Rawlings here that you like so much?' Tugger persisted.

Chanler's answer surprised him. 'I like her because she's a pirate,' he said.

'You mean like a thief?'

Chanler shook his head. 'No. And not just reckless, like Mark. I mean like a pirate captain, flying her own flag, taking no prisoners. The opposite of me.'

'Or me,' agreed Tugger. 'Or anybody else in here.' He gestured around the private club, where the members chatted at one another in a room designed by Stanford White; they looked and dressed and talked alike.

Chanler nodded. Yes, the first and most powerful rule of Society, he said, is that Society rules, that it is impossible to break those rules without dreadful penalties. 'But, of course,' he added, placing his long thin legs on the leather chair across from him, 'the rules only have power over those who agree to believe in them.' A portly man frowned fiercely at him, and Chanler quickly removed his feet from the chair. But, he added, there have always been pirates who did as they pleased and got away with it. One such pirate was Alva Vanderbilt. Diana Rawlings was another.

'And what did she do?' Tugger asked.

'She murdered her husband.' Chanler smiled. 'Nobody knows it, and I can't prove it, but I'm sure she did. And got away with it.'

Tugger frowned, his concern growing that Mark was right: Their friend was in the grip of a strange fixation.

Chanler squeezed his arm, his mild gray eyes brightened. 'That's what makes her so beautiful.'

'That she's a murderer?'

'That she's letting you know she's going to act on her desires. It's in her eyes. See how she looks right at you.'

Chanler took something from his pocket. It was a small framed photogravure that just that afternoon he'd come across at the antiques fair at the Armory. It was a picture of Diana Rawlings taken for the society pages some ten years after the death of her husband; she sat in a fashionable group at the races at Saratoga. Behind her in the group stood the artist Jacob Zanski, by then a successful man. 'And Jacob Zanski knew she was a pirate. He saw it from the beginning and put it in the portrait.'

Tugger, alarmed, looked from the photo to the painting. He saw a woman in a long golden gown, beaded with hundreds of small rubies, emeralds, and pearls, low-cut and strapless, except for two thin strands of rubies curling over her shoulders. Her head was a flame of auburn hair, piled high and sprinkled with rubies. She wore no necklace, and the white nakedness of her neck and bare arms was, even today, a shock to viewers. On her right hand, the one resting on the newel of the marble banister, she wore a bracelet of intricate design, of rubies twined in gold. The dress had cost more money than a thousand mill workers could earn in a year of long, backbreaking days at a thousand looms.

Chanler said the dress had caused a sensation at Mrs. Vanderbilt's ball. So had the fact that Diana Rawlings (who was not one of the Four Hundred) arrived unescorted by her husband (who was). In fact, no one had ever heard of Diana before she'd married DeWitt Rawlings six months earlier. His family had been surprised, and not at all pleased, and had tried to keep the marriage to a shop girl as quiet as possible. They'd thought DeWitt, an amateur archaeologist, would never marry anybody, much less a beauty half his age with no connections. But while Diana had arrived at the Vanderbilts' essentially uninvited, she'd been accompanied by the Reverend DeLancey, rector of a large Fifth Avenue church, who came dressed as El Cid, and by his wife, a lumber heiress, who came as Bo Peep. Between them, Mrs. Rawlings had walked past the police squads into the white limestone château, up the marble stairway lined by the rows of footmen in maroon knee britches, buckled shoes, and powdered wigs, who guarded every step. Beneath the circular frescoed ceiling, she'd offered her hand to Alva Vanderbilt as if she'd done so daily for the past dozen years, while she explained that her husband, DeWitt, sent his regrets; he'd been unexpectedly delayed returning from an archaeological trip to Greece.

Despite the shock of her décolletage, her beauty, and the fact that no one really knew who she was, Diana Rawlings then joined the thousand socialite guests dancing to an orchestra under a canopy of all the roses for sale that day in New York City. The moral standing of her escorts protected her as she climbed into a world where she was to live unchallenged until her death some sixty years later. If this Dido was all right with the Reverend and Mrs. DeLancey, well, then . . . And she managed to remain all right, from that night on, even when, the very next day, her husband was found lying dead on the terrace of the family's country house, having presumably fallen, or jumped, from a bedroom balcony. 'Or,' said Chanler, 'been pushed.'

Mark still hadn't returned with the girl. Tugger tried to stop himself from eating the mixed nuts the waiter kept replenishing. 'Channie, you do sound a little weird, you know that?'

'Oh, I'm not making this up. There were rumors even back then, but nobody ever — '

At that moment, Mark interrupted. 'Channie. Got a minute?'

Chanler turned and saw the young woman. She stood at the top of the stairs beside Mark and looked right at him. Even from a distance, he could see the shocking resemblance, even in the tailored black suit and pageboy haircut. She had the same slender figure and cream-white glow to her skin. The same auburn hair and the green, oddly tilted eyes that one couldn't look away from.

Mark was grinning as Chanler hurried to his feet, pulling Tugger with him. 'Right,' Mark said. 'Mattie, this is Tugger Whitelaw.'

'Tim,' insisted Tugger.

'And this is Chanler Swaine, the guy I've been telling you about.'

As she held out her hand, Chanler noticed the bracelet. He couldn't believe it. 'Hi, Chanler.' She smiled. 'Mark tells me you know all about my great-grandmother. Well, I don't know a thing. I don't think my dad ever mentioned her.' She laughed, a low conspiratorial chuckle.

'Your great-grandmother?'

'Diana Rawlings. There.' She pointed at the portrait. 'Look at that. Just like you said, Mark. It is my bracelet.' She spun the bracelet with its gold-tangled rubies, showing it to them. Tugger asked her where she'd gotten it. Mark told her she'd have to get used to Tugger; he was notorious for asking personal questions.

She answered. 'My dad gave it to me. He told me it had belonged to his family, but he didn't say it was in a famous painting. He wasn't much for old memories.' She spun the bracelet. 'So, Chanler, Mark says you can tell me everything?'

Chanler told her that Mrs. Rawlings's husband had been found dead the morning after the Vanderbilt ball. There were rumors of suicide, rumors that Diana had been having an affair, even rumors of murder.

Mattie laughed. 'Why do men think that just because a woman may be capable of adultery, she must be capable of murder too?'

'You gotta admit, Tug' — Mark grinned as later they followed Mattie and Chanler to the club dining room — 'she's got it. Like Bogie says, the stuff dreams are made of. Look at Channie!' Chanler was talking to the young woman with an animation unusual for him. She nodded, smiling as they went.

'I guess,' said Tugger. 'I don't know. I thought the idea was to get him away from this stupid painting, not bring it to life.'

A week after this first dinner together, Chanler invited Mattie Rawlings to be his date at the BGC. That made her one of their group. Only two months later, he proposed. They got along beautifully; it turned out that everything Chanler liked, Mattie liked as well. She shared his taste in restaurants, in politics, in movies, furniture, and friends. She liked to ballroom dance and jog in the park, she liked the History channel, and she collected things — old autographs, art deco lacquer. In fact, had Mattie been trained like Gigi since childhood to take her place as Chanler's mate, she couldn't have been more perfectly suited. She didn't even mind having dinner once a week with his mother, whose sarcasm had reduced earlier dates of Chanler's to tears; Mattie appeared to enjoy the undeclared war of thrusts and parries.

She had her own life too, in fact would occasionally be unavailable for an evening out or would go away for a weekend, and Chanler found this independence reassuring. Their only incompatibility was Mattie's pleasure in gambling; like Mark, she loved betting on long shots at Belmont, and Mark and she would occasionally go to the track together, where they seemed always to lose. It was a kind of recklessness that Chanler lacked but — he admitted to Tugger — secretly admired.

'Is she a pirate too?' Tugger asked.

Chanler responded, puzzled, 'A pirate?' He seemed to have forgotten his theories about Mrs. DeWitt Rawlings; her great-granddaughter had effaced her completely. She looked so much like her ancestor's portrait that Mark made a quip that went the rounds — that Chanler and Mattie were a match made in the fin de siècle. And in fact, Chanler grew so obsessed with her that he neglected his work at the brokerage firm where he had once been the odds-on favorite to be the first of their group to make partner. Instead, that honor went to Mark, who confessed he could use the raise; things were a little tight financially. 'Besides, what do you care, Channie? You're richer than God.'

'Not really,' Chanler modestly protested. He was, however, indisputably better off than Mark, and he congratulated his friend on his promotion. When Tugger claimed that Chanler was too decent to see how much less Mark had done to deserve the promotion, Chanler said he owed Mark a lot, for it was Mark who had given him Mattie.

Tugger sat looking at the portrait. 'Where did Mark say he met Mattie?'

'The Yale Club.'

'She went to Yale? When?'

'No, she was just there.'

'She and Mark were both in L.A. the year before.'

'It's a big town.'

'You know more about her family than she does — '

'What are you getting at, Tugger?'

Tugger blurted out: 'Channie, are you going to marry her?'

'Yes . . . Is that a problem?'

' . . . I hope not.'

But there were problems. Chanler's mother, alarmed by the speed of the engagement, let Mattie know in a general way of her fears that some lower-class girl would try to marry Chanler for his money. Mattie sweetly replied that she hoped Mrs. Swaine would do everything in her considerable power to thwart that tragedy. Even Mrs. Swaine, something of an East Side fixture and by her own proud admission a snob, could have no social objection to her son's choice. Mrs. Swaine still believed it took four generations to make a gentleman, which gave Mattie's father, DeWitt Rawlings IV, the rights to that title, even if he had drunk himself to death in a succession of cheap motel rooms, having long since squandered what little of the copper fortune his father hadn't managed to mislay in the Crash of '29. Society had lost track of the Rawlings since they'd moved west, and downhill. The Rawlings's house on Fifty-third Street had fallen to the wreckers' ball, their country estate was a girls' school, and who knew where the gold gown of Dido, so heavy with real jewels, had gotten to. Nevertheless, they had had a name, and that still meant something, at least to New Yorkers like Mrs. Swaine.

Mattie, the only child born to her father in his late middle age, was, she said, the last of the Rawlings. She worked at Sotheby's and roomed with two other pretty young women in a Chelsea walk-up the size of one of the bathrooms at the Parnassus Club. She had no great stake in either job or apartment but, nevertheless, the first three times Chanler proposed, she declined. Nearly a year went by before she said yes. It was this firm reluctance that finally won over his mother, who confessed to her minister that she'd originally thought Mattie a gold-digger, but the gold had been lying around for the picking a long time, untouched, and what fortune hunter of Mattie's generation would have the patience not to pounce at once.

Everyone seemed to like Mattie except, more and more obviously, Tugger. Finally Chanler had to warn his best friend to stop challenging Mattie with questions about her past. Tugger defended his reservations. Why should she object to such straightforward questions? He offered to resign as Chanler's best man, but Chanler told him not to be silly.

That Christmas, the engagement was announced at the BGC, to which Chanler and Mattie came dressed as Nick and Nora Charles, although everyone thought they were Fred Astaire and Ginger Rogers. Mrs. Swaine's friends were struck by Mattie's beauty and congratulated Chanler. In the end it was Mrs. Swaine herself who insisted on (and financed — Mattie didn't have a cent) the formal wedding at the Fifth Avenue church. She also paid for the big reception at the Parnassus Club. Her wedding present to

Chanler was to frame the life-size painting of Mattie he'd commissioned and to hang it in the town house — the bottom floors of which Mrs. Swaine planned to turn over to the newlyweds when they returned from their month-long honeymoon cruise in the Mediterranean.

The wedding itself was perfect. The trouble began at the reception. People commented on Tugger Whitelaw's toast to Chanler and Mattie, filled with curiously ominous fears for his friend's happiness. They couldn't help but notice his intense quarrel with the bride off in a corner (where no one could hear what they were arguing about), which was broken up by Mark, with whom Tugger also quarreled. Afterward, the best man abruptly left the party, despite his duties, presumably too upset over the loss of his sole fellow bachelor to stay. The older Mrs. Swaine then took the younger Mrs. Swaine aside for a few words about finances that the bride said she found insulting; Chanler's mother said they weren't accusations, merely clarification. All of Chanler's money was in Mrs. Swaine's control, not her son's. In the event of a divorce, or even an indiscretion, Mattie should expect to leave the marriage as unencumbered by wealth as she had entered it.

Later on, a drunken Mark offended Chanler's mother by his boorish conduct on the dance floor; he kept cutting in on the bride until Mrs. Swaine finally asked two friends to take him home. He kicked over a chair as they dragged him out. Chanler's mother announced to her minister that Mark Toral was no gentleman, he just looked like one — usually a successful substitute on social occasions, but only as long as one stayed sober. It was soon after this that Mattie realized that she'd lost her heirloom bracelet. She was as close to frantic as anyone had ever seen her. Chanler was distressed by her loss. The ballroom was searched to no avail. Sadly, despite its value, it wasn't insured.

By morning, as the newlyweds left to fly to Athens, Mattie had recovered her typical cheerfulness. She was even conciliatory toward Tugger when he showed up at the airport to apologize for his behavior at the reception. Mattie had even kissed Tugger on the cheek, then gone off to buy magazines so the friends could be alone. It was then that Tugger gave Chanler a special present; it was a daguerreotype of Mrs. DeWitt Rawlings that Tugger had located through an autograph dealer. Dated the night of the Vanderbilt ball, taken during that event, it showed her in her Dido gown, looking exactly like the portrait painted a year later, down to the rubies in the hair and the ruby bracelet. Tugger and Chanler embraced, reminding one another that they'd always be friends.

On the flight, Chanler didn't mention Tugger's gift. Nor did he ask what Mattie and Tugger had fought about at the reception. Chanler was never one to invade privacy, to gossip, to confide suspicions that he considered unjustified.

Two weeks after their honeymoon ship sailed out of Athens, Mattie gave Chanler a present as well. They'd had a good morning climbing among the ruins of Delos, then Chanler had returned to the ship for a swim while she went alone into Mykonos to do some shopping. She was gone so long she almost missed the last tender back to the ship. Now, as they pulled away from the island's postcard hills of white houses, the newlyweds stretched out on their private balcony on deck chairs whose cushions were as blue as the sky and the sea. 'Are you happy, Mr. Swaine?' Mattie asked him, raising her champagne flute to his. He nodded; he'd never been this happy. She toasted him. 'I was almost this happy one day in my life,' she confided. 'It was a doll, a stupid doll I wanted like crazy, a very expensive Madame Alexander doll, and my dad kept telling me we couldn't afford it.'

'But you got it?'

She smiled at him. 'I stole it . . . Does that shock you? I bet you've never stolen anything.'

He shook his head. 'I guess I never wanted anything that much, till I met you.'

Mattie leaned over, kissed Chanler, then handed him a cheerfully wrapped package. 'Here, I want to give you something for a change.'

He took her hand and kissed the wrist, near where she had once worn the ruby bracelet. She was still upset about its loss; no doubt, thought Chanler, because she had held on to so little of her past. It apparently had been a painful one; she'd once described 'memory lane' as 'a real nightmare alley.' He'd seen a few things in her apartment: family photos, her father's watch and cuff links, old books, a couple of letters her father had written her, and a few that his father had written him. Her present for Chanler was a part of that past. Among the jumble of odds and ends of furniture stored by her father in a friend's garage, she'd found an old suitcase. There was something in it she thought Chanler would enjoy seeing.

Chanler carefully opened the package,

taking out a battered travel journal, its leather covers cracked and dry. In faded ink, in thin, regular script, it was dated 1883 and inscribed *DeWitt Rawlings, Vol. 3*. Chanler read the first entry aloud.

> After the remarkable ruins at Mycenae, Eleusis is at first sight something of a disappointment. Still, it is fresh territory for us, and Trimmer is confident we shall have a successful dig. I miss Diana dreadfully. It is hard, as she says, that we should be separated these two months after so brief a time together. But I couldn't back out of this chance, having waited so long for a respite in my responsibilities to family business. Trimmer's team is the absolute best in the field, and working under them I am learning at such a great rate that Trimmer pleasantly jokes that all the new copper my father dug up has robbed the academy of a good digger of old bronze.

Chanler looked up, thrilled. Diana Rawlings's husband, DeWitt, the grandfather of Mattie's dad, had kept a diary on that Mediterranean voyage to ancient archaeological sites — the trip that had brought him back to the States, unknown to his wife, too late to attend Mrs.

Vanderbilt's ball. 'The perfect present,' said Chanler.

She smiled. 'But what else from the perfect wife? . . . Don't stay out here long. With that sunburn you'll get a chill. And a storm's coming.'

'Thank you.' He smiled.

Mattie turned, the white caftan caught by the Mediterranean breeze, blew a kiss. Then she was gone, headed to the ship's spa, to make herself beautiful for the captain's table tonight. He teased that it was a waste to spend so much time off at that spa; what could they do to improve her?

Chanler settled in his deck chair and re-opened the journal. On the surface DeWitt Rawlings was a contained, ironical man, whose meticulous notes about broken shards of the Peloponnesian past filled the bulk of his diary. But flaring up now and then from the yellowed pages were the man's two passions — his love of Greek art and his love of his young wife.

Diana says she has received not a single visit from anyone in my family. Their snobbery and cruelty disgust me. How can they not see her worth? I know they still think me mad for marrying her, and no doubt had Father not passed away before I met her, it might well have cost me his estate. But I would happily trade all the copper in this earth, and a thousand times more, to have her in my life. Before her there was nothing and, without her, nothing again.

As he read, Chanler could see that DeWitt Rawlings was not blind to his wife's shortcomings, her vanity, ambitions, propulsive desires; he simply loved her so much that everything in her nature gave him pleasure: *Diana has met a painter who has flattered her into a commission. How she likes to have her beauty appreciated. And why shouldn't she?* And then this:

Letter from Diana waiting here at the hotel, sent on from Athens. She talks of nothing but an idiotic ball Alva Vanderbilt is planning, at God knows what cost to poor Willie. My darling obviously would give her soul to be included and keeps hurling hints, heavy as cannonballs, that I might, even from this distance, somehow manage to get her invited, and adorned, no doubt, like Cinderella in some astonishing gown for which Lanouette will triple-charge her. I've decided to write Ted DeLancey to ask a favor. He and his wife go everywhere; indeed, one wonders when he has time to compose his sermons.

This morning, we unearthed a bronze mirror, nearly intact, with a figure of Eros at its base. A great excitement.

Chanler was mesmerized, reading the journal on the balcony, with the Mediterranean sun like a great blood orange set on the blue plate of the ocean. Here was the actual life only hinted at in the public records, the microfiche of old newspapers where he had first searched for the facts behind the painting. He read on, page after page of the dead man's diary, finding, among the lists of Attic amphora fragments, DeWitt's poignant hopes for children with Diana. Then, near the end of the entries, Chanler came to a page that stopped him cold. He shivered, looked up; the sun had gone down, and his burn was chilling him in the cooler air.

After hurriedly dressing, Chanler got out the little daguerreotype of Mrs. Rawlings that Tugger had given him at the airport and took it to the ship's library, where he'd noticed a magnifying glass beside a globe. He found it and carefully examined the figure of Diana Rawlings in the old photo. Chanler had guessed right. She had lied. At the brief inquest that followed her husband's death, she'd testified that she had not known that his ship had already docked before she left for the Vanderbilt ball, nor, she'd said, was there any indication that he'd come to their town house while she was away attending the ball. She said DeWitt must have gone for some reason straight to their country home, where he'd somehow fallen to his death. She said it was not until the police officers came with news of his accident that she'd had any idea her husband was not still off in the Mediterranean. None of that was true. Chanler had once checked the arrival time in New York of DeWitt Rawlings's ship and knew that Rawlings *could* have come to his town house that night in time for the ball. Now he knew he had to have been there!

Chanler went to the bridge and asked the captain a question: Would it be possible to verify a specific piece of historical maritime information? Chanler wondered if the time he'd once seen listed for a certain ship to dock in New York harbor on a certain day in 1883 was the scheduled time or the actual time? Yes, the captain thought it would be possible to assist Chanler, who was staying in the most expensive suite on the cruise. In fact, it took only fifteen minutes to learn that the ship had actually arrived ahead of schedule.

With the computer printout, Chanler hurried back up the stairs and along the hallway to their suite. The predicted rain was blowing in, the seas growing rough, and he had to catch his balance against the bulkhead as he went. As he came round a corner, he saw a dark-haired man heading into the elevator. Two women getting off it turned back to look at him; for an instant Chanler had the oddest sensation that the man was Mark Toral.

Back in the stateroom, he placed a ship-to-shore call to New York, to Tugger Whitelaw. He woke Tugger out of a deep sleep and there was a lot of static, so he wasn't sure how much Tugger understood about what he needed him to check out about Diana Rawlings's family. Tugger was happy to do it. In fact, Tugger had already done some research into the Rawlings family on his own. Furthermore, there was a lot he needed to talk to Channie about, though perhaps this wasn't the right time or the right way. Could they meet as soon as the Swaines returned from their cruise next week? Chanler set a lunch date at the Parnassus Club but warned Tugger that he wasn't going to listen to any more negative talk about Mattie. He'd hoped that Tugger's apology for that scene at the wedding reception was the end of it. Parenthetically, Chanler mentioned just seeing a guy aboard ship who'd reminded him of Mark, and he asked Tugger how Mark was doing. Tugger hadn't seen him lately; someone at the club had mentioned that Mark was on vacation somewhere. Tugger admitted that he and Mark hadn't really spoken since Chanler's wedding. 'We had sort of a falling out.'

'Oh?' Chanler said.

'About Mattie, to tell you the truth,' Tugger blurted out. 'Channie, I'm sorry, but I'm going to tell you this one thing and I don't care if you want to hear it or not,' Tugger said, and he told him.

There was a long pause. Then Chanler asked, 'Are you sure?'

'I'm sure. I took it to a guy at Tiffany's. If they don't know, who does?'

Chanler asked Tugger to fax him the information aboard the ship. The storm suddenly cut the connection and the operator wasn't able to get through again. Chanler sat on the bed, trying to decide what to say to Mattie. In the end, he decided to say nothing.

An hour later, when Mattie returned from the spa, Chanler was still seated on the bed in his khakis and T-shirt, looking at the journal.

'I guess you like your present,' she said.

' . . . Yes. Thank you. Did you read it?'

'Glanced at it,' she said, coming close. 'Why aren't you in your tux?'

Chanler held up the diary. 'Diana lied at DeWitt's inquest. I can prove it now.'

'What are you talking about?' She leaned over, took off his glasses, kissed him. 'You know, Mark was right. You're kind of nuts on the subject of my family.'

He put the glasses back. 'I know why she lied.'

'Why?'

'She killed her husband.'

Mattie's head pulled quickly back. ' . . . Channie, come on.'

'No, I'm serious. Diana Rawlings killed your great-grandfather. If that's who he was.'

Mattie stared at him with that strange, straight-on look that was so like the look of Mrs. Rawlings in the painting. 'What's that supposed to mean?' He didn't answer. 'First you're madly in love with her. Now you think she's a murderer. And she's just a painting.' Slowly she smiled and shrugged. 'Okay. So why do you think she killed him? Tell me while we get dressed.'

Chanler followed Mattie back to their bedroom. 'She was having an affair. And he found out.'

Mattie picked out a red dress. 'Oh? . . . Who with?'

'Jacob Zanski.'

'Who?' Mattie sat at the vanity, began applying make-up.

'I told you about him. Remember?'

'. . . Oh, right. The painter.'

'Yes. Zanski, who painted her portrait. They were lovers.' And sitting on the bed, Chanler read to her from DeWitt's journal.

> I cannot shake off Corinne's — ['His older sister, that would be your great-great-aunt,' Chanler explained] — disturbing letter. Her distasteful insinuations about Diana and this Zanski fellow . . . Why shouldn't she walk with him in the park, or picnic with him by the lake for that matter? But Corinne can't bear the thought that the bulk of Father's estate should go to Diana, or to our children if we have them. I've written my sister to keep her base suspicions to herself.

Mattie looked into her vanity mirror, at Chanler standing behind her. 'That's it?' She frowned. Both spoke to their reflections in the glass. 'All that means is her husband's sister tried to make him *think* she was having an affair. It doesn't mean she was. Why shouldn't they picnic in the damn park? And even if she was, so what?'

Chanler looked at her in the mirror. 'They'd been married less than a year.'

'Well, you know what I mean.' Mattie handed Chanler the pearls his mother had given her the night before the wedding. He fastened the clasp. 'What I mean is, how do you get from that to she murdered him?'

Chanler held up the journal. 'Listen. 'This evening in a shop in the Plaka, I found the most extraordinary bracelet, rubies set in twists of gold. Very Byzantine.' ' Chanler paused, looked up. 'The one you lost at our reception.' He read again. ' 'The shopkeeper, a fat, keen-eyed woman absurdly claiming direct descent from Agamemnon, soon had me at her mercy, and I bought the damn thing for Diana. So I've said my good-byes at the dig — Trimmer was so kind as to be disappointed — and we sail in the morning. My return should put a stop to Corinne's innuendoes. Perhaps I'll take Diana to Alva and Willie's party myself.' ' Chanler straightened his glasses, looked at Mattie.

Mattie shrugged at the mirror. 'I guess I don't get your point.'

His mild gray eyes moved down the line of her perfect neck to the white cream of her shoulder. 'You don't? Remember, Diana told everyone she didn't even know DeWitt had returned to the States before she went to the Vanderbilts'. But he brought the bracelet with him. He was bringing it to her. You see? She wore it the night of the ball. That means she had to have seen him that night.'

Mattie reminded Chanler that he'd told her himself that the portrait of Mrs. Rawlings as Dido at the Vanderbilt ball had been painted a whole year after the event. No doubt someone had found the bracelet in DeWitt's effects, had given it to his widow, and she'd added it to her costume when she'd sat for the painting.

Chanler shook his head. 'No. She wore it to Alva Vanderbilt's ball.'

'How do you know?'

'Tugger.'

'Oh, great. Tugger.'

Chanler then showed Mattie the daguerreotype of Mrs. Rawlings taken at the Vanderbilt mansion, the gift from Tugger that she had not yet seen. He pointed out the bracelet clearly visible on Diana's wrist.

'Tugger gave this picture to you at the airport? Why didn't he show it to me?'

Chanler made a gesture; it assumed that she was aware of Tugger's dislike of her and that Chanler wouldn't wish to remind her of that unpleasantness by mentioning Tugger at all. He said, 'She wore the bracelet to the ball. So what happened to DeWitt after he gave it to her? I have a theory about how she killed him.' He watched as Mattie slipped on the red dress. 'You gave me the proof, and I've worked it out.'

She turned for Chanler to do her zipper. 'You'll have to tell me later,' she said. 'We're going to be late.'

While Chanler was starting toward the shower, the phone rang; in the other room, Mattie told him to go ahead, she'd answer it. When he returned, she said it had just been their steward, reminding them they were to go to the captain's table.

At dinner, Mattie was at her most charming, and Chanler was generously congratulated on his marriage to so engaging a young woman.

'Yes,' Chanler said to the banker's wife to his right. 'I was in love with her before I even met her.' Months later, this woman told her husband back in Cleveland (when the 'Honeymoon Murder' made the papers even there) that she'd thought it such a romantic thing for a newly-wed to say.

Mattie left the table to return to their rooms to get casino chips she'd left in their safe; she wouldn't let Chanler go for her. She was talking with a stranger at their door when the steward appeared with a fax that had been sent to Mr. Swaine from the States. Mrs. Swaine said she'd take it to her husband. But when she returned to the dining room, she didn't mention the fax, nor the casino. She suggested they go to the Perseus Lounge at the stern of the ship instead. There were never many people there, and she loved listening to Chanler play his romantic old songs on the white baby grand.

Soon, with the bar closed, they were alone in the place with their bottle of champagne, the storm having driven the other passengers back to their cabins. Waves sprayed the decks and wind rattled the glass windows and doors. Although Mattie was cold, she didn't want to leave; she draped Chanler's tuxedo jacket over her shoulders. She kept filling his champagne glass as he answered her questions about what he'd learned of DeWitt and Diana Rawlings.

Chanler told her that the more he assembled the facts that he'd been unearthing for so long, the more they took the shape of a murder. The old rumors were true. Diana Rawlings was having an affair with the man who'd painted her portrait; in fact, now Chanler suspected she'd been involved with Zanski *before* she married DeWitt; DeWitt's sister Corinne had discovered (and written to inform her brother) that the painter's Battery studio was on the same block as the milliner's shop in which Diana McBride had worked. Zanski had talent but no money. Diana had ambition enough for two. She'd married DeWitt Rawlings so that, with his money and his name, she could make her way in Society, and make her lover's way as well. Perhaps that's as far as she planned the future.

But things went wrong. First, DeWitt's sister saw the lovers together. Worse, Diana found out she was pregnant and knew that if anyone calculated carefully enough (as apparently no one ever did, not until Chanler worked out the arithmetic a hundred years later), it would be clear when she delivered that she'd conceived while her husband was inconveniently on the other side of the Atlantic. So the child had to be Zanski's. Still, Chanler admitted, Diana might have somehow managed to squirm out of everything; DeWitt was deeply enamored of her and refused to listen to her detractors. But something catastrophic had happened the night of the Vanderbilt ball. Somehow, the betrayed husband had been confronted with evidence even he could no longer evade.

Chanler showed Mattie the computer printout that listed exactly when DeWitt's ship had docked in the New York harbor on March 26, 1883. It was a good six hours before Diana would have left with the DeLanceys to walk around the corner to the Vanderbilts' on Fifty-second Street.

'And that means?' asked Mattie, pouring him more champagne.

'That means DeWitt came home, completely unexpected, and caught Zanski and Diana in bed together or doing something he couldn't pretend was something else. Something that meant his sister was right. It was all over.'

Mattie jumped. With a sharp bang, the wind slapped open the glass door, sucking the flapping curtains out into the rain. Chanler had to throw himself against the door to get it closed. He was, he noticed, a little drunk, and he suddenly felt very sleepy. He suggested they go back to their cabin.

'No. Finish your story,' Mattie told him. 'It's fascinating. DeWitt came home that night and saw the lovers together . . . '

Removing his glasses to rub his eyes, Chanler nodded. 'Zanski left the room. DeWitt made it clear the marriage was over. Maybe he lost his temper and flung that bracelet at her. Diana saw herself losing everything. Social position. Wealth. A future for herself, for her unborn child, Zanski's child. I think she made her decision quickly. Her only hope was if no one ever knew he'd been there. Either the servants weren't at home or she avoided them. She pushed DeWitt down the stairs, or hit him with something. She killed him.'

Mattie nodded. 'To stop the divorce?'

'And everything that went with it.'

Mattie stared out at the black night. The wind smashed a deck chair against the glass, startling them. 'And then what?' she asked. 'She picks up the body, hails a hansom cab, hauls him out to their country house, and tosses him off the balcony? Come on!'

Chanler smiled at his wife sadly. 'No, I think Jacob Zanski did all that for her. He took care of it while she put on that gold gown, sprinkled rubies in her hair, and set out with Reverend and Mrs. DeLancey to the Vanderbilts' ball. Funny, if she hadn't been so vain that she couldn't resist wearing the bracelet, her secret would have been safe forever.'

Mattie laughed. 'Sweetheart, sometimes I think Diana Rawlings's life is more interesting to you than your own.' She yawned, turned the empty champagne bottle upside down in its bucket. 'So she steps over her husband's body and heads off to the Vanderbilts'. Pretty gutsy lady.'

'Very gutsy lady,' Chanler agreed.

'That invitation to the ball meant a lot to her . . . But then, maybe that sounds unbelievable to you; like you say, you never wanted anything that much.'

' . . . Except you.'

'Well, darling, you've got me.' She showed him the channel-set, multiple-carat diamond wedding ring they'd bought at Tiffany's. 'And Diana, did she get what she wanted?'

'I think she always did.' After her great triumph at the ball, Mrs. Rawlings had returned home at dawn and waited in bed to be brought the shocking news of her husband's demise. Of course, Chanler wasn't the first to suspect something wasn't right; even back then questions were raised. There were inconsistencies in the evidence, rumors of adultery. But in the end, DeWitt's death was ruled an unfortunate accident. And in the end, despite Corinne Rawlings's long legal battle to contest her brother's will, Diana and her newborn baby, DeWitt Rawlings the Third, inherited everything. Diana never married Jacob Zanski, and their son never knew his father was not a Rawlings but an immigrant portrait painter. Maybe the lovers didn't dare risk marriage. Or maybe their passion was killed by the murder they concealed. Maybe it just wore itself out.

'And that,' concluded Chanler, unsteadily rising to his feet, 'is the end of the story. Mrs. Rawlings died in her bed, a grande dame of ninety. Her son, DeWitt the Third, lost most of the family fortune in the twenties' Crash. His son DeWitt took care of the rest.'

'My dad.'

'So you tell us.' Chanler loosened his tie.

She turned to him. 'Are we talking about something we're not talking about, Chanler? I mean, that is your style.'

'We're talking about pirates,' Chanler said. He made his way to the curved glass of the stern, looked out at the storm waves spuming over the rail. He thought he saw the shape of a man on the observation deck behind some cable housing, but it made no sense that anyone would be out in that kind of weather, and when he looked again whatever he'd seen was gone.

Mattie asked, 'Does it change how you feel about your beloved Mrs. Rawlings, now that you've proven she's a killer?'

Chanler turned back, shook his head, his eyes on hers. 'No, it doesn't change a thing. Funny.'

'Funny,' Mattie said. 'So, what do you do about it, even if it's true? Everybody's dead. And the money's all gone. I didn't inherit a cent.'

'Just the bracelet. And you lost that.' He waited for her to say something, but she just looked at him curiously. Finally, he added, 'Here's something else that's funny. Zanski died in his early forties. In his will, he left a dozen paintings 'to his son.' But since he didn't have a son, as far as anybody knew, and since Diana certainly wasn't about to admit that her little boy was Zanski's son, all the paintings went to some distant cousin. You know how much the last Zanski portrait sold for at Sotheby's?'

She shook her head.

'No? . . . Three and a half million dollars,' Chanler replied. 'Actually, I thought you'd know, working there. I got that figure from a Sotheby's catalogue in your apartment.'

'Oh, maybe I knew it, I guess it didn't really register. Three and a half million? And he was so poor, she wouldn't marry him. Ironic.'

'Ironic. Also ironic that you seem to be a Zanski heir.'

She smiled at him. 'Maybe I ought to get in touch with the Zanskis, then. That is, if you think I'll be needing an income.'

Chanler staggered slightly when he took back the tuxedo jacket she held out; he'd drunk more champagne that he was used to. 'That's really ironic. You'd have to be a

Rawlings to be a Zanski.'

'Chanler, I don't know what you're talking about.'

He smiled at her. 'I'm not an idiot, Mattie; I just love you.'

'I love you too.' She moved against him, pulled him against the glass door, kissed him, then kissed him again. 'I'm going to the casino; see you back at the suite.' He took her arm, feeling suddenly queasy, and fell back into his seat.

Mattie asked if he was all right and, being told that he felt nauseated, suggested that he stand outside just for a minute to clear his head, then they'd go back to their cabin. He said no, he'd be okay, go on to the casino. Handing him the tuxedo jacket he'd dropped, she helped him tug the glass door open. But she didn't follow him onto the deck.

* * *

The croupier congratulated Mattie; she was unusually lucky, and a crowd gathered to watch her win.

Early the next morning, the storm behind them, just before they docked in Santorini, a horrified Mattie frantically called the steward. She couldn't find her husband anywhere!

She said she'd left him the night before in

the Perseus Lounge. She'd assumed he was still there when she'd returned from the casino and, as she'd felt a little seasick, she'd taken a sedative and quickly fallen asleep. When she awoke early that morning, she thought he'd already gone down for breakfast, perhaps even gone ashore. But he wasn't in the dining room, and no tenders had yet left the disembarking station. Besides, his boarding pass was on the bureau, and why would he leave without it? Back in their suite, she realized that there were no traces of his having come back at all last night. She was growing alarmed.

They paged Chanler throughout the ship. There were twelve decks and fifteen hundred passengers, but they searched everywhere. Nothing. They interviewed the morning bartender in the Perseus Lounge, who said when he'd come on shift he'd found an empty bottle of champagne overturned in an ice bucket, and wet curtains caught in the starboard door to the observation deck. They sent out radio messages to all other ships in the vicinity. No one had rescued a passenger fallen overboard.

A solemn captain and ship's doctor spoke privately with young Mrs. Swaine. It distressed the captain deeply to have to ask her whether there was any cause that might lead her husband to take his own life. Stricken, indignant, Mattie dismissed the possibility. Her husband had to be somewhere on the ship. They continued looking. Other passengers assured the honeymooning bride that their prayers were with her, that surely her husband would show up safe and sound. But at three that afternoon, one of the crew found Chanler's tuxedo jacket, still soaked, in a heap under an overturned chair, right beside the rail on the observation deck. And by dusk, when the ship had to set sail for its next port, a man's patent-leather dress shoe had washed ashore. Mattie identified it as Chanler's. Then they found bloodstains on the cable housing. The Santorini police arrived.

The captain felt he should prepare Mrs. Swaine for the probability that her husband — after drinking more than he was accustomed to — had walked out on deck for a breath of fresh air, tripped, and hit his head, disorienting him even further, recklessly climbed up on a railing (despite the posted warnings) and, losing his balance in the rough weather, fallen overboard. His cries unheard, he had been swept away to his death. Mrs. Swaine began to shake violently; the ship's doctor offered her tranquilizers, but she declined. She said she wouldn't give up hope for Chanler's return, but she would call his mother.

Chanler's mother took the next plane to Athens. She and Mattie were a comfort to each other; after a week, they were forced to accept the verdict of the Santorini police. Chanler was dead. His mother's only consolation was that her son's wife was pregnant with his child. She was very solicitous of Mattie, terrified that she would miscarry in her grief. Mattie phoned Chanler's best friend, Tugger Whitelaw, to tell him the news. She asked him to speak at Chanler's memorial service. As soon as she hung up, Tugger took six pages of notes to a friend at his firm who specialized in criminal law and who gave him the name of a homicide detective.

Two weeks after Chanler's memorial service, the detective, a good-looking young man from Queens, paid a call on the younger Mrs. Swaine at her mother-in-law's town house in the East Fifties. Mattie found him waiting for her in the living room, looking at her portrait in the gold BGC gown. It was, he said, a good likeness. The picture hung over the marble mantel, where it had been waiting to surprise Chanler on his return. The widow looked ill despite her lingering tan. Detective Eisenberg wondered if she'd mind a few questions. She wouldn't mind; she'd answered so many back in Greece. But questions about what?

The detective felt it only fair to tell her that certain accusations had been made by Mr. Timothy Whitelaw. Mattie confessed she was not surprised. Tugger had always been jealous of her, resented her taking Chanler away from him, and was spreading rumors about her even before the marriage. But as Mr. Whitelaw had been three thousand miles away from the site of her husband's accident, she hardly thought he could have anything useful to say about it.

Probably not, the detective agreed. But he guessed Mrs. Swaine knew how it was, how the system made them check things out, even things that probably weren't useful. Mrs. Swaine understood the detective's problem. How could she help? What was Tugger's accusation?

First the detective nonchalantly wondered if she would mind telling him a little about her background: for example, where she and her father, DeWitt Rawlings IV, had lived in California, where she'd gone to school, when she'd first come to New York. He appeared to be almost uninterested in her answers to his bland questions. Mattie noted that she could hardly see the point in them, but she answered pleasantly enough; after about twenty minutes, however, she admitted she was still under an emotional strain, and she hoped Mr. Eisenberg would excuse her.

'No problem. I just got a couple more things here.'

Mattie politely sat back down.

'How 'bout this guy, Mark Toral? What's your relationship with him?'

'I don't care for the insinuation.' She stood back up. 'I assume it originated with Mr. Whitelaw.'

'What insinuation?'

'Don't be coy, Mr. Eisenberg. Mark and I dated a few times years ago. Nothing serious. I haven't seen him since my wedding day.'

Eisenberg looked from her to the painting. 'You sure? See, Mr. Toral is kinda telling us something a little bit different.'

Mrs. Swaine blinked just once, then said that she didn't care what Mr. Toral might or might not be telling them. And now she would ask the detective to leave. He stood, rummaging through his jacket pockets until he found a balled-up handkerchief. Mattie's face stayed perfectly still as Eisenberg pulled out the bracelet of rubies twisted in gold. 'Mr. Whitelaw says he found this thing of yours at your wedding reception.' Eisenberg pointed at the portrait, where the same bracelet circled Mattie's perfect white wrist.

Mattie reached for the bracelet. 'Found it? I suspect he stole it.'

'Could be. He admits he wanted it real bad. Had an idea about it. Maybe,' Detective Eisenberg said, 'you could help me out with that. According to Mr. Whitelaw — '

She surprised him by interrupting. 'It's fake.'

Detective Eisenberg lost his bearings for a moment, not expecting the admission. 'You admit you told folks that this was a bracelet your dad inherited from some turn-of-the-century lady named Diana Rawlings, and that wasn't true?' She nodded. 'Well, then you know what the problem is. Mr. Whitelaw's appraiser at Tiffany's claims it's a couple of years old. And it's paste.'

'That's right.' Mattie looked at the young man coolly. Finally she said, ' . . . So?'

'So.' He smiled.

'So, what's this got to do with Mark Toral?'

'That's what I need you to come to the station and tell me, Mrs. Swaine. Mr. Whitelaw's got his ideas. And I've had a lot of talks with your friend Mark and he's says he was on that honeymoon ship, whereas you'd think three would be a crowd. Which I guess is what he was thinking too. But the version I really want to hear is yours, ma'am. For instance, how 'bout telling me what's your real name?'

'Mrs. Chanler Swaine,' she replied.

'Yeah.' He nodded at her slowly. 'I guess that's true.'

Mattie walked to the door. 'I think I'll call my attorney, Mr. Eisenberg. Would you excuse me?'

'No problem.' He sat down, facing the portrait.

In the end, Mattie confessed to a number of things. But not the murder. And only the murder was a crime. Besides, Mark Toral had already confessed to that, before his lawyer could stop him. Tugger told him that he should have known from his love of film noir that he didn't have anywhere near the nerves of Mattie Rawlings Swaine — born Madeline Gart — and that she'd throw him over in the end. Mark insisted Mattie knew nothing about his killing Chanler and she agreed with him, but they put her on trial anyhow. Many were sympathetic to Mattie, especially the elderly Mrs. Swaine, who'd lost her only child and lived for the birth of her grandchild. Mattie asked their friends to forgive Tugger's animosity to her; he'd lost his best friend and was irrational from grief. She could understand.

'The Honeymoon Murder,' the papers

called it. Tugger sat in the courtroom day after day, taking notes as Mattie admitted the things Tugger had helped the prosecution already prove. Of course, she and her defense team put a very different construction on them. In their version Mattie had been a poor, hardworking young woman seduced by a good-looking sophisticate (Mark) into playing a prank on his friend Chanler (by pretending to be descended from Diana Rawlings). In their version, during the playing of this prank, she'd fallen in love with Chanler and broken off with Mark. But she'd been too ashamed to confess her original lie and so allowed Chanler to go on believing she was a Rawlings when she was no more real than the bracelet. She'd tried over and over to say no to his marriage proposals, feeling unworthy, but she'd loved him so much. She cried when she said that. Her defense attorney told her she was fantastic on the stand.

The prosecution told a very different story. According to the prosecution, Madeline Gart had met Mark at a cigar and martini club in Los Angeles and had promptly started an affair with him, one of many she'd had, despite her youth. Mark had just been let go from his job in his uncle's brokerage firm for buying a stock he was sure was going to double, with funds he was sure no one would find out didn't belong to him; his uncle covered the loss. Madeline was at a shop in Beverly Hills, selling to naive millionaires in search of a heritage overpriced antiquarian prints and autographs, many of them forged, some of them by her — by no means her first con, despite her youth. She had a knack for such things.

Mark fell in love; he wanted to marry Mattie. She declined, and he didn't take it well. The second time he came to her apartment and caused a scene, she had her neighbor throw him in the pool. She refused to answer his calls when he tried to apologize.

Around this time, the alcoholic DeWitt Rawlings IV came into Mattie's store to try to sell off little bits of his past, just enough to allow him to finish drinking himself to death. From Rawlings, Mattie learned how amazingly she resembled the portrait of his grandmother Diana that was hanging in a place called the Parnassus Club back in New York. He invited her out for a drink and, sensing something big yet undefined in this connection, Mattie said yes. The lonely, childless, dying old man developed a kind of crush on her; she would listen for hours to all the stories about his once-grand family, including the old rumors about the famous painter Jacob Zanski. One day he brought Mattie his grandfather's 'Mediterranean journal' and she read it, much more closely than she'd admitted to Chanler. If she'd noticed the implication that Mrs. Rawlings was a murderer, it didn't interest her. What interested her was that Mrs. Rawlings had slept with Zanski. She got an idea. If she could 'prove' that Diana's son, DeWitt Rawlings III, was really the son of Jacob Zanski, and 'prove' that she, Mattie, was the daughter of DeWitt Rawlings IV, then Mattie was in line to inherit, not Rawlings money (there wasn't any), but Zanski money (there were dozens of Zanski portraits still in the private collection of the family of a distant cousin who'd wrongly inherited them, and they were worth millions of dollars each). Rawlings grew quite dependent on Mattie in his last months; she was very sweet to him, his only visitor. She had pictures taken of them together. She pored over his letters, photos, little mementos, and the day he died, she took them all. She was in a way his only heir. For with Rawlings now in no position to argue, Mattie was set to become a Zanski by claiming to be Rawlings's daughter; she worked on the plan patiently for over a year, including the forging of the legal documents and personal letters needed to make her case.

And here — as the prosecutor said — here's the thing about successful con artists like Madeline Gart. After all that preparation to file her claim to be the true Zanski heir, she threw the whole plan away. Why? Because something better came along, something simpler and quicker and much, much less risky. That something was Chanler Swaine.

By this point Mark had returned to New York, but he wasn't over Mattie. He called her, sent her roses, told her he was back on his feet: A college friend (Chanler) had helped him secure a job in the best brokerage firm in Manhattan. Mark wanted Mattie to move to New York and marry him. She said no, but she didn't hang up. Then one night during their phone talk, Mark happened to mention his friend Chanler's fascination with the painting of Diana Rawlings in the Parnassus Club, where Mark, too, was now a member; he mentioned it to Mattie because she'd told him she was supposed to resemble the portrait, and he wanted her to know that she certainly did.

According to the prosecution, it was this news about Mark's very wealthy friend's peculiar obsession with Diana Rawlings that gave Mattie her next idea.

To Mark's delight, she decided to come

East. She found a job at Sotheby's. (Her recommendations — most of them forged — were impressive.) She and Mark resumed their affair. Although she refused to live with him, they went out nearly every night; they both had expensive tastes in restaurants and a reckless habit of betting extravagantly on horses with large odds. Soon Mark was playing the market to try to cover his credit cards; it didn't work. It was then that Mattie told him the new plan. It was simple. Since Mark was always trying to find a girl for the reluctant Chanler, it would be easy for him to introduce Chanler to Mattie Rawlings. His bizarre infatuation with the portrait would make things even easier. She would marry Chanler, divorce him, keep half his assets and, after a decent interval, return to Mark. Mark didn't like the part that involved her marrying Chanler, but by now he would do anything Mattie wanted. She had Mark bring her to the Parnassus Club, where they took a photograph of the portrait of Diana Rawlings in order to have a cheap copy made of the bracelet in the picture.

Chanler was smitten the moment he saw her in the Parnassus Club. The rest, said the prosecutor, was as easy as Mattie predicted: She seduced Chanler Swaine through her resemblance to Mrs. Rawlings, whose descendant she pretended to be. She married Chanler Swaine for his money. But when she learned that Chanler's mother would stop her from getting the money if she divorced Chanler or was caught out in an affair, she had to change her plan. Now, claimed the prosecutor, she needed to maneuver her lover, Mark Toral, into killing her husband. She began by telling Mark at the wedding reception that she was going to try to make the marriage to Chanler work.

The day after Mattie and Chanler left on their honeymoon, a disconsolate Mark flew to Athens and, according to his confession, tracked down their ship. He admitted to a fatal passion for Mattie that made the reality of her marriage to another man unbearable. He began calling the ship and, finally, at Mykonos, she agreed to meet him, which she did on her island 'shopping trip.' It was then that she told Mark that divorcing Chanler would not solve their problems; his mother had taken care of that. She was going to stay with her husband, and Mark had to leave them alone. Forever. Then she kissed him. And kissed him again. How, she whispered, could she ever give him up? She agreed to meet him onboard and gave him Chanler's pass so he could board the ship. According to the prosecutor, she knew exactly what she was doing. That night, his passion and jealousy heated to a boil, Mark called Mattie, and they arranged to meet. But when Mattie met Mark at the suite (where the steward saw him and later identified him from a photograph), she told him Chanler had grown suspicious; they couldn't risk ever being together again. Not ever. It was over. This was not something Mark was willing to accept and, according to the prosecutor, Mattie knew that. The question was, did she know that Mark was following them, was hiding out on the stern deck, when she took Chanler back to the deserted Perseus Lounge; did she get him drunk and lure him outside? There was no doubt that that was when Mark saw his chance, knocked Chanler out, and shoved him over the railing, then sneaked off the ship with the early-morning crowd headed for the Santorini shops. DNA analysis showed traces of Chanler's blood on Mark's jacket sleeve. And Mark admitted the crime to Detective Eisenberg.

The prosecutor told the jury that there was no doubt that Mattie had put Mark up to the murder. Her defense team told the jury that Mattie was a victim; she had followed Mark to New York because she loved him. Once there, she'd agreed, at his request, to play a foolish but innocent trick on his friend Chanler by pretending to be a Rawlings. But in the process, she'd fallen in love with Chanler, broken off with Mark, and accepted Chanler's marriage proposal. It wasn't her fault that Mark wouldn't give her up. He'd caused such a scene at her wedding that she'd had to ask him to leave (many witnesses confirmed this). She had no idea Mark had somehow sneaked aboard the ship with them in Santorini, and certainly no idea that his violent obsession would lead him to murder her husband. Mattie broke down when she said this, blaming herself for Chanler's death.

The jury believed the defense team. They felt sorry for Mattie, just as the defense advised them to do. There the poor young widow sat, after all, pregnant with her dead husband's baby. After some hours of deliberation, they found Mattie not guilty. Mark would not testify against her. Tugger couldn't get him to see that Mattie had used him. Mark still thought they were in love. Mattie walked out of the courtroom, pausing to nod at Tugger Whitelaw, who turned his back on her. A few days later, Mark was sentenced to ten years in prison for second-degree murder. It was a good deal; there were, after all, no witnesses, no corpse, and possibly no premeditation. The judge agreed with the press, who didn't believe Mark had murdered Chanler for money but on the spur of the moment, driven to the act by his jealousy over Mattie. Mark had the looks of a man who'd murder for love.

Naturally Mattie stayed in the Swaine town house with her mother-in-law. Sadly, the elder Mrs. Swaine, broken by grief, died of a sudden stroke before ever seeing the grandchild she'd been living for. The baby was a boy, with (Tugger heard) very blue eyes. Tugger told Mark about the child when he visited him at the prison. Mark hadn't heard about the birth and was upset when Tugger told him how much the boy looked like him. Mattie, Mark admitted, hadn't kept in touch.

About a year later, Tugger started dating a young woman who worked at the courthouse, someone he'd known back in his hometown in Maryland. She called him Tim. She didn't run with his old group, and slowly Tugger drifted away as well, although a few friends from Yale did give him a bachelor party when he (the last of the bachelors) married the young woman.

He took her once to eat at the Parnassus Club and, on their way out, he ran into Mattie Swaine, hosting a dinner to plan the upcoming BGC. She was chair of the invitation committee, and the chair always hosted the dinner that decided what the year's good cause should be. Mattie was seated beside her fiancé, one of the old group, one of the wealthiest — and although Mattie had plenty of money of her own by now, Tugger suspected she didn't feel it was enough. From the time of the trial, this young man (another friend of Chanler's) had been a staunch supporter of Mattie's innocence, absolutely sure that she had had nothing to do with Mark's 'craziness.' A few months ago, the young man had warned Tugger that if he didn't quit talking against Mattie, they'd have to stop seeing each other. So Tugger walked past the table without speaking to him. To his surprise, Mattie called out, 'Tugger,' and asked if they could talk for a second. She smiled. 'You're looking good, Tug.'

'Yes, I've lost some weight,' Tugger said. 'You oughta go see Mark, Mattie. I mean, after all, he killed Channie for you; it's the least you could do.'

She smiled at him. 'Never one to beat around the bush, were you?'

'No.'

It was a diamond bracelet that Mattie now wore. It looked real, and no doubt this one was. She pointed at her wrist. 'Tug, you remember that fax you sent Chanler on the ship, about how I'd faked Diana Rawlings's bracelet? I'm just wondering, had you told him about it before you sent the fax?'

'Yes. He called me that night.'

'I thought so. He was acting funny.'

Tugger shook his head. 'Is that why you had him murdered? He knew the truth about you?'

She smiled again. 'You think it would have made any difference to Channie? That's *why* he loved me.' She pointed over at the painting above the green marble mantelpiece, *Mrs. Rawlings as Dido. Mrs. Vanderbilt's Ball, 1883*. 'That's why he loved *her*. That was the whole point, Tugger; you didn't get it.'

'I don't think Mark got it either.'

She nodded. 'Mark always had a serious problem with impulse control. He had no patience. He wanted what he wanted and he could never wait.'

Tugger smiled. 'I think he's going to feel that way about getting his son back, too.'

He left her standing there and was convinced that he'd shaken her; not much maybe, and not for long, but he felt good about it.

Tugger's wife was waiting. She looked back at Mattie Swaine, standing alone near the painting of Diana Rawlings. 'I see what you meant. If you hadn't told me,' she said to

Tugger, 'I would have thought they were the same woman.'

He put his arm through his wife's as he led her out of the room. He said, 'They were.'

Ed McBain

The question asked most frequently of writers is 'Where do you get your ideas?' Stephen King says, 'Utica. There's a little shop that sells them.' It's the question we all want answered, and it's the one many authors would like answered, too. They mostly don't know.

This little story by Evan Hunter, using his famous pseudonym, does have a recognizable genesis. He was recently married to a lovely woman who brought many things to their marriage — including a small dog. While the dog and the husband get along wonderfully now, it was not mutual love at first sight. What most of us might fantasize about in the quiet of the night becomes a story idea for an author.

Although this bizarre tale is quite different from his best-selling 87th Precinct sagas, it should come as no surprise at all. He is one of the most versatile writers alive, having written children's stories, science fiction, serious popular fiction, films, and, currently, a Broadway-bound musical, The Night They Raided Minsky's.

Barking at Butterflies

By Ed McBain

Damn dog barked at everything.

Sounds nobody else could hear, in the middle of the night the damn dog barked at them.

'He's protecting us,' Carrie would say.

Protecting us. Damn dog weighs eight pounds soaking wet, he's what's called a Maltese poodle, he's protecting us. His name is Valletta, which is the capital of Malta. That's where the breed originated, I suppose. Some sissy Maltese nobleman must've decided he needed a yappy little lapdog that looked like a white feather duster. Little black nose. Black lips. Black button eyes. Shaggy little pipsqueak named Valletta. Who barked at everything from a fart to a butterfly. Is that someone ringing the bell? The damn dog would hurl himself at the door like a grizzly bear, yelping and growling and raising a fuss that could wake the dead in the entire county.

'He's just protecting us,' Carrie would say.

Protecting us.

I hated that damn dog.

I still do.

He was Carrie's dog, you see. She rescued him from a husband-and-wife team who used to beat him when he was just a puppy — gee, I wonder why. This was two years before we got married. I used to think he was cute while she was training him. She'd say, 'Sit, Valletta,' and he'd walk away. She'd say, 'Stay, Valletta,' and he'd bark. She'd say, 'Come, Valletta,' and he'd take a nap. This went on for six months. He still isn't trained.

Carrie loved him to death.

As for El Mutto, the only thing on earth *he* loved was Carrie. Well, you save a person's life, he naturally feels indebted. But this went beyond mere gratitude. Whenever Carrie left the house, Valletta would lie down just inside the door, waiting for her to come home. Serve him a hot pastrami on rye, tell him, 'Come, Valletta, time to eat,' he'd look at me as if he'd been abandoned by the love of his life and never cared to breathe again. When he heard her car in the driveway, he'd start squealing and peeing on the rug. The minute she put her key in the lock, he jumped up in the air like a Chinese acrobat, danced and pranced on his hind legs when she opened the door, began squealing and leaping all around her until she knelt beside him and scooped him into her embrace and made comforting little sounds to him: 'Yes, Valletta, yes, Mommy, what a good boy, oh, yes, what a beautiful little puppyboy.'

I used to joke about cooking him.

'Maltese meatloaf is delicious,' I used to tell Carrie. 'We'll pluck him first, and then wash him real good, and stuff him and put him in the oven for what, an hour? Maybe forty-five minutes, the size of him. Serve him with roast potatoes and — '

'He understands every word you say,' she'd tell me.

Damn dog would just cock his head and look up at me. Pretended to be bewildered, the canny little son of a bitch.

'Would you like to be a meatloaf?' I'd ask him.

He'd yawn.

'You'd better be a good dog or I'll sell you to a Filipino man.'

'He understands you.'

'You want to go home with a Filipino man?'

'Why do you talk to him that way?'

'In the Philippines they *eat* dogs, did you know that, Valletta? Dogs are a delicacy in the Philippines. You want to go home with a Filipino man?'

'You're hurting him.'

'He'll turn you into a rack of Maltese

chops, would you like that, Valletta?'

'You're hurting *me*, too.'

'Or some breaded Maltese cutlets, what do you say, Valletta? You want to go to Manila?'

'Please don't, John. You know I love him.'

Damn dog would rush into the bathroom after her, sit by the tub while she took her shower, lick the water from her toes while she dried herself. Damn dog would sit at her feet while she was peeing on the toilet. Damn dog would even sit beside the bed whenever we made love. I asked her once to please put him out in the hall.

'I feel as if there's a *pervert* here in the bedroom watching us,' I said.

'He's not watching us.'

'He's sitting there *staring* at us.'

'No, he's not.'

'Yes, he is. It embarrasses me, him staring at my privates that way.'

'Your privates? When did you start using *that* expression?'

'Ever since he started staring at it.'

'He's not staring at it.'

'He is. In fact, he's *glaring* at it. He doesn't like me making love to you.'

'Don't be silly, John. He's just a cute little puppydog.'

One day, cute little puppydog began barking at *me*.

* * *

I came in the front door, and the stupid little animal was sitting smack in the middle of the entry, snarling and barking at me as if I were a person come to read the gas meter.

'What?' I said.

He kept barking.

'You're barking at *me*?' I said. 'This is *my* house, I *live* here, you little shit, how *dare* you bark at me?'

'What is it, what is it?' Carrie yelled, rushing into the hallway.

'He's barking at me,' I said.

'Shhh, Valletta,' she said. 'Don't bark at John.'

He kept barking, the little well-trained bastard.

'How would you like to become a Maltese hamburger?' I asked him.

He kept barking.

* * *

I don't know when I decided to kill him.

Perhaps it was the night Carrie seated him at the dinner table with us. Until then, she'd been content to have him sitting at our feet like the despicable little beggar he was, studying every bite we took, waiting for scraps from the table.

'Go ahead,' I'd say, 'watch every morsel we put in our mouths. You're *not* getting fed from the table.'

'Oh, John,' Carrie would say.

'I can't enjoy my meal with him staring at me that way.'

'He's not staring at you.'

'What do you call what he's doing right this minute? Look at him! If that isn't staring, what is it?'

'I think you're obsessed with this idea of the dog staring at you.'

'Maybe because he *is* staring at me.'

'If he is, it's because he loves you.'

'He doesn't love me, Carrie.'

'Yes, he does.'

'He loves *you*.'

'He loves you, too, John.'

'No, just you. In fact, if you want to talk about obsession, *that's* obsession. What that damn mutt feels for you is *obsession*.'

'He's not a mutt, and he's not obsessed. He just wants to be part of the family. He sees us eating, he wants to join us. Come, Valletta, come sweet puppyboy, come little Mommy, come sit with your family,' she said, and hoisted him off the floor and plunked him down on a chair between us.

'I'll get your dish, sweet babypup,' she said.

'Carrie,' I said, 'I will not have that mutt sitting at the table with us.'

'He's not a mutt,' she said. 'He's purebred.'

'Valletta,' I said, 'get the hell off that chair or I'll — '

He began barking.

'You mustn't raise your hand to him,' Carrie said. 'He was abused. He thinks you're about to hit him.'

'*Hit* him?' I said. 'I'm about to *kill* him!'

The dog kept barking.

And barking.

And barking.

I guess that's when I decided to do it.

* * *

October is a good time for dying.

'Come, Valletta,' I said, 'let's go for a walk.'

He heard me say 'Come,' so naturally he decided to go watch television.

'Is Daddy taking you for a walk?' Carrie asked.

Daddy.

Daddy had Mr. Smith and Mr. Wesson in the pocket of his bush jacket. Daddy was going to walk little pisspot here into the woods far from the house and put a few bullets in his head and then sell his carcass to a passing Filipino man or toss it to a wayward coyote or drop it in the river. Daddy was going to tell Carrie that her prized purebred mutt had run away, naturally, when I commanded him to come. I called and called, I would tell her, but he ran and ran, and God knows where he is now.

'Don't forget his leash,' Carrie called from the kitchen.

'I won't, darling.'

'Be careful,' she said. 'Don't step on any snakes.'

'Valletta will protect me,' I said, and off we went.

The leaves were in full voice, brassy overhead, rasping underfoot. Valletta kept backing off on the red leather leash, stubbornly planting himself every ten feet or so into the woods, trying to turn back to the house where his beloved mistress awaited his return. I kept assuring him that we were safe here under the trees, leaves dropping gently everywhere around us. 'Come, little babypup,' I cooed, 'come little woofikins, there's nothing can hurt you here in the woods.'

The air was as crisp as a cleric's collar.

When we had come a far-enough distance from the house, I reached into my pocket and took out the gun. 'See this, Valletta?' I said. 'I am going to shoot you with this. You are never going to bark again, Valletta. You are going to be the most silent dog on earth. Do you understand, Valletta?'

He began barking.

'Quiet,' I said.

He would not stop barking.

'Damn you!' I shouted. 'Shut up!'

And suddenly he yanked the leash from my hands and darted away like the sneaky little sissydog he was, all white and furry against the orange and yellow and brown of the forest floor, racing like a ragged whisper through the carpet of leaves, trailing the red leash behind him like a narrow trickle of blood. I came thrashing after him. I was no more than six feet behind him when he ran into a clearing saturated with golden light. I followed him with the gun hand, aiming at him. Just as my finger tightened on the trigger, Carrie burst into the clearing from the opposite end.

'No!' she shouted, and dropped to her knees to scoop him protectively into her arms, the explosion shattering the incessant whisper of the leaves, the dog leaping into her embrace, blood flowering on her chest, oh dear God, no, I thought, oh dear sweet Jesus, no, and dropped the gun and ran to her and pressed her bleeding and still against me while the damn dumb dog barked and barked.

He has not barked since.

* * *

For him, it must seem as if she's gone someplace very far away, somewhere never even remotely perceived in his tiny Maltese mentality. In a sense this is true. In fact, I have repeated the story so often to so many people that I've come to believe it myself. I told her family and mine, I told all our friends, I even told the police, whom her brother was suspicious and vile enough to call, that I came home from work one day and she was simply gone. Not a hint that she was leaving. Not even a note. All she'd left behind was the dog. And she hadn't even bothered to feed him before her departure.

Valletta often wanders into the woods looking for her.

He circles the spot where two autumns ago her blood seeped into the earth. The area is bursting with fresh spring growth now, but he circles and sniffs the bright green shoots, searching, searching. He will never find her, of course. She is wrapped in a tarpaulin and buried deep in the woods some fifty miles north of where the three of us once lived together, Carrie and I and the dog.

There are only the two of us now.

He is all I have left to remind me of her.

He never barks and I never speak to him.

He eats when I feed him, but then he walks away from his bowl without once looking at me and falls to the floor just inside the entrance door, waiting for her return.

I can't honestly say I like him any better now that he's stopped barking. But sometimes . . .

Sometimes when he cocks his head in bewilderment to observe a floating butterfly, he looks so cute I could eat him alive.

Joyce Carol Oates

As a writer of serious literary fiction, both in the novel and short-story form, Joyce Carol Oates has achieved extraordinary success by any standards of measurement.

In recent years, it seems that an avid interest in reading mystery fiction has influenced her enough so that she has begun to write in the mystery genre — broadly defined, true, but still genuine mystery fiction — with greater and greater frequency.

Having already written psychological suspense novels under the Rosamond Smith pseudonym, as well as a gothic and a fictional account of the murder of Mary Jo Kopechne at the hands of Ted Kennedy, she has recently written My Heart Laid Bare, *an epic novel about a family of nineteenth-century con artists, and numerous short stories about crime and punishment. She has had a story selected for each of the first two annual editions of* Best American Mystery Stories.

There is no reason to think she won't have one in every issue. As one of the shining literary lights of our age, and one of the hardest-working, most dedicated authors in America, she will have earned the honor.

The Vampire

By Joyce Carol Oates

1.

Through the rifle scope the woman's head silhouetted by light drifts like a wayward balloon.

Staring into darkness. Into him.

No. She can't see. The part-shuttered windowpanes, the bright-lit room behind her, would reflect light.

Seeing her own face, her fleshy torso.

Seeing her eclipsed eyes. Seeing nothing.

Now she's sighted through the rifle scope from the rear of the tall narrow house where there's a shallow ridge of grassy earth.

Through the rifle scope hair-fine lines crossing to indicate that lethal spot at the very base of the skull.

His forefinger on the trigger. Squeezing.

Except now seen at an angle, in fact barely seen, through the rifle scope as she moves through the kitchen into that alcove off the kitchen, what is it — the pantry. She's in the pantry. Where there's a second, waist-high refrigerator and a freezer.

That freezer stocked with venison. One of Carlin's fans brought them. Just a token of my esteem. My admiration for your good work. Bless you.

Through the rifle scope the woman's eyes glisten.

Through the rifle scope she's seen now from beneath. Not twelve feet away. Yet (there's music playing inside the house, loud) she hasn't heard a sound, no footstep. His quickened breath, a faint steaming breath in the just-freezing air she hasn't seen and will not see.

No moon tonight. Yes, a moon, a crescent moon (he's checked the newspaper, the weather box), but massed cumulus clouds, gusty autumn, and no moonlight to expose him. In his night clothes. Night-camouflage. Hooded canvas jacket purchased for this night. The color of night.

Beneath the side window, spongy leafy earth. He knows he's leaving footprints, which is why he'd purchased, at a Sears in Morgantown, not the same store in which he'd purchased the jacket, a pair of rubber boots two sizes larger than his own.

Which he'll dispose of hundreds of miles away from the house in which the dead woman will be discovered, encircled by footprints in spongy leafy earth.

Through the rifle scope — is the woman smiling? Smiling!

She's speaking on a cellular phone tucked into the crook of her neck. That slow sensuous smile. Greedy gloating smile. Incisors damply glistening.

Through the rifle scope the crossed hairs, that fleshy face, smiling.

Through the rifle scope moving about idly as she speaks on the phone. Unconsciously caressing her breasts. Smiling, and laughing. Speaking to a lover. One of the widow's lovers. *Since your death. Since she's begun to feed*.

Through the rifle scope the woman's head large as a dinner plate. He wonders will it shatter like a dinner plate. He wonders whether anyone will hear the shattering.

In Buckhannon, West Virginia. On a moon-shrouded autumn night.

How many months, now it's been more than a year, since Carlin Ritchie's death he isn't sure. He'd count on his fingers except his forefinger is in use.

But his arms ache! This heavy rifle he isn't used to, the long barrel. Purchased especially for tonight. His arms, his shoulders, his backbone, and his wrists ache. His jaws ache from that fixed grimace he isn't conscious of, next time he sees his face, examines his stubbled face in a mirror (in a motel near Easton, Pennsylvania) he'll see the creases etched in the skin as with a knife blade. How he's aged.

Through the rifle scope, a woman's torso. Shapely breasts, shoulders. He'd caressed, once: he knows. In layers of clothing, gypsy-clothing Carlin called it, admiring, lovesick, velvets and silks and Indian muslin, long gauzy skirts swishing against the floor. Even at home, by herself, she's in costume. Through the rifle scope laughing like a girl, eager, shrewd, wetting her lips, unconsciously stroking her breasts. Through the rifle scope on display as if she knows (but of course she can't know) she's observed.

On TV it looked as if she'd dyed her hair a darker, richer red. Tincture of purple. Yet streaks of silvery-white, theatrical as bars of paint. *How does it feel? Widow? His name, his memory. Dedicating her life*.

Through the rifle scope, that life. Will it shatter, like crockery? Will any neighbors hear?

But the nearest neighbors are at least a quarter mile away. And this wind tonight. A low rumbling, a sound of thunder in the mountains. No one will hear.

Through the rifle scope she's moving

toward the stairs. Still talking on the phone. Slow hip-swaying walk. She's gained how many pounds since becoming a widow, twenty pounds, twenty-five, not a fat woman but fleshy, ample. Solid. Those solid breasts. Skin that exudes heat. Burning to the touch. He knows!

His finger on the trigger. For in another minute she'll have climbed the stairs. In another minute she'll be out of the rifle sight. He's anxious, on the veranda. Peering through a side window. Risking being seen. Boots trailing mud. Nudging the barrel of the rifle against the very glass. This wide, old-fashioned veranda on which Carlin lay. *Don't want to die. Yes, but I'm ready. I want to be brave. I'm a coward, I want to be brave. Help me*. On this moonward side of the house if there were a moon this October night, which there isn't. *Like God watching over me* Carlin said *if there's a God but I guess there is not*.

Which is why, through the rifle scope, or not, we die.

2.

It might be that I know of a murder soon to be committed, and it might be that I don't. I mean — I don't know if the murder will be committed, if the murderer is serious. (Though he surely seems serious.) Does this make me an accessory? Am I involved, whether I wish to be or not? I don't mean just legally, I mean morally. What's the right thing to do here? Say I make a call to the potential victim, what do I say? 'Ma'am, you don't know me, but your life is in danger. You're hated, and you're wanted dead.' The woman would say, 'Is this some kind of joke? Who are you?' I'd say, 'It doesn't matter who I am. Your life is in danger.' She'd be getting upset, maybe hysterical, and what could I tell her, really? How could I save her, if the man who wants to kill her is determined to kill her? I surely couldn't give her his name. Even if that makes me an accessory. And I surely couldn't inform the police, any police. And anyway — does such a woman deserve to be saved?

My cousin Rafe has said *There are folks who deserve to die because they don't deserve to live, it's that simple. They must be stopped in their paths of destruction*.

I've known about this murder, this potential murder, for less than a week. Never did I ask for such knowledge. I'm not a man who thinks obsessively. I mean, I'm not a man who broods. I'm a tool-and-die designer, I'm skilled at my job, working with my brains and my hands, and when I'm working I'm focused like a laser beam — I put in an eight-hour day (we're on computers now doing three-dimensional design) and when I'm through for the day, I'm through. Like, wiped out. And now knowing of this murder-to-be, I'm having trouble concentrating at work. I'm having trouble driving my car. Even eating. Trying to listen to my wife, to tune in to something besides my thoughts. *She is one of these, an emissary of Satan. A vampire. Must be stopped*. My life at home is a quiet life. We've been married a long time and neither of us will surprise the other except if my wife knew my thoughts she'd be surprised, shocked. Last night was the worst yet. Trying to sleep. Kicking at the bedclothes like they're something trying to smother me and grinding my molars (a habit I'd gotten into when our two boys were young teenagers making our lives hell, but I hadn't done for years) so my wife wakes me, frightened — 'Honey, what is it? What's wrong?' She switches on the light to look at me and I try to hide my face. I know what she's thinking: I might be having a heart attack — her father died of a heart attack at around my age, forty-four. That's young, but not too young. My own father had a saying — *You're never too young to die*. And it's true; my heart is pounding so hard you can feel the bed shake and I'm covered in cold sweat and shivering and for a minute I don't even know where I am. I'd had a few drinks before going to bed and my mind's like cobwebs. I tell her, 'Nothing! Nothing is wrong. Leave me alone.'

What the hell can I tell my wife, who loves me, and who I love, that when she woke me up I was crouched in the dark outside some house I'd never seen before, in some place I'd never been, peeking at a woman inside the house through a long-range rifle scope? A woman who's a total stranger to me? And my finger on the trigger of the rifle? Me, Harrison Healy, who's never even touched a gun in my life, let alone aimed it at another human being?

3.

I never asked for such knowledge, God knows. It was my cousin Rafe spilled it into me like you'd tip something poisonous into a stream.

There I was at the county courthouse. Kind of anxious and self-conscious, first time I'd been summoned for jury duty in my life. And practically the first person I see in this big drafty windowless room in the basement where we're told to wait is my cousin Rafe. Rafe Healy. Who's two years younger than me, at least three inches taller, and thirty pounds heavier — a tall, husky, sort of shuffling man in overalls, a gingery beard and thinning hair sticking up around his head so he looks like (my wife used to say when we saw Rafe, which hasn't been lately) an accident getting ready to happen. Rafe commands attention in any situation because of his height and girth and his mode of dress and that look in his face like a beacon turned on high — his pebbly eyes sort of shining out. He's always looked younger than his age, even with that scruffy beard and hair and the hard-drinking life he's led. And the drugs. Rafe's an artist, you'd have to call him; he does clay pots, ceramics, latch hook rugs, and quilts. He's been written up in magazines and has had exhibits in museums, even in New York. You don't think of a man making quilts, but Rafe Healy is said to be one of the leading quilters in the United States. Nobody in the family knows what to make of him. Mostly, they're sort of embarrassed. You could be switching TV channels seeing what's on and there on PBS there's Rafe Healy's broad earnest sunburned face, he's being interviewed standing in front of a quilt that looks like a constellation in the night sky, saying something weird like *I need to talk to myself when I'm working. Otherwise I'd disappear into my hands, I'd cease to exist.* My wife disapproves of Rafe for a number of reasons and I can't argue she's wrong. Mainly it has to do with Rafe and drugs. Maybe ten, twelve years ago we were on friendly terms and we'd have Rafe over for dinner and he'd think nothing of taking out a pipe, smoking some sweetish-stale-smelling weed right in our living room, and looking surprised when Rosalind got upset and told him to put it out. Another time he showed up for dinner bringing a woman with him, an Amazon-type 'sculptress' in soiled overalls just like Rafe's, loud and sassy. You just don't behave that way if you have any manners, Rosalind says. She's possibly a little jealous of Rafe and me, for we'd grown up like brothers when Rafe's father, who was my dad's younger brother, was killed (in a car crash) and Rafe's mother wasn't well enough (mentally) to keep him so he came to live, age four, with my family. I was older than Rafe and so felt protective of him until he passed me by physically and in other ways, already in junior high school. And in high school he ran with a wild crowd, had a reputation for being hot-tempered and already a drinker, quick to get into fights. Nobody would've figured him for an artist in those years, except Rafe always had a strange imagination, a sort of impassioned exaggerated attitude, as likely to burst into tears if something made him sad as he was to lash out with his fists, face boiling up like a tomato ready to burst, if something made him angry. By sixteen he'd been arrested more than once for brawling, usually with older guys in some tavern or another, and my parents couldn't handle him though they loved him, we all loved him — it was just Rafe was too much for any ordinary family to deal with. So he moved out. Left town. Bummed around for years, up into Canada, Alaska, Oregon, and California and back to the East and somehow he wins a scholarship to the Shenandoah School of the Arts, in Virginia — when he hadn't even graduated from high school! — so that was a real surprise, and nobody in the family knew how to take it except possibly me. I told Rafe when he visited I was proud of him and Rafe said, I remember his words clear as if he'd uttered them just yesterday and not twenty years ago, 'Hell, pride's a risky thing. It 'goeth before a fall.' ' And he glowered at me like I'd said the wrong thing, making him think worried thoughts.

The past fifteen years or so, Rafe's been living just outside town. On a forty-acre rundown farm, beautiful hilly countryside we've been told (we've never visited), with people coming and going, fellow artists, so it's said that Rafe Healy is living in some sort of hippie-style commune, which I frankly doubt — Rafe was never one to tolerate anybody's bullshit. He's a hard worker, maybe a little obsessed. For an artist, as I see it, is one who works nonstop — nobody's paying him for an eight-hour day. You'd have to be a little crazy to work so hard, or maybe it's the hard work that makes you a little crazy. What's sad is that I'm living in town, a half hour's drive from Rafe's place, and we never see each other, who'd once been so close. About five years ago there was a TV documentary about the famous West Virginia artist Carlin Ritchie, who had some sort of wasting disease, and it was a surprise to see my cousin Rafe included in a segment on Ritchie's generation of 'crafts' artists, and to see that Rafe was apparently a friend of Ritchie's; they'd all been at the Shenandoah School together. It made me a little dazed to think of something you could call 'history' (if only 'art history') and Rafe Healy included in it (if only in a brief segment). I called for Rosalind to come and see this on TV, but by the time she got there the part about Rafe was over. I said, 'I don't care what you think of Rafe, I'm proud of him. He's my cousin.' And Rosalind, who's got this sweet, prim little face and placid eyes but never misses a beat, says, 'Makes no difference whose cousin he is. Even if he was mine. He's a loose, careless, dangerous man of no true morals and he isn't welcome in this house, if that's what you're edging toward.' And back in April, just this year, there was Rafe Healy honored at the White House! And this is on network TV, and a big spread on the front page of our local paper so Rosalind, like everybody else in the vicinity, can't ignore it. But she says, 'There were fifty other 'artists' honored at the ceremony, it couldn't have been too selective. Don't tell me there are fifty great artists like Rembrandt or Picasso living in the United States at one time. And there's absolutely no morals at the White House. So Rafe Healy would fit in just fine.' I can't argue my wife is wrong but a few weeks ago for her birthday I brought home a sea-green ceramic bowl purchased at a crafts store in town, she's blinking back tears lifting it from the wrapping paper saying, 'Oh, Harrison — I never saw anything so beautiful.' And she looks at me surprised like I could select something so beautiful for her, and kisses me. How many times she's admired this bowl, and showed it off to visitors, and examined it, running her fingers over the potter's initials on the bottom, RH, she's never caught on whose work it is. And I'm surely never going to tell her.

All this was passing swiftly through my head when I saw Rafe in the jury selection room, a big tall fattish man with gingery hair and beard, bib overalls splattered with what looked like paint or manure, and the other potential jurors, and the brisk efficient ladies who run the jury selection, looking at him like he's either a freak or somebody of local renown, or both. He'd sighted me and came excitedly over to me, shaking my hand so hard I couldn't help but wince, and if I hadn't blocked him he would've hugged me, cracking a rib or two, with everybody in the room gaping at us. Rafe was so happy to see me he was practically crying. His big bulgy pebble-colored eyes shining with tears. We went out into the corridor and before we'd even exchanged greetings, caught up on news, Rafe was leading me out of earshot of others, puffing hard, saying, 'Oh, Jesus. Harrison. This place is like a prison. A morgue. I'm scared here. It's a bad sign I'm here. I don't want to be here.' I said, 'Well, I don't want to be here, either. Nobody does. It's called 'jury duty.' ' Rafe just kept on, in a voice more hoarse and cracked than I remembered, but in that same intense manner, like he's in his head so much, and you're inside his head, too, so he doesn't need to listen to anything you might actually say, 'Harrison, listen. I was up all night. My brain is about to explode. I need to work, I need to use my hands — I work in the morning from six-thirty till noon and I couldn't work this morning worrying about coming here, I didn't even know if I could find the courthouse, it's not even nine A.M. and we have to be here until five P.M. and I'm scared I'm going to explode. All week it's going to be like this, and if I'm seated on a jury it could be longer. I'm not a man who belongs on a jury, not at this time in my life. Oh Jesus.' He whimpered like he felt actual pain. Here I hadn't seen Rafe in years and already I was feeling that mixture of impatience and affection he used to stir in me, that feeling that, in whatever intense mental state he's in, if you can get him to listen to you, which he will sometimes do, you can have a calming effect on him, so it makes you want to try. I said, 'Rafe, it isn't the end of the world, for God's sake. Chances are you won't be seated on a jury, there's two hundred ninety of us and they won't be needing any more than seventy, somebody said.' Rafe was gripping my upper arm; he'd walked me to the far end of the corridor, which was just a deadend, an EMERGENCY EXIT ONLY door with warning red light, DO NOT OPEN ALARM WILL SOUND. He was saying, puffing, his eyes swerving in their sockets, 'I tried to get another postponement but I failed. I tried to get an exemption, I pleaded 'I can't be a juror, I believe in *Judge not lest ye be judged* — I believe in *Let he who is without sin cast the first stone*.' But all I could get when I called the number was a recorded message! I never spoke to a living human being! And that lady who's in charge, she warns me I'll be in contempt of court if I address any judge like that and if I walk out of here like I'm thinking of doing. I don't mind paying the five-hundred-dollar fine but there's a chance I'd be 'incarcerated,' too. Harrison, I feel like I'm going to burst.' Rafe's face was heavy with blood, a nerve or artery was twitching on his forehead, his eyes blinking in virtual panic. I didn't know whether to laugh at him or take him seriously. That was the way of Rafe Healy — of artists, I suppose — they draw you into their moods no matter how extreme, you can see something's truly possessing them, they're in pain and you want to help. I said, leading Rafe back toward the jury selection room the way you'd lead a dazed, upright bear back to his cage (we'd been summoned inside, though I doubt Rafe noticed), 'Come on, Rafe. If I can do it, you can do it. Just calm down. Can't you make some sketches while you're waiting? Work on your art?' As if I'd insulted him Rafe said, 'Work on my *art*? In a place like this? Where I'm being detained against my will? Fuck you, Harrison. I thought you were my friend.'

But he allowed me to lead him back inside the jury selection room where we picked up plastic JUROR badges to pin to our shirts. I was JUROR 121 and Rafe was JUROR 93. We sat in uncomfortable folding chairs and watched, or anyway looked at, a fifteen-minute TV documentary on the justice system in the country, which must've been prepared for junior-high kids, and then we were made to listen to a forty-minute monotone recitation on jury selection by a middle-age female court officer who looked as if she'd been living in this windowless musty-smelling underground space most of her life, and then we were told to wait 'until such time as your jury panel is called.' A TV set was turned on loudly, to what appeared to be a morning talk show. All this while Rafe was breathing quickly, wiping at his damp face with a wadded tissue, sighing and squirming in his seat. He reminded me of one of those hyperactive children no one knows how to treat except to dose with drugs. As Rafe said, he seemed about to burst. What if he had a stroke? A heart attack? He was making me anxious. I'd brought along the morning paper, and tried to read it, and an old back issue of *Time* someone had discarded, but couldn't help but glance sidelong at my poor cousin, with concern. The twitchy nerve or artery in his forehead was throbbing. I wondered if he was on a drug, but, no — if he'd taken any drug it would've been one to calm him down. And he hadn't been drinking, he was stone cold sober. That was the problem, I thought. Whatever was troubling Rafe (which had to be more than just jury duty) was pure and unalloyed, as real to him as a fever burning in his veins.

Every ten minutes or so Rafe would jump up, excuse himself to the court officer to use the men's room, or get a drink from a fountain in the corridor, or just pace out there like a trapped beast. I'd see him glance through the doorway at me, and I knew he wanted me to join him, but I stayed where I was. I'd been nerved-up well into my twenties but I was grown up now, or God knows I tried to be.

If you've ever been drafted for jury duty, you know that what you do, like the lady told us, is wait. You sit, or you stand, and you wait. You're relaxed, or you're restless, but you wait. You wait until you're officially discharged for the day. Somewhere in the courthouse there are judges preparing for trials, at least in theory, and an army of potential jurors has to be in readiness for their use; a juror is a disposable unit, just a badge and a number. In fact, the judges are hearing motions, talking and arguing with their fellow lawyers; prosecuting and defense attorneys are trying to work out pleas and settlements in order to avoid trials. Guilt or innocence doesn't much matter, except to the defendant. Everyone else is a lawyer, and the lawyers are drawing salaries. The court system is a factory that works most efficiently when what happens today is exactly what happened yesterday. I suppose I sound cynical and I'm not a cynical man but this is the wisdom I came away with after my week of jury duty and it's been confirmed by others who've had the identical experience, though nobody who hasn't had it can comprehend — 'But it must be exciting, to be on a jury. At a trial.' That's what everybody says who doesn't know better. The truth is, most potential jurors are never seated on a jury and don't get within fifty feet of any trial. A trial means that a deal between the lawyers couldn't be worked out. If things moved smoothly in the justice system, there would be no trials. Potential jurors would be summoned, hundreds of us, made to sit like zombies in rows and wait hour after hour, day after day, until the week of jury duty is concluded, and we're sent back home with phony thanks and the promise that our payment will be mailed to us within six weeks — a salary of five dollars per day.

Maybe if Rafe had understood this, and hadn't exaggerated the likelihood of being a juror at an actual trial, he wouldn't have confessed to me what he did, and I'd have been spared these miserable hours, a roaring in my ears and my stomach in knots. For in my soul I'm like a newborn baby *not knowing what to do*. It's like my conscience is a sheet of transparent glass and I can't figure out if it's there or not, if it exists. How do I know what's the right thing to do? But even if I do nothing I will have done something. *I'm trapped*.

4.

At 1:10 P.M. our panel of jurors was released for a forty-minute lunch, with severe warnings from the court officer to return on time, and Rafe and I were about the first out of the courthouse; Rafe might've looked like a shambling bear in those overalls, and his facial expression sort of dazed and glassy-eyed, but like a bear the man could move fast when motivated. In the open air he laughed wildly. 'Freedom! We can breathe! Let's celebrate, man.' I didn't think it was a wise idea to drink right then, but like when we were kids I found myself going along with Rafe, Rafe's enthusiasm, so we ended up in a tavern a block from the courthouse. Rafe downed his first beer straight from the can, rubbed his knuckles over his bloodshot eyes, and said, lowering his voice so no one else could hear, 'Harrison. It's meant for me to tell you. I got to tell somebody. I'm going to explode if I don't.' I asked Rafe what was it, feeling a tinge of alarm, and Rafe leaned over the table toward me and said with a grimace, as of pain, 'I'm being forced to — kill someone. I think. I don't have a choice.'

I wasn't sure I'd heard right. I laughed. I wiped my mouth. Moisture glistened in my cousin's beard that was threaded with gray. I heard myself asking, 'Rafe, what?' and he didn't reply for so long I thought he'd decided not to tell me; then he said, his eyes fixed on mine with that look of his of profound sadness, yet with excitement glimmering beneath, that I remembered from when we were kids, and struck a spark of excitement in me, despite my good judgment, 'There are folks who deserve to die because they don't deserve to live. It's that simple. They must be stopped in their paths of destruction.'

'Folks? . . . What folks?'

'From the beginning of time they must've lived. Victimizing the innocent. Do you believe in Satan?'

'Satan?'

'I'm not sure if I believe in Satan myself. Probably I don't. You know how we were brought up — your mom would take us to that Lutheran church, and the minister talked of 'Satan' but you had the idea he didn't really mean it. Like a man speaks of 'death' — 'dying' — but has no idea what he's saying. But I do believe in evil. I believe that there are individuals among us who are evil, who've chosen evil, who might believe in Satan themselves and are emissaries of Satan in their hearts.' Rafe was speaking quickly in his low, hoarse voice, and gripping my wrist in a way I didn't like as if to keep me where I was, in the booth listening to him. A waitress brought us more beers, set down plates before us, and Rafe scarcely noticed. He said, breathing quickly, 'I believe in vampires.'

'Rafe, what? *Vampires*? . . . '

'What the hell's wrong with you? Everything I say you repeat like a parrot! Not actual vampires, of course — mortal men — and women — who are vampires. Who destroy others. Suck away their lives. And even after their deaths — their victims' deaths — a vampire can continue. A man's work, a man's reputation — he can't protect it if he's dead. I'm thinking of a man, a good man, a man who was a great artist, a man who was my friend, who trusted me, a man now dead, who can't protect himself, whom I must protect.' These were like prepared words, uttered with passion. I didn't know how to reply. I felt like an empty vessel waiting to be filled.

So Rafe began telling me about Carlin Ritchie, who'd died the previous summer (I guess I knew that Ritchie had died, there'd been tributes to him in the media) at his mountain place in West Virginia that his second wife had made into a shrine for him; he'd died in 'suspicious circumstances' and since his death his widow was stealing his art, his reputation, claiming the two of them had been 'collaborators' on the important work Ritchie had been doing the last five or six years of his life; she'd hidden away a dozen silk screens — 'Carlin's Appalachia series, some of the best work he'd ever done' — that Carlin had designated in his will should go to Rafe Healy. 'She's taken from me! Stolen from me! Who was a friend of Carlin's, who loved him like a brother! Not just me but other old friends of his, she'd prevented from seeing him the last months of his life, this vicious woman, this vampire, sucking a helpless man's blood, and it goes on and on after his death — 'Janessa Ritchie' she calls herself. I've tried to reason with her, Harrison. I'm not the only one, there's Carlin's first wife, and his grown children, relatives of his — she's cut us all out. She wants him for herself. Herself alone. A great American artist, an artist people loved, now he's dead and can't protect himself — it's killing me, tearing me apart. I have to stop her.'

'Stop her — how?'

'A gun, I think. Rifle. I'm not a man of violence, no more than Carlin was, but — it's like there's a cancer inside me, eating me up. The vampire has got to be *stopped*.'

I was astonished. I was shocked. My cousin Rafe telling me such things! I saw he was serious, dead serious, and I didn't know what to say. There was this queer tawny light coming up in his eyes I'd never seen before. I didn't have much appetite for lunch but sat there staring as Rafe devoured his, a sandwich and french fries doused with ketchup, ducking his head toward his plate, turning it slightly to one side, his incisors tearing at the thick crust of a roll, slices of rare-done roast beef.

5.

This is what Rafe told me, over the broken-up course of the next three days.

'The last time I saw Carlin Ritchie, at his place in Buckhannon, West Virginia, that she'd made into a tourist shrine before he even died, it was eight weeks before she killed him, I swear he pleaded with his eyes — *I'm not ready to die. Rafe, don't abandon me*! Putting out his hand to me. His good hand, the left. Squeezing my fingers. Jesus, I loved that man! Even when I don't remember too clearly, I know I've been dreaming about him. Like last night. And the night before. *Rafe? Rafe? Don't abandon me, okay*?

'How I knew he'd died, a friend called. Mutual friend. 'Carlin's dead, she's killed him,' my friend was screaming. I made calls, I turned on the TV but there was nothing, got a copy of *The New York Times* and there was the obituary across the full top of the page — CARLIN RITCHIE, 49, 'PRIMITIVE' ARTIST, DIES IN WEST VIRGINIA. Now I saw it was real, I started sobbing like a baby.

'That's bullshit that Carlin was a 'primitive' artist. He was a born talent, no one could capture the human face, eyes, soul like Carlin, but he'd trained himself too; there was a phase, when he was in his twenties, he turned out these ugly, wrenching silk screens modeled after Goya. At the Shenandoah School, we were just kids then, Carlin was the 'classicist' — *You can't overcome the past unless you know it*. And he'd quote Blake — *Drive your cart over the bones of the dead*.

'Yeah. The last lines of an obituary tell you who the survivors are. Carlin's first wife was named, and his three grown kids. Then — 'Janessa Ritchie, his widow.' *His murderer*.

' 'Janessa'? — that isn't even her name, her name's something like Agnes, Adelaide — and she'd been married at least once before, and wasn't so young as everybody thought. I found this out later. I never did tell Carlin. He was crazy in love with her, enthralled by her — wouldn't listen to a word against her even from his old friends. Even from his kids. They're the ones who're hurting — she'd gotten him to change his will, leaving her mostly everything and naming her the executor of his estate. Carlin never spent much, money didn't seem to mean anything to him except as a means of buying art supplies, but we're talking millions of dollars here. And the way she's marketing him — we're talking double-digit millions. She's gonna suck that name for all it's worth.

'Sure I knew Carlin's first wife, his family, not intimately but I knew them and counted myself a friend. Carlin had married his high-school sweetheart, both of them just kids when they started having babies. They were together for twenty-six years. Nobody could believe they'd broken up, Carlin was living with another woman — 'That just can't be. Carlin isn't that type' was what everybody said. And it was true, Carlin wasn't. But *she* was — the vampire, I mean. Just took him over. Like she'd put her hand, her nail-polished talons, on the man's living heart.

'No, I don't cast any blame on Carlin. I believe he was enthralled — enchanted. Like under an evil spell. He'd been sick with m.s. — that's multiple sclerosis, in case you don't know — 'mucho shit' Carlin called it — struck him down when he was twenty-nine, just starting to sell his work, make a name for himself, win prizes — and he's in a wheelchair, like that. Except he gets better, he's in remission for a while, then struck down again, can't use his legs, then he's into some holistic health regimen and actually improves — back in remission is what they call it, though in fact, as Carlin said, nobody knows what m.s. actually is, it's like a syndrome, what works for one person doesn't work for another, one person shrivels away and dies in five years and another person can be on his feet, walking and healthy for twenty years — *it can't be calculated. Like life*. But Carlin was lucky, I think it had to do with his attitude, his heart — he just wasn't going to let that disease eat him away.

'First time any of us knew about 'Janessa' — it was a summer arts festival in Virginia, and there was Carlin Ritchie, a guest of honor, without his wife — surrounded by admirers, one of them this strange-looking young woman, this slender sort of snaky-sexy girl, with a constant, nervous smile, showing her gums and white, slightly protruding teeth, enormous dark eyes, you'd have to call them beautiful eyes though they were sort of weird, with bluish, hooded lids, and a way of staring like she was memorizing you. Carlin was embarrassed being with her, that shamed, lovesick look in his face, but he introduced us, saying Janessa's a photographer from New York, very talented, and I thought Oh yeah? and didn't say much. The girl looked about twenty. (In fact, she was over thirty.) She wasn't embarrassed in the slightest. Her eyes hooked on to mine, and her skin gave off a musky heat. She pushed her hand into mine like a squirmy little creature, and there's the pink tip of her tongue between her teeth — Jesus! Did I feel a charge. She said, 'Rafe Healy! I'm sure honored to meet *you*.' Like there was some immediate understanding between us and even Carlin was out of it. I was disgusted by her, but I have to admit sort of intrigued, at that time it wasn't altogether clear how serious Carlin was about her, whether they were a couple, or just together in Virginia. Nobody would've predicted Carlin would leave Laurette for her, after all they'd been through together, and Carlin making money now, famous. I watched Carlin and the girl for the rest of the week, keeping my distance, so Carlin would get the message I didn't approve, not that I'm a puritan or anything, not that I even take marriage all that seriously, most marriages at least — you make vows to be broken, is my experience. But the last night of the festival I got drunk and spoke to Janessa in private, I said, 'You know, Carlin Ritchie is a married man, a devoted family man, he hasn't been well and his wife has taken care of him and before he began to make money she supported him for years, and they've got three kids — keep that in mind.' And Janessa says, all eager and girlish, wide-eyed, laying her hand on my arm and giving me goose bumps, 'Oh, Rafe, I know!' like she knew me, she'd been calling me 'Rafe' for years, ' — Carlin has told me all about that wonderful woman, 'My first love' he calls her.' Janessa lowered her eyes, and made this simpering face like she knew she was being naughty, flirtatious and naughty, but couldn't help it, ' — but I'm thinking, Rafe, y'know? — I'd rather be Carlin Ritchie's last love than his first.'

'With his medication, Carlin wasn't supposed to be drinking. He'd had a whole life practically before he got sick when he drank — serious drinking. Without Laurette around he'd relapse, and in this situation he was drinking, and people were worried about him, but not Janessa — I watched the two of them walk off together, from a party, it was late, past three A.M., Carlin was leaning on the girl, and she had her arm around his waist, she was skinny but strong, practically holding him up, and Carlin was a tight-packed, heavy little guy, those muscular shoulders and torso, but Janessa supported him walking up this hill to the cabin Carlin was staying in, a white-birch log cabin, and I stood in the shadows watching, I don't believe I was drunk but stone cold sober, watching after those two, after they'd gone inside the cabin, and the cabin lights were off.

'Next thing we knew, Carlin was separated from Laurette. He was living with Janessa in New York, going to parties, gallery openings, being photographed by Avedon for *The New Yorker* — Carlin's haggard-homely face, like a kid's, yet he was beautiful in his way, his unique way, like his Appalachian Faces silk screens that made him famous — there's something about faces like that, that touch you deep in the heart. A few of Carlin's friends turned against him, but not me — I'd forgive him anything, almost. Also, I'm not so innocent myself, with women. I wasn't anyone to judge. I never judged *him* — only *her*. It happened pretty fast that Carlin divorced Laurette and married Janessa, let her take over running his life, his exhibits, his correspondence, his finances; let her talk him into buying the house in Buckhannon and renovating it, the shrine to Carlin Ritchie, having it painted lavender with purple trim, and putting up a spike fence with a gate and a little bronze plaque CARLIN RITCHIE RESIDENCE PRIVATE PLEASE so admirers could take pictures of it from the road — 'Jesus, Carlin, it's like you're on display, marketing yourself, how can you tolerate it?' I asked him, I was frankly pissed, and Carlin said, embarrassed, 'It's got nothing to do with *me*. It's just the idea. Janessa says — 'People love your art, so they want to love you. You can't deny them.' 'Hell you can't deny them,' I said, ' — you denied them in the past.' Carlin said, in a flat, sad voice, 'Well — the past is past.' We were talking over the phone, Carlin was in his studio, it was about the only way we could talk and even then Janessa was monitoring his incoming calls, lifting the receiver so you'd hear a hissing breath. Most of the time when Carlin's friends called, Janessa would answer the phone with this mock-girlish greeting, 'Oh *hel*-lo! Of course I know who you are. Of course Carlin would love to speak with you. But — ' and she'd explain how it was a day Carlin had worn himself out in the studio, or a day he hadn't been able to use his legs, or focus his eyes; a day he was 'fighting the demon' — meaning the m.s. More and more when we called we'd be told that Carlin 'isn't available, regretfully.' His sons complained they were told repeatedly, the last fifteen months of their father's life, that he 'isn't available, regretfully.' Yet there was a steady stream of photographers, interviewers, TV and videotape crews traveling to the Carlin Ritchie residence in Buckhannon, from as far away as Japan and

Australia, and these people, you can be sure, who never failed to include 'Janessa Ritchie' in their profiles, were always welcome.

'When Carlin left Buckhannon it wasn't ever to visit his old friends as he used to. After he married that woman, he never came to see me again. She'd take him to arts festivals, to fancy events where Carlin was the guest of honor, black-tie evenings in New York and Washington, but she'd never take him to the Shenandoah summer festival, or anywhere ordinary. Carlin went as a star, or he didn't go at all. She demanded high fees for him, and he seemed embarrassed but proud, too; he'd never forgotten his West Virginia background, he'd been born in a small town twenty miles from Buckhannon, just a crossroads, and his folks were poor; despite the Carlin Ritchie legend that's sprung up, Carlin hadn't been happy in his childhood, I happen to know; not as happy as I was — and I'd lost both parents. (But I had good, kind, generous stepparents, you could say. And even a brother close to my heart.) Janessa wouldn't ever let Carlin talk about his real home, his real folks, everything had to be pretense, sentiment. In Carlin's best work there was always a melancholy tone, like Hopper's paintings, but with more texture and subtlety than Hopper, sort of dreamy, meditative, after-the-fact — posthumous, almost. Like these Appalachian people and places were really gone, vanished. And Carlin Ritchie was remembering them. (And Janessa started taking these phony, posed pictures in West Virginia, 'companion pieces' she called them to Carlin's art, and when he was too sick to prevent her, and after his death, she published them side by side with his work claiming she'd been his 'collaborator' for all of their marriage. Carlin Ritchie's 'collaborator'! But that wouldn't be the worst.)

'The last time I saw Carlin in public, it was a black-tie awards ceremony at the American Academy in New York. Carlin was a member of the Academy, and I was getting an award. And some other friends of ours, from the old days at Shenandoah, the days of our youth, were there. And celebrating. But, hell, we couldn't get within twenty feet of Carlin. He'd cast sort of wistful, embarrassed looks at us — but he was in his wheelchair, and Janessa had him surrounded by rich, important people — 'Carlin's privileged patrons' she called them. It would be revealed afterward that she'd been selling Carlin's work, drawing up actual contracts, before he'd created it; she was getting the poor bastard to sign contracts, naming her as agent, without knowing what he was signing

— he'd always been a careless kind of guy with contracts and money, worse even than I am. We got drunk on champagne and watched our friend Carlin in his tux that made him look embalmed, in his wheelchair that was an expensive motorized chair but guided by this white-skinned female in a black velvet gown cut so low her breasts were almost falling out, strands of pearls around her neck, looking like the real thing, not cultured, surely not West Virginia-type costume-jewelry pearls, her glossy red hair upswept on her head and her face beautiful, radiant — this was the second Mrs. Ritchie? No wonder photographers loved snapping her and poor Carlin, sunken-chested in his chair, wearing thick glasses now, and his right hand palsied, lifting his ghastly-hopeful smile and managing to shake hands with his left hand as 'privileged patrons' hovered over him. Janessa wasn't a skinny strung-out anorexic-type any longer, she'd packed on serious, solid female flesh and looked good enough to eat. Her face was pale as a geisha's and made up like a cosmetic mask, flawless — crimson mouth, inky-black mascara accentuating her big eyes, flaring eyebrows that looked as if they'd been drawn on with Crayola. She didn't look any age at all now — like Elizabeth Taylor in those glamour photos you used to see on the covers of supermarket tabloids, generic female vamp-beauty. Totally phony, but glamorous as hell. I have to admit that Carlin looked happy enough that night, under the sharp eye of Janessa, and her shapely bust nudging the back of his head so if he was nodding off (on medication, probably) he'd wake up with a startled smile. I managed to get near enough to him to shake his hand — hell, I leaned over to hug the guy, and Carlin hugged me, hard, like a drowning man — though the second Mrs. Ritchie didn't like this at all. Carlin was saying, almost begging, 'Rafe? Where've you been? Why don't you visit me anymore? Come see me! Come soon! Next week! Show me what you're doing these days, man! I'm into some new, terrific work — I'm gonna surprise you, man!' while that bitch Janessa is smiling a tight, angry smile, pushing Carlin's wheelchair away saying, 'Mr. Healy, you're over-exciting my husband. He's on medication, he doesn't know what he's saying. *Excuse us*.' And she'd gotten him to an elevator, blocking me from entering with them, though there was plenty of room, and there was the artist Robert Rauschenberg in the elevator; Janessa recognized a famous name and it was like she'd been shot with pure adrenaline, her big hungry eyes glistened, her sexy mouth lost its stiffness, her breasts sort of burgeoned out, there she was cooing and cawing over Rauschenberg, saying how she'd loved his 'big wild collage paintings' since she was a young girl, all the while blocking me, and pretending not to be aware of me, while Carlin looked on, confused and anxious — it would've been a comic scene on TV, but in real life, if you had to live through it, it wasn't so pleasant. Anyway, you know me, I kept pushing onto the elevator, nudging up against Janessa, her perfume in my nostrils like rotted gardenias, and I was trying to talk to Carlin, and Janessa loses control and slaps at me, actually slaps at me, and says, 'Damn you! You're harassing my husband, and you're harassing me! We don't know you! I'm going to call a security guard if you don't let us alone!' I say, 'What the fuck do you mean, you don't know me? I'm Carlin's friend — who the fuck are *you*?' So maybe I was a little drunk, and belligerent, and my black tie was coming untied, but Janessa provoked me, and I'd like to haul off and hit her, except she starts screaming, 'Help! Police!' so I back off the elevator quick; everybody's glaring at me, even Rauschenberg.

'It's then I realize that that woman, 'Janessa,' is my sworn enemy. And she's Carlin's enemy, too. Though the poor guy wasn't in any condition to know it.

'The last time I saw Carlin Ritchie in private, it was at his place in Buckhannon, West Virginia, that I'd visited only once before. This was about eight weeks before Carlin died. I'd gotten a call from him, inviting me down; he was trying to sound in good spirits on the phone, but his voice was weak, and I had the distinct idea that our conversation was being monitored by Janessa, but I was damned happy to hear from my friend, and if I figured anything I figured that Janessa was embarrassed at her treatment of me and worried I might make trouble somehow. So she was allowing Carlin to invite me to Buckhannon. And this was more or less what it was, I think. Also she was preparing to murder him and may have believed she needed some credible witness beforehand, to testify that the poor guy was in bad shape. 'Lost the use of his legs!' as she'd say, in this wailing breathy voice like it was a total surprise to her, or to Carlin, that he wasn't walking just then.

'So I drove to Buckhannon, grateful to be invited if it was only for overnight, and I loaded the van with some of my new quilts to show Carlin, who'd always been a strong supporter of my work, even if it was totally different from his own, and there was Janessa opening the door for me in this weird Disney-type theme house, 'West Virginia gingerbread classic-Victorian' was how she described it in interviews, 'an exact duplicate of Carlin's family home lost in the Depression' — bullshit you'd think Carlin would be ashamed of, but he had to endure it; and instead of my enemy, Janessa was now my friend, or so it seemed — hugging me with her strong, fleshy arms, dazzling me with her perfume and a wet high-school-girl kiss right on the mouth — 'Rafe Healy! We've been missing you! Come *in*! How long can you *stay*?' (Like she hadn't worked it out with me that a single night was the limit.) You'd have thought the scene was being televised; here's Mrs. Carlin Ritchie the gracious hostess, in some long, floor-length, swishing Indian skirt, layers of gauze and silk, red hair tumbling down her back, welcoming an artist-friend of her husband's, a woman who'd sacrificed her professional photography career to tend to a crippled husband she adored. And Rafe's a sap, a sucker; she kisses me on the mouth and pokes me with her tongue and Jesus! — I feel such a charge I'm thinking I'll forgive this female anything. It's a total surprise to me that the mood between us is completely different from what it had been in New York, in that elevator, which I understand now is typical of a certain kind of psychopath, the most devious kind, who isn't predictable from one occasion to another but is coolly improvising, trying out different methods for deception, manipulation, and control. (This would explain what Carlin's children said of her: that sometimes, when they'd spoken with their father on the phone, in the days she'd allowed it, they could hear Janessa screaming at him, or at someone, in the background, while at other times she was cooing and welcoming, saying how nice it was of them to call, how happy their father would be hearing from them — 'And that makes me happy, too!')

'This visit with Carlin, this final visit, was painful to me, but very powerful, memorable — it was like I was in the presence of a saint, yet a saint who was also a good-hearted guy, a friend, with no pretensions, no sense of who he was, what stature he'd attained. Just Carlin Ritchie I'd known since we'd been kids together at Shenandoah, groping our way into our 'careers.' It shocked me to see how he'd lost more weight and seemed to have resigned himself to the wheelchair. His legs looked shriveled, even his socks were baggy. But his mind was clear, sharp. He told me he was supposed to be taking a certain medication, Janessa would be upset if she learned he'd skipped it that day, 'But it makes my head fuzzy, and my tongue so thick I can't talk — so the hell with it, right? For now.' We spent most of the visit out on the veranda where Carlin could lie back on a wicker divan, it was a mild May evening, and it pissed Janessa off that Carlin wanted just to eat off plates, no formal dinner like she'd planned in the dining room, and no Polaroids — 'Janessa is the most posterity-minded individual I've ever known,' Carlin told me, winking, 'she'd snap me on the toilet if I didn't lock the door.' Janessa laughed, hurt, and said, 'Well, somebody's got to be posterity-minded around here. This is a living archive, and you're 'Carlin Ritchie' lest you forget. You're not *nobody*.' Looking sort of bold-provocative at me, like she's saying Rafe Healy is *nobody*. After a while Janessa got bored with us and went inside; I'd catch glimpses of her through a curtained window, drifting around, talking on a cellular phone, simpering, laughing so it seemed to me she must have a boyfriend, sure she's got a boyfriend, a female like that, and poor Carlin a cripple. But I was grateful she'd let us alone, and I could see Carlin was, too. He'd never say a word against that woman but there was a sad-ironic tone of his, a way he'd shrug his shoulders when she said some preposterous thing, his eyes locking with mine like we were boys and some adult female was bullshitting us. But then he'd say, a few minutes later, talking about his new work, 'Rafe, I don't know how I would continue, without Janessa. She hires my assistants, she screens my calls, my business — the world.' I wanted to retort, 'Well, Laurette would know, if you don't.' But I didn't. I knew better. The vampire had her fangs in him deep, there must've been an anesthetic effect, a comforting delusion. I get drunk for more or less the same reason, maybe I shouldn't judge. We just sat out there on Carlin's veranda and talked. Must've been three hours — and Janessa fuming and stewing inside. Carlin wasn't supposed to drink, but he had a couple of beers, and I put away a six-pack at least. It was like we both knew this might be the final time we saw each other. I said, 'Carlin. I wish the fuck there was something I could do, y'know? Like donate a kidney. A spleen transplant. Hell — half my cerebral cortex.' And Carlin laughed, and said, 'I know you do, Rafe. I know.' 'It's a goddam thing. It's fate, it's unfair. Like, why *you*?' I said. My eyes were stinging with tears, I was about to bawl. Carlin groped out for me with his left, good hand and said, like he was feeling a little impatient with me, he'd worked through this logic himself and was impatient I hadn't yet, 'But my fate was to be 'Carlin Ritchie' one hundred percent. It's one big package deal.' Then he started telling me how 'we' — meaning himself and Janessa — were making 'plans of expediency.' For when, finally, he got too sick. Which might be coming a little more quickly than he'd hoped. Stockpiling pills, barbiturates. It would have to be, Carlin said, without his doctors knowing. Without anyone 'legal' knowing. No one in his family — 'They're old-style Baptists, they don't hold with taking your life, let alone your death, in your own hands.' I was shocked to hear this, I said, 'Carlin, what? You're planning — what?' Carlin said, lowering his voice, 'I don't want to be a burden on Janessa. Not any more than I am. When — if — I become 'incontinent,' as it's called, I know what to do.' 'Carlin, I don't like to hear such talk. You're young, for Christ's sake — not even fifty.' 'That's the problem, man, I'm young enough to be around, in a vegetable state, for a long time.' 'You've got more work to do — lots of work to do. What the fuck are you telling me, you're thinking of pulling out?' 'Rafe, I didn't tell you what I did, I didn't share it, for you to condemn me,' Carlin says, with dignity, ' — I didn't invite you even to have an opinion. I'm telling you. That's that.' So I sat there, shaking. I'm an aggressive guy I've been told, I talk before I think, so I tried to absorb this, tried to see Carlin's logic. I could see it, I suppose. Back inside the house, that was lit up like a movie set, Janessa was watching TV and it sounded like she was still talking on the phone. Carlin said apologetically that he'd been thinking, a few years ago, of asking me to be his estate executor if something premature happened to him — 'Laurette was real enthusiastic' — but now of course things were different; Janessa was to be his executor. I swallowed hard and said okay, I could see that, I understood. Carlin said, embarrassed, 'You know how Janessa is — she loves me so. She's a little jealous of me and some of my old friends. I can't blame her, she's a hot-blooded woman, y'know? She's an artist too. She gave up her art for me.' 'Did she.' 'She gave up the possibility of having children, she said, for me.' 'Did she.' 'She doesn't want me to suffer, she says. She's worried sick about me, it's almost more upsetting to her than to me, that I might suffer. 'Interminably' as she says.' 'So you're stockpiling barbiturates for her,' I said, sort of meanly, ' — you don't want her to suffer.' Carlin blinked like he didn't exactly get this, and I said, louder, 'She's rehearsing your death, is that it? She's urging you to die? Has she picked the date yet?' Carlin said quickly, 'No, no — my wife isn't urging me to do anything. It's my own best interests she has in mind. If — when — it comes time I can't walk, can't move, can't eat, can't control my bowels — I don't want to live, man.' 'But that won't be for a long time. That might be never.' 'It might be next month.' 'I might beat you to it, Carlin. It's like shooting dice.' Carlin finished his beer, or tried to — a trickle of beer ran down his chin. He said, shrugging, 'Okay, I don't want to die. Yes, but I'm ready. I want to be brave. Fuck it, I'm a coward, I want to be brave. Help me.' 'Help you? How?' But Carlin laughed, and repeated what he'd said, adding something about God watching over him — 'If there's a God but I guess there is not. We've got to grow up sometime, right?' And I said, uneasy, not knowing what the subject was any longer, 'Hell, no. Not me.' And we both laughed.

'That visit in May of last year was the last time I saw Carlin Ritchie alive, though I tried to speak with him on the phone once or twice. But Janessa always answered the phone, saying in this breathy little-girl voice, 'Who? Oh — you. Well, I'm truly sorry, Rafe Healy, but my husband isn't taking calls today.' 'When do you think he will be taking calls, Mrs. Ritchie?' I asked, trying to keep my voice steady, and she said, as rehearsed as if she was being taped for posterity, 'That's in the hands of the Lord.' '

* * *

At this point, my cousin Rafe paused. He'd come close to breaking down. And I was feeling kind of strange myself — exhausted by Rafe's story, but excited, too. And a little suspicious just suddenly.

We weren't at the tavern near the courthouse, nor in the basement corridor of the old building. As it happened, we were having a few beers in a bar called Domino's; it was early evening of the second day of jury duty, and our panel of jurors had been dismissed that afternoon still without being summoned to any courtroom. Since Rafe had begun telling me his story, though, the hours flew past, and neither of us seemed to mind our enforced idleness. I was so caught up in Rafe's words I could feel pity for Carlin Ritchie, whom I'd never known, as intense as any I'd ever felt for anyone, and I could feel hatred fermenting in my heart for that woman Janessa. I could sympathize why Rafe hated her so but I wouldn't have gone so far as to wish her dead — that's a pretty extreme state after all.

The evening before I'd come home late, past 7:00 P.M., having stopped at Domino's with Rafe, and Rosalind was waiting for me, worried — 'Since when does jury duty last so long? Were you called for a trial?' I'd decided not to tell her about meeting up with Rafe at the courthouse, and I knew it was futile to pretend to this sharp-nosed woman that I hadn't stopped at a bar and had a few beers, so I told her, yes, I'd been selected for a trial, and it was a damned ugly trial, and we were forbidden to talk about it until it was over — 'So don't ask me, Rosalind. Please.' 'A trial! You actually got chosen!' Rosalind cried. 'Is it a . . . murder case?' 'I told you, Rosalind, I can't discuss it. I'd be in contempt of court.' 'But, honey, who would know? *I* wouldn't tell.' 'I would know. I've given my word, I've sworn on the Bible to execute my duties as the law demands. So don't tease me, I'm not going to say another word about it.' And I was feeling so nerved-up, anyway, about the ugly story my cousin was telling me, it didn't really seem that I was lying to Rosalind; there was a deeper truth, lodged in my heart, my cousin's secret he was sharing with me, which I would never tell to another living soul.

But Rafe was shifting his shoulders in that way he'd had when he was a kid, and you knew he wasn't telling all of the truth. So I said, on a hunch, 'Rafe, back up just a bit. To the last time you saw Carlin Ritchie. That visit in Buckhannon.' 'Why? I already told you about Buckhannon.' 'But was there anything more? Between you and Mrs. Ritchie, maybe?' 'That's a crude accusation,' Rafe said. 'Fuck you, man.' 'Well — was there? You'd better tell me.' 'Tell you what, man?' Rafe was defying me, but his pebble-colored eyes were clouded and evasive, and I kept pushing, until finally he admitted yes, there was more. And he wasn't proud of it.

* * *

'Already, by eleven P.M., Carlin was exhausted. Where in the old days he's stay up much of the night talking art and ideas and drinking, now I could see he was ready for bed when Janessa came to fetch him. She wheeled him away to a specially equipped room at the rear of the house, and when she returned she said with a sigh and a sad-seeming smile, 'That poor, brave man. Thank you for making this pilgrimage, Rafe Healy.' Pilgrimage! Like I was some kind of fawning pilgrim. I thought

Fuck you, lady and should've gone off to bed myself (I was staying in a guest room upstairs) except I let her talk me into having a nightcap with her — 'Just one. For old time's sake. So there's no hard feelings between us.' There was this coquettish way about the woman, yet an edge of reproach, too, as if she knew full well how certain people valued her, and was defying them, yet wanted them to like her, at least be attracted to her, just the same. So she pours us both bourbon. She's wearing a gauzy cream-colored dress like a nightgown, and her hair in ringlets like a little girl's, and her eyes like an owl's ringed in mascara, and there was this hungry, ugly lipstick mouth of hers I couldn't stop staring at. *Yes, I knew I should've gotten the hell out of that house. All I can say is, I was drunk, I was a fool*. Janessa slipped her arm through mine and led me around showing off the house, which had been her idea, she boasted, a 'shrine of memories' for Carlin while he was still in good-enough condition to appreciate it. I said, 'Hell, he'll be in good-enough condition to appreciate lots of things, for a long time,' but she wasn't even listening. This cold, sickish sensation came over me that, to her, Carlin Ritchie was already dead and she was the surviving widow, the proprietor of the shrine, keeper of the legend. Executor of the estate. Heiress. She'd been drinking earlier in the evening, too. She showed me this display-case room, a parlor, which was papered in deep purple silk wallpaper with recessed lighting in the ceiling, photos of Carlin from the time he was a baby till the present time (except there was no evidence of Carlin with his first wife or his children), an entire wall covered with framed photos of Carlin and Janessa, posed in front of his artworks or at public ceremonies shaking hands with important people. I flattered the woman by saying, 'Is this the President of the United States?' and she said, pleased, yet a little rueful, 'Yes, it sure is. But it was Carlin he made a big fuss over, not me.' I laughed, and said, 'Janessa, the President would've made a bigger fuss over you, if it hadn't been such a public occasion,' and she laughed hard at that, she liked that kind of humor.

'After that, things got a little confused.

'I mean — I know how it ended. I sure do. But how it got to where it ended — that's confused.

'We were in the living room, which was mostly darkened. And having another bourbon. And this hot-skinned, good-looking woman is sort of pressing up against me like she doesn't know what she's doing. And I'm not supposed to catch on till it's too late.

She's complaining how Carlin's family is spreading slander about her, then she's boasting how Carlin's art was fetching higher and higher prices now it was being marketed more professionally — 'Thanks to my intervention. *He'd* be happy giving it away.' She's complaining, or boasting, how so many folks make the pilgrimage to Buckhannon, a lot of them bringing gifts like needlepoint-Bible pillows, glow-in-the-dark crucifixes, a hundred pounds of venison steak Carlin's too kindly or too weak to decline — 'So it's jamming our freezer. Can you believe it?' 'Well, if people love him,' I mumbled, or words like that. Janessa starts saying how lonely she is amid all this commotion, and how frightened, 'like a little girl,' of the future. How painful it is, married to a man who's not really a man any longer — 'My husband, but not my lover. And I'm still *young*.' There's the pink tip of her tongue between her teeth, and suddenly she's in my arms, and we're kissing, panting like dogs like we'd been waiting for this for hours, for all of our lifetimes and now there's nothing to hold us back. Except — I'm pushing her away, disgusted. The taste of her mouth was like something rotten. Like you'd imagine old, stale blood — ugh! If I'd been drunk I was stone cold sober now, on my feet and out of there, upstairs to get my duffel bag and back down again and there's this furious, shamed woman saying, 'You! God damn you! Who do you think you are, you!' — she slapped at me, shut her fist, and punched like a man; I pushed her away and she lunged back like a wildcat, clawing me in the face, and I was a little scared of her, knowing she'd have loved to murder me, she'd been so insulted, but she wasn't strong enough to do any real injury, didn't have time to rush into the kitchen for a knife, shouting after me from the veranda as I pulled away in my van, 'You fucker! You sorry excuse for a man! Don't you ever darken this house again! You're no better than he is — cripple! *Cripple*!' And a few weeks later, Carlin Ritchie was dead.

6.

On the third day of jury duty, which was a Wednesday, our panel of jurors was taken at last upstairs to the fifth floor, to a judge's courtroom, where there was an aggravated-assault case to be tried. After a ninety-minute voir dire session, during which time neither JUROR 93 (Rafe Healy) nor JUROR 121 (Harrison Healy) was called, meaning that Rafe and I just sat, sat, sat in enforced silence, Rafe so tense I could feel him quivering, a panel of twelve jurors and two alternates was seated, and the rest of us were dismissed for lunch with a severe warning to be back in the courthouse in forty minutes. Rafe groaned in my ear thank God he hadn't been chosen, he wasn't in any mental state to be questioned by any judge.

I wanted to say *If you're so torn up about this, maybe you shouldn't be planning to commit a murder. Maybe you're not a murderer*. But I never said a word. It was like I didn't want to interfere with this strange, scary thing that was happening in my cousin's soul, of such magnitude and danger it could never have happened (I was certain) in mine, as if I didn't have the right, but could only be a witness.

Again we went to the tavern up the street. Again we had several quick beers, to soothe our nerves. Rafe held out his big, burly hand — 'Jesus, Harrison: I got the shakes.' But he only laughed. He said, 'I hope you don't think too lowly of me, Harrison, for behaving like I did. With that vicious woman.' I said, truthfully, 'I believe you did the right thing. Getting out like you did.' 'I drove all night to get back home. I was so disgusted with myself! And with her, for making a fool of me like she did. Jesus, the taste of her! — it's still with me, I swear.' Rafe wiped at his mouth and ordered another beer to assuage that taste; it was almost so I could taste something rotten and bloody-stale on my own lips.

Rafe continued with his story, and now I already knew parts of it, and could feel I'd lived through some of it myself, and was feeling tense and agitated at what was to come. It was like I'd been with him when he opened *The New York Times* to see CARLIN RITCHIE, 49, 'PRIMITIVE' ARTIST, DIES IN WEST VIRGINIA. And Carlin's photo, taken how many years before. The county coroner ruled 'complications caused by multiple sclerosis' but the actual cause of death, as Rafe hadn't been surprised to learn from the Ritchie family, was that, during a siege of bad health, and depression, Carlin had 'accidentally' ingested a lethal quantity of alcohol and barbiturates. 'And guess what? Janessa hadn't been there. Carlin had been alone. For the first time in years, the second Mrs. Ritchie had left her husband out of her sight long enough to travel to New York.

'So she'd killed him and would get away with it. For who was to blame *her*?

'Now, the wake. Harrison, you are not going to believe the wake.

'The wake was held in the shrine-house in Buckhannon, and — Jesus! — what a mob scene. I'd been prepared for Janessa to forbid me to come, and every other old friend of Carlin's, but that wasn't the case — Janessa hired an assistant to call us, wanting to make sure that as many people came to the wake and funeral as possible. Even Carlin's first wife and children were invited. We were advised to fly into Charleston, secure a motel room, rent a car, and drive to Buckhannon, which is what most of us did. I was in a state of shock, though I'd known what was coming. I'd about written off Carlin as a doomed man, after that visit. Though the Ritchie family was claiming he hadn't been that sick, only just depressed because he hadn't been able to work for some time. 'He was too young to die. There were doctors who'd given him hope. How could Carlin do such a desperate thing?' I knew, but I wasn't going to say. I was feeling sick and guilty myself, as if I'd betrayed Carlin, left him with the vampire to die. And Janessa was the bereaved widow, with her dead-white powdered skin and black velvet gown, even a black velvet band around her throat, and her hair streaked at her temples with silver. She stood at the door greeting everyone like a hostess. Her eyes were manic-bright and her mouth crimson like a wound. Seeing me, she pressed herself into my arms with a wail, as if we were old, intimate friends. We were on camera: There was a German documentary film-maker on the site, who'd apparently been interviewing Carlin up to a few days before his death. There were 'selected' journalists from *Vanity Fair, People, The New York Times;* from England, France, Japan, and Israel. The interior of the house was packed with people, most of them strangers to me. There were flowers everywhere. What appeared to be a lavish cocktail buffet had been set up in the dining room, and white-costumed caterer's assistants were serving. The shock, and I mean it was a shock, was Carlin himself — I mean, Carlin's body. It was lying, in an expensive tuxedo, on the white lace spread of a brass four-poster bed (the marital bed, carried down from upstairs) in the parlor. Dozens of candles reeking incense had been lighted. Exclusively white lilies were banked around the bed. I stood there trembling, staring at my friend who'd been made to appear younger and healthier, you could say more garish with health, than he'd looked in years. Pancake make-up skillfully disguised the hollows beneath his eyes, his sallow cheeks were rouged. 'It's like Carlin is only just sleeping, and he'll be waking any minute to say *What's going on here*?' — this remark was repeated numerous times. I said it myself. I said it seriously, and I said it as a joke. I was in that metaphysical-drunk stage where the saddest truth in the world can be the funniest. Photos were being taken of Carlin Ritchie's beautiful grieving widow, standing at the bier-bedside, her fingers linked with those of her dead husband. A tape of mournful country-and-western rock music played. Janessa was taking photos herself, avidly. From time to time she disappeared to freshen her make-up, which was elaborate and effective; at some point she changed into another black dress, low-cut, taffeta, with a startling slit up the side to mid-thigh. Later that night she called for testimonials from 'those who'd known and loved Carlin' and I was one who stood by the four-poster bed speaking of Carlin Ritchie's great talent, his great spirit, and his great courage, and tears ran down my cheeks and others wept with me, as at a gospel ceremony. Janessa pushed into my arms, embraced me hard, her talon fingernails in my neck — 'Rafe Healy! I thank you in Carlin's name.' The wake continued through the night. The problem with grief is it reaches a peak, and another peak, and quickly you begin to repeat yourself. What is spontaneous becomes a performance. Repeated. More people arrived, distraught and needing to expend their shock, grief, loss.

They wept in the widow's arms. Some wept in my arms. Food had fallen underfoot in the dining room, but fresh platters were being hauled in from the kitchen, and bottles of whiskey, bourbon, wine. Carlin had always appreciated a good party, hadn't stinted when it came to quality, and he'd have been proud of this one. Except there was an encounter, caught on videotape, between some Ritchie relatives and Janessa, and there was an encounter between Laurette (who proudly called herself 'Laurette Ritchie') and Janessa, and harsh words were said. Carlin's twenty-seven-year-old daughter, Mandy, screamed and slapped Janessa — 'You stole Daddy! Like a thief! He'd be alive this minute but for you!' — and had to be carried, hysterically weeping, out of the house. The German film-maker hurried after her. More mourners pushed into the parlor, there was a roaring of motorcycles in the drive. Near dawn, Janessa requested several old friends of Carlin's to lift him from the bed and place him in a casket beside the bed, and we were a little unsteady on our feet, shy about touching our dead, embalmed, sleeping-looking friend with the rouged cheeks and shoe-polish hair; also Carlin was heavier than he appeared. I said under my breath, 'Man, what'd they inject you with? Lead?' My buddies laughed. We were sweating like hogs but Carlin was cold. You could feel the cold lifting from him. I believe he was sucking the heat from our hands as cold water will do. Janessa had her camera, taking flash shots of us. I muttered, 'Fuck you, you bitch, a man has died for fuck's sake, we must respect him.' My buddies muttered, 'Amen!' But Janessa chose not to hear. She gave her camera to someone so that her picture might be taken beside us, fitting Carlin into his casket, which was silver-onyx-mahogany, purchased in Charleston and shipped to Buckhannon. We were having a hard time keeping from laughing, fitting poor Carlin into the silk-cushioned casket, and everybody looking on, gaping and drinking. Carlin's toupee was askew, and Janessa hurriedly adjusted it, and I was trying to remember if I'd realized that my friend had been wearing a toupee in life but I couldn't. The funeral was scheduled for nine A.M. but didn't take place until 10:20 A.M. Some folks, driving from the Ritchie house to the cemetery a mile away, became lost, or disappeared. Yet others appeared. A raw-boned preacher from the Gospel Church of Jesus of Buckhannon, whom Carlin hadn't known, spoke at the grave site, quoting Scripture. This was 'Americana' for the foreign journalists, I suppose — Carlin hadn't belonged to any church, though he'd been baptized Baptist. I tried to interrupt the preacher to say what Carlin had said — 'I believe in God but not in man believing in God' — but everybody hushed me. I was pissed, and would've left before the casket was lowered into the grave, but Janessa gripped my arm in her talon-claws and held me there. She'd been glancing at me at the grave site, using her eyes on me; I wondered if she was worried that Carlin might've told me of the plan to stockpile barbiturates and I might tell the authorities. Sure, the woman was guilty of aiding and abetting a suicide, probably under West Virginia law she'd be vulnerable to arrest, but no one could prove her involvement, any good lawyer would've gotten her off. Anyway that wasn't her truest crime, an act of murder. And soul-murder. But what she wanted from me was that I'd stay for the funeral luncheon at the Buckhannon Inn and come back to the house that afternoon — 'There's just a select few of Carlin's artist-friends I'm inviting; Heinz Muller wants to interview you and wrap up his film.'

'When I left Buckhannon that day, which was immediately following the funeral, I could not have believed that I would ever plan to return. For any purpose possible.

'Yet now I'm being called. It's Carlin calling me. He'd been the one to own firearms, as a kid. He'd been a hunter, with rifle and shotgun.

'Only a few weeks after Carlin's death, it began to happen. Her calculated acts. Not honoring Carlin's will, getting a lawyer to help her break it, contesting the provisions Carlin had made for his first wife and his children, refusing even to surrender the artworks he'd left to museums in West Virginia and to certain of his friends, like me. Those silk screens Carlin wanted me to have — from his Appalachia series — she's claiming she doesn't have. People try to excuse her — 'Poor Janessa, she's devastated with grief. Cries all the time, she says.' Bullshit. But this isn't the worst.

'This behavior, it's mean, cruel, vicious, conniving — criminal. But you wouldn't wish to kill because of it. At least, I wouldn't.

'What's unforgivable in her, what's purely evil, is that she's a vampire. She's sucking from the living, and from the dead. On TV, for instance, interviewed by Barbara Walters. Network TV. And she's reminiscing of Carlin Ritchie's last years, how they collaborated together on mostly everything, Carlin had even worked from sketches she'd provided him, and suggestions; saying theirs was 'one of the great loves of the century, like Georgia O'Keeffe and Alfred Stieglitz.' Work of Carlin's he'd done years before he met her, work he'd had in his studio but hadn't shown, turns out it's 'collaborative.' Janessa Ritchie is 'co-artist.' Right there on TV, her hair dyed almost purple, with grief-streaks of silver, and the big owl-eyes brimming with tears as Barbara Walters pretends to take this bullshit seriously. There's even a journal of Carlin's Janessa reads from, conveniently not handwritten but typed, a so-called log of the final year of his life — 'My heart is full! My love for Janessa and for my work is God's grace! I will die not out of sorrow or despair but out of love, in the ecstasy of pure love, knowing my soul is complete.' And her and Barbara Walters practically bawling together. I came close to kicking in my TV, I was so furious.

'Furious, and sick in my soul. For *my* soul is sure not complete!

'Now she's being invited everywhere. 'Janessa Ritchie' is as famous as Carlin, almost. Exhibits in Berlin, Paris, London. This exhibit at the Whitney — it's up right now. Go and see for your own eyes. Big features in glossy magazines — *The New Yorker*, *Mirabella*, even *Art in America*, where you'd expect the editors to be more discerning. Some people in the art world have called her to protest, Carlin's ex-dealer drew up a letter, which dozens of us signed, and which was sent certified mail to her, but none of it does any good, and it won't. To stop a creature like her you must destroy her. Trying to reason with her, pleading, even threats of lawsuits — none of that will work. This exhibit at the Whitney — that did it, for me. Tipped me over. It's more of this 'collaborative' bullshit except this time Janessa has dared to put her name to art that was Carlin's, that he hadn't finished and signed. The title of the exhibit is 'The Ritchies' — like she, the woman who killed him, the vampire, is an equal of her victim! It's a nightmare. It's like the media know what's happening but go along with it, Janessa's a glamorous woman, they can champion 'an exemplary female artist,' as she's been called.

'I wasn't invited to the champagne opening at the Whitney, of course. But I got in anyway. I saw what was on the walls and walked right up to her, the bitch, the thief, the 'grieving widow'; she's lovey-dovey with this guy who's Carlin's new dealer at a wealthy uptown gallery, and she's dressed in sexy black silk, spike-heeled shoes, and textured black stockings, she's put on more weight, in her bust and hips, fleshy but not fat, and sexy, though her skin is powdered dead-white and looks bloated like a corpse that's been in water. And that crimson mouth that's wider than ever, thick with greasy lipstick. *Ugh! — I remember the taste of her*. She sights me coming at her and I see the guilty panic in her eyes, though right away she puts on this pose of innocence so I'm the one who comes off badly. I say, 'Goddamn you, woman, what do you mean claiming this work is yours? It's Carlin's and you know it,' and she says to her companion in this scared little-girl voice, 'He's a deranged man! I don't know who he is! He's been threatening me for months!' and I say, 'Don't know who I am! I'm Carlin's friend. I'm here to speak for him. To tell the world that you are thieving from him, and betraying him. Jesus, woman, didn't you love that man at all?' But by this time two security guards are on me and I'm being hustled out onto the street — Madison Avenue. And I know better than to stick around and get arrested by some real cops.

'So what'd I do — drove home here. Sick in my heart. Wanting to commit a murder right then if only I had the power. I saw Carlin on that veranda, as dusk came on, wrapped in a flimsy blanket, shivering, trying to smile at me, pleading. *I don't want to die. Yes, but I'm ready. Help me.*'

We were still in the tavern, but it was almost time to return to the courthouse. Rafe had showed me a newspaper photo of 'Janessa Ritchie' and she looked just like he'd said: glamorous, fleshy, with hungry eyes and mouth. I felt my heart beating hard and heavy, Rafe's hot, angry blood streaming through my veins. He said, 'Every day it gets worse. It's hanging over me always. Can't sleep, can't work. And this week of jury duty — at the courthouse — in that atmosphere — it's like somebody is fucking with me, y'know? — mocking me. Every defendant who's on trial had the courage to do what he needed to do — there's that way of thinking. But Rafe Healy doesn't have the courage, so far, to do what I need to do.'

I could see how agitated he was, so I paid the bill for both of us and got him out of there, walking in the sunshine and trying to talk to him, reason with him. It was like we'd been imprisoned together in a small cell that, even though we were in the open air now and in the eyes of observers free, unconfined men, continued to press in upon us. I said, 'Maybe it's a sign, Rafe? If you don't have the 'courage'? That you shouldn't do it? That you should just forget about it? Since your friend is dead anyway — '

Rafe stopped on the sidewalk, glared at me like I was his mortal enemy. 'Fuck you, man, what're you saying? Carlin's *dead*, that means — what? I should abandon him?'

'No, Rafe. Only just that — '

'She's a vicious, evil woman. I swear, an emissary of Satan. That's more and more clear to me, Harrison. Last night I was in my studio, trying to work, drinking and trying to work, and my hands shook so badly I couldn't do a thing — I heard her laughing at me, and saw those eyes, I tasted that mouth sort of nuzzling at me, teasing. She's moving onto me, now. The vampire's moving onto me.'

'Rafe, that isn't right. You know that isn't right. Listen to you.'

At the courthouse steps, Rafe wiped his face on his sleeve, tried to compose himself. Just since Monday, I believed he'd lost some weight. There were knifelike vertical creases in his cheeks. He said, 'I believe you're right. I can hear my own voice, and it's become a deranged voice. I'm not me — I'm a deranged man. And it's that woman who's to blame. So long as she lives, I am her victim.'

7.

You could rent a car. Two cars. In sequence. The first you'd rent at an airport, perhaps in New Jersey. You'd leave your van in a parking lot. The second car you'd rent in Pennsylvania. And drive to Buckhannon, West Virginia, to arrive there by first dark. Because you would need to seek your target in a lighted house, yourself hidden in darkness. But wait: Before this, at a Sears or Kmart in any large mall (some distance from your home), you could purchase a dark jacket with a hood. Rubber boots a size or two larger than your own. Gloves. But wait: Before this, you will need to buy the rifle. The rifle with the scope. Ammunition. You're going deer hunting, you'll tell the salesclerk. You'll purchase the rifle upstate, where hunting is common, and you'll need to practice shooting at a target. Somewhere private. Maybe we could practice together. I don't mean that I'd be coming with you to West Virginia. I could not do that. But I could help you. I could buy the rifle, possibly. I could give you moral support. I can see you are in need of moral support. I'm your cousin but we're closer than most cousins. You could say I'm your lost brother. And I'm lonely.

Rosalind woke me, gently. Telling me I'd been grinding my teeth.

A bad dream? she asked, and I said, No. Not a bad dream. Not at all.

8.

Thursday afternoon at 2:25 P.M., Rafe's luck runs out. Juror 93 is called to take his seat in a jury box — our panel of jurors was sent up to a sixth-floor courtroom where there's a murder case scheduled, a nasty case it looks to be, burly black man with a downlooking, gnarled face accused of having killed his wife. Rafe shudders and gives my arm a quick scared squeeze as he stumbles out of his seat to step forward. Poor Rafe: Everybody's staring at him, he's unsteady on his feet as a sleepwalker (or a drunk: He'd had at least six beers at lunch, in spite of my telling him to go easy), the tallest of all the jurors and, judging by the look in his mottled face, the shyest. He's wearing his bib overalls, which look as if he's been sleeping in them (I wouldn't doubt he has), and his beard and hair are scruffy. I'm worried that my cousin will get into trouble if it's discovered he's been drinking while on jury duty: Does that mean contempt of court? I'd been drinking, too, but not as much as Rafe, and I believe I'm fully sober.

This trial will be for first-degree murder. Which is to say, it's a capital case. New York State reinstated the death penalty a few years ago, by lethal injection.

As Rafe Healy passes by the defense counsel's table, the defendant turns to stare at him. It's the first time in the approximate ninety minutes we've been in this courtroom that the defendant, a muscular, near-bald man of about fifty, has roused himself to take such an interest. But Rafe, a vague dazed smile on his face, or a grimace of the lips that might be mistaken for a smile, makes it a point not to look at him.

Not many jurors, Caucasians or persons of color (as we're told they wish now to be called), are anxious to be assigned to this case. Downstairs the rumor circulated that it could last for weeks. And there's death-penalty trial that follows, if the verdict is guilty. I swear Rafe was actually praying, moving his lips during the voir dire as potential jurors were questioned one by one, a few retained in the jury box but most dismissed. Now JUROR 93 is seated in the box being asked occupation? ('self-employed craftsman' — which makes a few people smile) and whether he's associated in any way with the case, heard anything about it, or believes he might be in any way disqualified to remain on the jury, and Rafe is staring pained at the judge, moving his lips but not speaking. I'm feeling — Jesus! — just so excruciatingly embarrassed for my cousin, and anxious for him; I'm worried as hell what he's going to say. *I can't sit in judgment of any murderer. I am not the man*. The way Rafe and I've worked it through these past few days, less than a week but it feels like we've been together for a long, long time, there are times when murdering another human being isn't just not-wrong but morally and ethically right. The law just can't cover that. The judge rephrases his question, and again Rafe tries to answer, but can't seem to speak; his face is mottled now like he's got a sudden case of measles, and his eyes are glassy. 'Mr. Healy, is something wrong? Mr. Healy?' the judge inquires, concerned; he's a middle-age man, friendly-seeming most of the time though he's been a little impatient with some of the jurors who'd clearly wanted to be dismissed, and now with Rafe he doesn't know how to proceed. Is this juror just being difficult, to be excused, or is there something really wrong with him? I raise my hand like a kid in school and say, 'Excuse me? Your Honor? That man is my cousin and he's kind of a — nervous type? He's on medication, I think — probably he shouldn't be here.' Now everybody's staring at *me*.

But it's okay. It's the right, inspired thing. The judge contemplates me for a minute, frowning, then thanks me for the information and calls Rafe over to speak with him in private. After a few minutes' consultation (I'm watching Rafe's earnest face and hoping to hell he isn't uttering any sort of blunt truth, only just improvising a reasonable excuse to get him out of here) JUROR 93 is formally dismissed for the day.

In fact, it will be for the rest of the week. Rafe Healy is finished with jury duty, probably forever.

For me, the remainder of the voir dire passes in a blur. I keep waiting for my number to be called, but it isn't. By 5:20 P.M. the jury box is finally filled, twelve jurors and two alternates and the rest of us dismissed for the day.

I'd been wondering if Rafe would be downstairs waiting for me, but he isn't. But he's in the parking lot, leaning against the fender of my car. 'Jesus, Harrison! You saved me up there. Man, I'm grateful.' Rafe actually hugs me, it's that weird. But I know I did the right, shrewd thing. It just seems like my brain's been revved up lately, like a machine working faster and more efficiently. Things falling into place.

9.

It's past 8:00 P.M. by the time I get home, Thursday night. Should've called Rosalind from the bar but forgot. And the woman's in my face as soon as I get in the door asking how's the trial? and I say, Trial? What trial? (Goddamn, I'd kind of forgotten what I'd told her the other day) then — 'Oh, that. It's pretty ugly stuff, like I said. I'll be glad when it's over.' Rosalind says, with that blinking little frown of hers that isn't an accusation, but means to make you think along those lines, 'I looked everywhere in the paper but I didn't find anything. About any trial that sounded like yours.' I say, beginning to get pissed at her, 'Look, Rosalind, I explained to you I can't discuss it. Didn't I explain to you I can't discuss it?' and she says, 'It's got to be something terrible for you to get drunk every night on the way home, like you haven't done for twelve years,' and I say, 'What? You've been counting?' like it's a joke, or I'm willing to grant her the possibility that it's a joke. I'm an hour late for supper, but what the fuck, I get a beer from the refrigerator and Rosalind's pulling at my arm in that way I don't like, and she knows I don't like, saying, 'Don't be ridiculous, Harrison, you can hint about it, can't you? Is it a murder case? Some kind of murder case?' I'm drinking from the can saying nothing trying to walk away and the woman keeps pushing, 'Is it a woman killed, and a man on trial? Is it some pervert? It isn't a child killed, is it? And some disgusting pervert on trial? Just wink your left eye, honey, and give me a clue,' and I'm beginning to lose it, I say, 'Look, we could both be in trouble if I breathe a word of this trial to anyone, including even my fellow jurors, before the judge gives permission, didn't I explain that to you? Can't you comprehend? Violating the judge's order is called contempt of court and you can be jailed,' and she's in my face persisting, in that way she used to do with the boys, and that pisses me for sure, saying, 'Harrison? Come *on*. Just wink your left eye if — ' And I shove her back against the edge of the kitchen table, and she gives a little scream of pain and surprise and I'm out of the kitchen, I'm slamming out of the goddamned room, I'm shaking, muttering to myself words I've never heard myself speak aloud in this house, in such a voice, I'm thinking I've never touched my wife, or any woman, in anger in my life, never in anger like this, like flame, never until now and it feels right, it feels good, it feels goddamned good.

Like Rafe knows.

Anne Perry

When this story found its way to my desk, the author acknowledged that she thought it was the best short story she had ever written. She is right. This wonderfully evocative tale of the trenches in World War I and the terrible crime it reports will haunt your memory for a long time to come.

It doesn't seem, at first blush, to be a crime story at all, but as you continue along you will learn that it surely is.

This is a different era for Anne Perry, who has achieved great success with her Victorian era mystery novels, but it must have been important to her as she has produced such a vivid account of the place and time.

Perhaps the reason for the power of this unusual tale is that it was inspired by a real-life person. The kindly but strong chaplain who understands the obsession of an officer who wants to be a hero was based very closely on the author's grandfather.

Heroes

By Anne Perry

Nights were always the worst, and in winter they lasted from dusk at about four o'clock until dawn again toward eight the following morning. Sometimes star shells lit the sky, showing the black zigzags of the trenches stretching as far as the eye could see to left and right. Apparently now they went right across France and Belgium all the way from the Alps to the Channel. But Joseph was only concerned with this short stretch of the Ypres Salient.

In the gloom near him someone coughed, a deep, hacking sound coming from down in the chest. They were in the support line, farthest from the front, the most complex of the three rows of trenches. Here were the kitchens, the latrines and the stores and mortar positions. Fifteen-foot shafts led to caves about five paces wide and high enough for most men to stand upright. Joseph made his way in the half dark now, the slippery wood under his boots and his hands feeling the mud walls, held up by timber and wire.

There was an awful lot of water. One of the sumps must be blocked.

There was a glow of light ahead and a moment later he was in the comparative warmth of the dugout. There were two candles burning and the brazier gave off heat and a sharp smell of soot. The air was blue with tobacco smoke, and a pile of boots and greatcoats steamed a little. Two officers sat on canvas chairs talking together. One of them recited a joke — gallows humor, and they both laughed. A gramophone sat silent on a camp table, and a small pile of records of the latest music-hall songs was carefully protected in a tin box.

'Hello, Chaplain,' one of them said cheerfully. 'How's God these days?'

'Gone home on sick leave,' the other answered quickly, before Joseph could reply. There was disgust in his voice, but no intended irreverence. Death was too close here for men to mock faith.

'Have a seat,' the first offered, waving toward a third chair. 'Morris got it today. Killed outright. That bloody sniper again.'

'He's somewhere out there, just about opposite us,' the second said grimly. 'One of those blighters the other day claimed he'd got forty-three for sure.'

'I can believe it,' Joseph answered,

accepting the seat. He knew better than most what the casualties were. It was his job to comfort the terrified, the dying, to carry stretchers, often to write letters to the bereaved. Sometimes he thought it was harder than actually fighting, but he refused to stay back in the comparative safety of the field hospitals and depots. This was where he was most needed.

'Thought about setting up a trench raid,' the major said slowly, weighing his words and looking at Joseph. 'Good for morale. Make it seem as if we were actually doing something. But our chances of getting the blighter are pretty small. Only lose a lot of men for nothing. Feel even worse afterward.'

The captain did not add anything. They all knew morale was sinking. Losses were high, the news bad. Word of terrible slaughter seeped through from the Somme and Verdun and all along the line right to the sea. Physical hardship took its toll, the dirt, the cold, and the alternation between boredom and terror. The winter of 1916 lay ahead.

'Cigarette?' The major held out his pack to Joseph.

'No thanks,' Joseph declined with a smile. 'Got any tea going?'

They poured him a mugful, strong and bitter, but hot. He drank it, and half an hour later made his way forward to the open air again and the travel trench. A star shell exploded high and bright. Automatically he ducked, keeping his head below the rim. They were about four feet deep, and in order not to provide a target, a man had to move in a half crouch. There was a rattle of machine-gun fire out ahead and, closer to, a thud as a rat was dislodged and fell into the mud beside the duckboards.

Other men were moving about close to him. The normal order of things was reversed here. Nothing much happened during the day. Trench repair work was done, munitions shifted, weapons cleaned, a little rest taken. Most of the activity was at night, most of the death.

''Lo, Chaplain,' a voice whispered in the dark. 'Say a prayer we get that bloody sniper, will you?'

'Maybe God's a Jerry?' someone suggested in the dark.

'Don't be stupid!' a third retorted derisively. 'Everyone knows God's an Englishman! Didn't they teach you nothing at school?'

There was a burst of laughter. Joseph joined in. He promised to offer up the appropriate prayers and moved on forward. He had known many of the men all his life.

They came from the same Northumbrian town as he did, or the surrounding villages. They had gone to school together, nicked apples from the same trees, fished in the same rivers, and walked the same lanes.

It was a little after six when he reached the firing trench beyond whose sandbag parapet lay no-man's-land with its four or five hundred yards of mud, barbed wire, and shell holes. Half a dozen burnt tree stumps looked in the sudden flares like men. Those gray wraiths could be fog, or gas.

Funny that in summer this blood- and horror-soaked soil could still bloom with honeysuckle, forget-me-nots, and wild lark-spur, and most of all with poppies. You would think nothing would ever grow there again.

More star shells went up, lighting the ground, the jagged scars of the trenches black, the men on the fire steps with rifles on their shoulders illuminated for a few, blinding moments. Sniper shots rang out.

Joseph stood still. He knew the terror of the night watch out beyond the parapet, crawling around in the mud. Some of them would be at the head of saps out from the trench, most would be in shell holes, surrounded by heavy barricades of wire. Their purpose was to check enemy patrols for unusual movement, any signs of increased activity, as if there might be an attack planned.

More star shells lit the sky. It was beginning to rain. A crackle of machine-gun fire, and heavier artillery somewhere over to the left. Then the sharp whine of sniper fire, again and again.

Joseph shuddered. He thought of the men out there, beyond his vision, and prayed for strength to endure with them in their pain, not to try to deaden himself to it.

There were shouts somewhere ahead, heavy shells now, shrapnel bursting. There was a flurry of movement, flares, and a man came sliding over the parapet, shouting for help.

Joseph plunged forward, slithering in the mud, grabbing for the wooden props to hold himself up. Another flare of light. He saw quite clearly Captain Holt lurching toward him, another man over his shoulder, deadweight.

'He's hurt!' Holt gasped. 'Pretty badly. One of the night patrol. Panicked. Just about got us all killed.' He eased the man down into Joseph's arms and let his rifle slide forward, bayonet covered in an old sock to hide its gleam. His face was grotesque in the lantern light, smeared with mud and a wide streak of blood over the burnt cork that blackened it, as all night patrol had.

Others were coming to help. There was still a terrible noise of fire going on and the occasional flare.

The man in Joseph's arms did not stir. His body was limp and it was difficult to support him. Joseph felt the wetness and the smell of blood. Wordlessly others materialized out of the gloom and took the weight.

'Is he alive?' Holt said urgently. 'There was a hell of a lot of shot up there.' His voice was shaking, almost on the edge of control.

'Don't know,' Joseph answered. 'We'll get him back to the bunker and see. You've done all you can.' He knew how desperate men felt when they risked their lives to save another man and did not succeed. A kind of despair set in, a sense of very personal failure, almost a guilt for having survived themselves. 'Are you hurt?'

'Not much,' Holt answered. 'Couple of grazes.'

'Better have them dressed, before they get poisoned,' Joseph advised, his feet slipping on the wet boards and banging his shoulder against a jutting post. The whole trench wall was crooked, giving way under the weight of mud. The founds had eroded.

The man helping him swore.

Awkwardly carrying the wounded man, they staggered back through the travel line to the support trench and into the light and shelter of a bunker.

Holt looked dreadful. Beneath the cork and blood his face was ashen. He was soaked with rain and mud and there were dark patches of blood across his back and shoulders.

Someone gave him a cigarette. Back here it was safe to strike a match. He drew in smoke deeply. 'Thanks,' he murmured, still staring at the wounded man.

Joseph looked down at him now, and it was only too plain where the blood had come from. It was young Ashton. He knew him quite well. He had been at school with his older brother.

The soldier who had helped carry him in let out a cry of dismay, strangled in his throat. It was Mordaff, Ashton's closest friend, and he could see what Joseph now could also. Ashton was dead, his chest torn open, the blood no longer pumping, and a bullet hole through his head.

'I'm sorry,' Holt said quietly. 'I did what I could. I can't have got to him in time. He panicked.'

Mordaff jerked his head up. 'He never would!' The cry was desperate, a shout of denial against a shame too great to be borne. 'Not Will!'

Holt stiffened. 'I'm sorry,' he said hoarsely. 'It happens.'

'Not with Will Ashton, it don't!' Mordaff retorted, his eyes blazing, pupils circled with white in the candlelight, his face gray. He had been in the front line two weeks now, a long stretch without a break from the ceaseless tension, filth, cold, and intermittent silence and noise. He was nineteen.

'You'd better go and get that arm dressed, and your side,' Joseph said to Holt. He made his voice firm, as to a child.

Holt glanced again at the body of Ashton, then up at Joseph.

'Don't stand there bleeding,' Joseph ordered. 'You did all you could. There's nothing else. I'll look after Mordaff.'

'I tried!' Holt repeated. 'There's nothing but mud and darkness and wire, and bullets coming in all directions.' There was a sharp thread of terror under his shell-thin veneer of control. He had seen too many men die. 'It's enough to make anyone lose his nerve. You want to be a hero — you mean to be — and then it overwhelms you — '

'Not Will!' Mordaff said again, his voice choking off in a sob.

Holt looked at Joseph again, then staggered out.

Joseph turned to Mordaff. He had done

this before, too many times, tried to comfort men who had just seen childhood friends blown to pieces, or killed by a sniper's bullet, looking as if they should still be alive, perfect except for the small, blue hole through the brain. There was little to say. Most men found talk of God meaningless at that moment. They were shocked, fighting against belief and yet seeing all the terrible waste and loss in front of them. Usually it was best just to stay with them, let them speak about the past, what the friend had been like, times they had shared, just as if he were only wounded and would be back, at the end of the war, in some world one could only imagine, in England, perhaps on a summer day with sunlight on the grass, birds singing, a quiet riverbank somewhere, the sound of laughter, and women's voices.

Mordaff refused to be comforted. He accepted Ashton's death; the physical reality of that was too clear to deny, and he had seen too many other men he knew killed in the year and a half he had been in Belgium. But he could not, would not accept that Ashton had panicked. He knew what panic out there cost, how many other lives it jeopardized. It was the ultimate failure.

'How am I going to tell his mam?' he begged Joseph. 'It'll be all I can do to tell her he's dead! His pa'll never get over it. That proud of him, they were. He's the only boy. Three sisters he had, Mary, Lizzie, and Alice. Thought he was the greatest lad in the world. I can't tell 'em he panicked! He couldn't have, Chaplain! He just wouldn't!'

Joseph did not know what to say. How could people at home in England even begin to imagine what it was like in the mud and noise out here? But he knew how deep shame burned. A lifetime could be consumed by it.

'Maybe he just lost sense of direction,' he said gently. 'He wouldn't be the first.' War changed men. People did panic. Mordaff knew that, and half his horror was because it could be true. But Joseph did not say so. 'I'll write to his family,' he went on. 'There's a lot of good to say about him. I could send pages. I'll not need to tell them much about tonight.'

'Will you?' Mordaff was eager. 'Thanks . . . thanks, Chaplain. Can I stay with him . . . until they come for him?'

'Yes, of course,' Joseph agreed. 'I'm going forward anyway. Get yourself a hot cup of tea. See you in an hour or so.'

He left Mordaff squatting on the earth floor beside Ashton's body and fumbled his way back over the slimy duckboards toward the travel line, then forward again to the front and the crack of gunfire and the occasional high flare of a star shell.

He did not see Mordaff again, but he thought nothing of it. He could have passed twenty men he knew and not recognized them, muffled in greatcoats, heads bent as they moved, rattling along the duckboards, or standing on the fire steps, rifles to shoulder, trying to see in the gloom for something to aim at.

Now and again he heard a cough, or the scamper of rats' feet and the splash of rain and mud. He spent a little time with two men swapping jokes, joining in their laughter. It was black humor, self-mocking, but he did not miss the courage in it, or the fellowship, the need to release emotion in some sane and human way.

About midnight the rain stopped.

A little after five the night patrol came scrambling through the wire, whispered passwords to the sentries, then came tumbling over the parapet of sandbags down into the trench, shivering with cold and relief. One of them had caught a shot in the arm.

Joseph went back with them to the support line. In one of the dugouts a gramophone was playing a music-hall song. A couple of men sang along with it; one of them had a beautiful voice, a soft, lyric tenor. It was a silly song, trivial, but it sounded almost like a hymn out here, a praise of life.

A couple of hours and the day would begin: endless, methodical duties of house-keeping, mindless routine, but it was better than doing nothing.

There was still a sporadic crackle of machine-gun fire and the whine of sniper bullets.

An hour till dawn.

Joseph was sitting on an upturned ration case when Sergeant Renshaw came into the bunker, pulling the gas curtain aside to peer in.

'Chaplain?'

Joseph looked up. He could see bad news in the man's face.

'I'm afraid Mordaff got it tonight,' he said, coming in and letting the curtain fall again. 'Sorry. Don't really know what happened. Ashton's death seems to have . . . well, he lost his nerve. More or less went over the top all by himself. Suppose he was determined to go and give Fritz a bloody nose, on Ashton's account. Stupid bastard! Sorry, Chaplain.'

He did not need to explain himself, or to apologize. Joseph knew exactly the fury and the grief he felt at such a futile waste. To this was added a sense of guilt that he had not stopped it. He should have realized Mordaff was so close to breaking. He should have seen it. That was his job.

He stood up slowly. 'Thanks for telling me, Sergeant. Where is he?'

'He's gone, Chaplain.' Renshaw remained near the doorway. 'You can't help 'im now.'

'I know that. I just want to . . . I don't know . . . apologize to him. I let him down. I didn't understand he was . . . so . . . '

'You can't be everybody's keeper,' Renshaw said gently. 'Too many of us. It's not been a bad night otherwise. Got a trench raid coming off soon. Just wish we could get that damn sniper across the way there.' He scraped a match and lit his cigarette. 'But morale's good. That was a brave thing Captain Holt did out there. He wanted the chance to do something to hearten the men. He saw it and took it. Pity about Ashton, but that doesn't alter Holt's courage. Could see him, you know, by the star shells. Right out there beyond the last wire, bent double, carrying Ashton on his back. Poor devil went crazy. Running around like a fool. Have got the whole patrol killed if Holt hadn't gone after him. Hell of a job getting him back. Fell a couple of times. Reckon that's worth a mention in dispatches, at least. Heartens the men, knowing our officers have got that kind of spirit.'

'Yes . . . I'm sure,' Joseph agreed. He could only think of Ashton's white face, and Mordaff's desperate denial, and how Ashton's mother would feel, and the rest of his family. 'I think I'll go and see Mordaff just the same.'

'Right you are,' Renshaw conceded reluctantly, standing aside for Joseph to pass.

* * *

Mordaff lay in the support trench just outside the bunker two hundred yards to the west. He looked even younger than he had in life, as if he were asleep. His face was oddly calm, even though it was smeared with mud. Someone had tried to clean most of it off in a kind of dignity, so that at least he was recognizable. There was a large wound in the left side of his forehead. It was bigger than most sniper wounds. He must have been a lot closer.

Joseph stood in the first paling of the darkness and looked at him by candlelight from the open bunker curtain. He had been so alive only a few hours ago, so full of anger and loyalty and dismay. What had made him throw his life away in a useless gesture? Joseph racked his mind for some sign that should have warned him Mordaff was so close to breaking, but he could not see it even now.

There was a cough a few feet away, and the tramp of boots on duckboards. The men were stood down, just one sentry per platoon left. They had returned for breakfast. If he thought about it he could smell cooking.

Now would be the time to ask around and find out what had happened to Mordaff.

He made his way to the field kitchen. It was packed with men, some standing to be close to the stoves and catch a bit of their warmth, others choosing to sit, albeit farther away. They had survived the night. They were laughing and telling stories, most of them unfit for delicate ears, but Joseph was too used to it to take any offense. Now and then someone new would apologize for such language in front of a chaplain, but most knew he understood too well.

'Yeah,' one answered his question through a mouthful of bread and jam. 'He came and asked me if I saw what happened to Ashton. Very cut up, he was.'

'And what did you tell him?' Joseph asked.

The man swallowed. 'Told him Ashton seemed fine to me when he went over. Just like anyone else, nervous . . . but, then, only a fool isn't scared to go over the top!'

Joseph thanked him and moved on. He needed to know who else was on the patrol.

'Captain Holt,' the next man told him, a

ring of pride in his voice. Word had got around about Holt's courage. Everyone stood a little taller because of it, felt a little braver, more confident. 'We'll pay Fritz back for that,' he added. 'Next raid — you'll see.'

There was a chorus of agreement.

'Who else?' Joseph pressed.

'Seagrove, Noakes, Willis,' a thin man replied, standing up. 'Want some breakfast, Chaplain? Anything you like, on the house — as long as it's bread and jam and half a cup of tea. But you're not particular, are you? Not one of those fussy eaters who'll only take kippers and toast?'

'What I wouldn't give for a fresh Craster kipper,' another sighed, a faraway look in his eyes. 'I can smell them in my dreams.'

Someone told him good-naturedly to shut up.

'Went over the top beside me,' Willis said when Joseph found him quarter of an hour later. 'All blacked up like the rest of us. Seemed okay to me then. Lost him in no-man's-land. Had a hell of a job with the wire. As bloody usual, it wasn't where we'd been told. Got through all right, then Fritz opened up on us. Star shells all over the sky.' He sniffed and then coughed violently. When he had control of himself again, he continued. 'Then I saw someone outlined against the flares, arms high, like a wild man, running around. He was going toward the German lines, shouting something. Couldn't hear what in the noise.'

Joseph did not interrupt. It was now broad daylight and beginning to drizzle again. Around them men were starting the duties of the day: digging, filling sandbags, carrying ammunition, strengthening the wire, resetting duckboards. Men took an hour's work, an hour's sentry duty, and an hour's rest.

Near them somebody was expending his entire vocabulary of curses against lice. Two more were planning elaborate schemes to hold the water at bay.

'Of course that lit us up like a target, didn't it!' Willis went on. 'Sniper fire and machine guns all over the place. Even a couple of shells. How none of us got hit I'll never know. Perhaps the row woke God up, and He came back on duty!' He laughed hollowly. 'Sorry, Chaplain. Didn't mean it. I'm just so damn sorry poor Ashton got it. Holt just came out of nowhere and ran after him. Obsessed with being a hero, or he'd not even have tried. I can see him in my mind's eye floundering through the mud. If Ashton hadn't got caught in the wire he'd never have got him.'

'Caught in the wire?' Joseph asked, memory pricking at him.

'Yeah. Ashton must have run right into the wire, because he stopped sudden — teetering, like — and fell over. A hell of a barrage came over just after that. We all threw ourselves down.'

'What happened then?' Joseph said urgently, a slow, sick thought taking shape in his mind.

'When it died down I looked up again, and there was Holt staggering back with poor Ashton across his shoulders. Hell of a job he had carrying him, even though he's bigger than Ashton — well, taller, anyway. Up to his knees in mud, he was, shot and shell all over, sky lit up like a Christmas tree. Of course we gave him what covering fire we could. Maybe it helped.' He coughed again. 'Reckon he'll be mentioned in dispatches, Chaplain? He deserves it.' There was admiration in his voice, a lift of hope.

Joseph forced himself to answer. 'I should think so.' The words were stiff.

'Well, if he isn't, the men'll want to know why!' Willis said fiercely. 'Bloody hero, he is.'

Joseph thanked him and went to find Seagrove and Noakes. They told him pretty much the same story.

'You going to have him recommended?' Noakes asked. 'He earned it this time. Mordaff came and we said just the same to him. Reckon he wanted the Captain given a medal. He made us say it over and over again, exactly what happened.'

'That's right.' Seagrove nodded, leaning on a sandbag.

'You told him the same?' Joseph asked. 'About the wire, and Ashton getting caught in it?'

'Yes, of course. If he hadn't got caught by the legs he'd have gone straight on and landed up in Fritz's lap, poor devil.'

'Thank you.'

'Welcome, Chaplain. You going to write up Captain Holt?'

Joseph did not answer, but turned away, sick at heart.

He did not need to look again, but he trudged all the way back to the field hospital anyway. It would be his job to say the services for both Ashton and Mordaff. The graves would be already dug.

He looked at Ashton's body again, looked carefully at his trousers. They were stained with mud, but there were no tears in them, no marks of wire. The fabric was perfect.

He straightened up.

'I'm sorry,' he said quietly to the dead man. 'Rest in peace.' And he turned and walked away.

He went back to where he had left

Mordaff's body, but it had been removed. Half an hour more took him to where it also was laid out. He touched the cold hand and looked at the brow. He would ask. He would be sure. But in his mind he already was. He needed time to know what he must do about it. The men would be going over the top on another trench raid soon. Today morale was high. They had a hero in their number, a man who would risk his own life to bring back a soldier who had lost his nerve and panicked. Led by someone like that, they were equal to Fritz any day. Was one pistol bullet, one family's shame, worth all that?

What were they fighting for anyway? The issues were so very big, and at the same time so very small and immediate.

* * *

He found Captain Holt alone just after dusk, standing on the duckboards below the parapet, near one of the firing steps.

'Oh, it's you, Chaplain. Ready for another night?'

'It'll come, whether I am or not,' Joseph replied.

Holt gave a short bark of laughter. 'That doesn't sound like you. Tired of the firing line, are you? You've been up here a couple of weeks; you should be in turn for a step back any day. Me too, thank God.'

Joseph faced forward, peering through the gloom toward no-man's-land and the German lines beyond. He was shaking. He must control himself. This must be done in the silence, before the shooting started up again. Then he might not get away with it.

'Pity about that sniper over there,' he remarked. 'He's taken out a lot of our men.'

'Damnable,' Holt agreed. 'Can't get a line on him, though. Keeps his own head well down.'

'Oh, yes.' Joseph nodded. 'We'd never get him from here. It needs a man to go over in the dark and find him.'

'Not a good idea, Chaplain. He'd not come back. Not advocating suicide, are you?'

Joseph chose his words very carefully and kept his voice as unemotional as he could.

'I wouldn't have put it like that,' he answered. 'But he has cost us a lot of men. Mordaff today, you know?'

'Yes . . . I heard. Pity.'

'Except that wasn't the sniper, of course. But the men think it was, so it comes to the same thing, as far as morale is concerned.'

'Don't know what you mean, Chaplain.' There was a slight hesitation in Holt's voice in the darkness.

'Wasn't a rifle wound, it was a pistol,' Joseph replied. 'You can tell the difference, if you're actually looking for it.'

'Then he was a fool to be that close to German lines,' Holt said, facing forward over the parapet and the mud. 'Lost his nerve, I'm afraid.'

'Like Ashton,' Joseph said. 'Can understand that, up there in no-man's-land, mud everywhere, wire catching hold of you, tearing at you, stopping you from moving. Terrible thing to be caught in the wire with the star shells lighting up the night. Makes you a sitting target. Takes an exceptional man not to panic, in those circumstances . . . a hero.'

Holt did not answer.

There was silence ahead of them, only the dull thump of feet and a squelch of duckboards in mud behind, and the trickle of water along the bottom of the trench.

'I expect you know what it feels like,' Joseph went on. 'I notice you have some pretty bad tears in your trousers, even one in your blouse. Haven't had time to mend them yet.'

'I daresay I got caught in a bit of wire out there last night,' Holt said stiffly. He shifted his weight from one foot to the other.

'I'm sure you did,' Joseph agreed with him.

'Ashton didn't. His clothes were muddy, but no wire tears.'

There were several minutes of silence. A group of men passed by behind them, muttering words of greeting. When they were gone the darkness closed in again. Someone threw up a star shell and there was a crackle of machine-gun fire.

'I wouldn't repeat that, if I were you, Chaplain,' Holt said at last. 'You might make people think unpleasant things, doubts. And right at the moment morale is high. We need that. We've had a hard time recently. We're going over the top in a trench raid soon. Morale is important . . . trust. I'm sure you know that, maybe even better than I do. That's your job, isn't it? Morale, spiritual welfare of the men?'

'Yes . . . spiritual welfare is a good way of putting it. Remember what it is we are fighting for, and that it is worth all that it costs . . . even this.' Joseph gestured in the dark to all that surrounded them.

More star shells went up, illuminating the night for a few garish moments, then a greater darkness closed in.

'We need our heroes,' Holt said very clearly. 'You should know that. Any man who would tear them down would be very unpopular, even if he said he was doing it in the name of truth, or justice, or whatever it was he believed in. He would do a lot of harm, Chaplain. I expect you can see that . . . '

'Oh, yes,' Joseph agreed. 'To have their hero shown to be a coward who laid the blame for his panic on another man, and let him be buried in shame, and then committed murder to hide that, would devastate men who are already wretched and exhausted by war.'

'You are perfectly right.' Holt sounded as if he were smiling. 'A very wise man, Chaplain. Good of the regiment first. The right sort of loyalty.'

'I could prove it,' Joseph said very carefully.

'But you won't. Think what it would do to the men.'

Joseph turned a little to face the parapet. He stood up onto the fire step and looked forward over the dark expanse of mud and wire.

'We should take that sniper out. That would be a very heroic thing to do. Good thing to try, even if you didn't succeed. You'd deserve a mention in dispatches for that, possibly a medal.'

'It would be posthumous!' Holt said bitterly.

'Possibly. But you might succeed and come

back. It would be so daring, Fritz would never expect it,' Joseph pointed out.

'Then you do it, Chaplain!' Holt said sarcastically.

'It wouldn't help you, Captain. Even if I die, I have written a full account of what I have learned today, to be opened should anything happen to me. On the other hand, if you were to mount such a raid, whether you returned or not, I should destroy it.'

There was silence again, except for the distant crack of sniper fire a thousand yards away and the drip of mud.

'Do you understand me, Captain Holt?'

Holt turned slowly. A star shell lit his face for an instant. His voice was hoarse.

'You're sending me to my death!'

'I'm letting you be the hero you're pretending to be and Ashton really was,' Joseph answered. 'The hero the men need. Thousands of us have died out here, no one knows how many more there will be. Others will be maimed or blinded. It isn't whether you die or not, it's how well.'

A shell exploded a dozen yards from them. Both men ducked, crouching automatically.

Silence again.

Slowly Joseph unbent.

Holt lifted his head. 'You're a hard man, Chaplain. I misjudged you.'

'Spiritual care, Captain,' Joseph said quietly. 'You wanted the men to think you a hero, to admire you. Now you're going to justify that and become one.'

Holt stood still, looking toward him in the gloom, then slowly he turned and began to walk away, his feet sliding on the wet duckboards. Then he climbed up the next fire step and up over the parapet.

Joseph stood still and prayed.

Shel Silverstein

A prolific author and illustrator, Shel Silverstein writes regularly for Playboy *and other magazines. His impossible-to-categorize books, such as* The Light in the Attic *and* Where the Pavement Ends, *make the bestseller lists with regularity.*

The Guilty Party

By Shel Silverstein

Judge Vernon Hobbs had been known for some unusual and unorthodox rulings.

There was the occasion when Leon Poole and Maurice Stebner came before him for a judgment on a 1938 De Soto.

It seems they had bought the vehicle together from Orville Clayton's lot with Leon's three hundred dollars, eighty-seven of which was owed by Orville to Maurice to settle a wager on the World Series. Maurice then did what was disputed to be six hundred and forty-two dollars worth of repair and restoration, for which he demanded full payment or the De Soto.

Judge Hobbs suggested joint ownership or selling the damn thing and splitting the profits — but by then there was so much bad blood between the boys, as to who said what, and who promised which, and who indeed was the De Soto's rightful owner.

'Well then,' said Judge Hobbs, 'I am gonna render a decision based upon the wisdom of Solomon. Is either one of you boys versed in

or acquainted with the Biblical tale of Solomon and the two mothers?'

The boys had to admit that Scripture was not their long suit.

'Good,' said Judge Hobbs, 'I wouldn't want either of you anticipating my ruling, which is — that the aforementioned De Soto be cut in half, and one half awarded to each of the claimants. Leon, is that all right with you?'

'Fine with me,' said Leon.

'And Maurice, do you find this acceptable?'

'I'll go for that,' said Maurice, 'but who gets the front half and who gets the back half?'

'I'll take the front half,' said Leon.

'The hell you will,' shouted Maurice, 'the front half's got the engine, the radio, the hood ornament, and the — '

'Order,' called Judge Hobbs, banging down the claw hammer he used as a gavel. 'I'm amending my decision — the De Soto will be split lengthwise — thereby giving each of you an equal — '

'Well, who gets the driver's side?' demanded Leon. 'That's got the mahogany wheel, the transmission, gearshift, the — '

'And who's supposed to saw that damn engine in half?' Leon whined. 'You try cuttin' *through a windshield and an engine, with a chain saw, and you're sure as hell gonna mess up a — '*

Judge Hobbs banged his hammer.

'Well,' sighed Judge Hobbs, 'I can see from the incredible willingness of both claimants to gladly destroy this unique and classic example of automotive art that neither one of them is the rightful owner. And the court hereby impounds said vehicle as property of the court to be used at the court's discretion on various court business on weekends and holidays, and if there is any question as to the right of the court to impound said De Soto, I'm sure that something can and will be found in the trunk or glove compartment to justify my decision. These proceedings are concluded — everybody go home.

'And that,' said Judge Hobbs later, as he and Clarence Sawyer his bailiff, sat sipping some good apricot brandy, 'is the last time I try to render a verdict based upon anybody's wisdom but my own.'

* * *

It was too damn hot.

Judge Hobbs leaned back in his swivel chair and turned up the fan as high as it would go. He didn't want to lean too far back. They might see that he was wearing short pants underneath his robe. That might be interpreted as being unjudicial or, at best, undignified.

Carefully, Judge Hobbs rolled up the brief that lay upon his desk. The fly was on the rim of the coffee cup. One swat — *justice* — swift and sure. But *was* it just? What was the fly doing but exercising its nature? What was young Billy Ray doing but exercising his? But if that were the case, who deserved to be punished for anything?

Judge Hobbs closed his eyes and tapped the rolled papers against his palm. He hoped that this would look contemplative. The fly was moving down the inside of the cup now. As long as it stayed there it was safe. Did the sonofabitch know that?

'All right,' said Judge Hobbs, unrolling the brief and flattening it out, 'all right, let's proceed with these — *Clarence*, will you turn that damn thing off.'

'I got the sound down, Judge,' said the bailiff.

'Well, I can still hear it,' said Judge Hobbs. 'What's the score, anyway?'

'Eight to two, Bluebirds, top of the fifth — they just brought in that Binky Lewis. He's as wild as a — '

'Well, I think that Lewis boy might be able

to hold a six-run lead,' said Judge Hobbs, wiping his neck with his handkerchief.

'Judge, they got two men on and — '

'Damn it, Clarence, at least turn the *sound* off — and announce these proceedings — in a proper and official manner.'

Clarence snapped off the sound and stood up, pouting.

'Hear ye, hear ye, first district court, Menasha County, now in session, *Honorable* Vernon Hobbs presiding — all rise.'

He had hit the *Honorable* a little too hard.

'Too hot to rise,' said Judge Hobbs, throwing Clarence his stern look. 'Stay sittin'.'

'The state versus William Raymond Brockley,' continued Clarence. 'The charge, sexual battery, assault with a deadly weapon, kidnapping, resisting arrest — '

'All right,' said Judge Hobbs, 'I'm tired of list'nin'.'

The fly had taken off.

Judge Hobbs turned toward Billy Ray. Damn, the boy was too good-looking to have to force anyone into anything.

'Billy Ray, you've decided to forgo and dispense with a trial by a jury of your peers.'

'Yes, sir,' said Billy Ray.

'Well,' said Judge Hobbs, 'that may be a wise decision, since most of your peers around here would like to see you strung up slow and sliced down a piece at a time. A few of 'em might even be blood-related to Eunice Tillman.'

'The young lady is in critical condition at Baptist Hospital,' said Lew Porter, district attorney and proprietor of Porter Brothers General Contracting, Roofing, and Aluminum Siding, 'and is at this time physically and emotionally unfit to attend this hearing. Therefore, Your Honor, the state requests a one-week postponement until the young lady — '

'The young *lady*'s condition has been upgraded to stable,' interjected Buddy Linz, defense attorney and co-owner of Buddy's Four Alarm Chili And Pit Bar-B-Cue.

'Well, I think we can proceed ahead,' said Judge Hobbs. 'I want to get this over and done with as soon as possible.'

Lew Porter stood up. How did he manage to look so dry and unwrinkled in a three-piece suit on a day like this?

'Your Honor,' said Lew Porter, 'the state will prove that on the night of — '

'*Attempt* to prove,' snapped Judge Hobbs. Lew Porter sighed.

'*Attempt* to prove that on the night of April seventeenth, the accused, Billy Ray Brockley, did willfully and forcibly — '

'Come to think of it, Lew, you don't even have to attempt to prove anything,' said Judge Hobbs. 'Sit back down — I have all the pertinent facts right here.' He tapped the rumpled brief. 'This don't look like that big of a deal.'

'We know you'll render a fair and impartial judgment, Your Honor,' said Buddy Linz.

Lew Porter groaned and sat back down.

Judge Hobbs had the reputation of being one of the goodest and oldest of the county's good old boys, two of his favorite expressions being 'Boys will be boys' and 'Let he who has never been young cast the first stone.' Also Judge Hobbs had been heard to remark on more than one occasion that it didn't serve much purpose slappin' young people in jail.

'In the spring the sap will rise,' he would sigh, his eyes looking back a long time ago. 'The fruit turns ripe and the pickers come. That's nature — you can't stop it or slow it down.'

'All right,' says Judge Hobbs, tossing the brief aside and turning to Billy Ray Brockley, 'Billy Ray, you've been advised by counsel that my decision will be binding?'

'Yes, sir,' said Billy Ray.

''Cause I sure as hell don't want to hear no bitchin' or moanin' later that I been too severe — or too lenient — and I sure as hell don't want to hear the word *appeal* interjected anywhere into these proceedings. I mean I don't want to even sniff the word *appeal*, and anybody — defense attorney or prosecutor — who even breathes or whispers that word is gonna find me somewhat prejudicial in my rulings on his future cases — is that understood? All right, you wanted my decision on this case and you'll get it — and abide by it. Billy Ray — how do you plead to these charges?'

'I didn't do it.'

'You didn't meet Eunice Tillman at the VFW Blue Moon Dance on the night of . . . April seventeenth?'

'I met her.'

'You didn't dance with her?'

'We danced . . . awhile.'

'You didn't get her drunk?'

'You don't have to get Eunice drunk,' said Billy Ray. 'She's always — '

'You didn't drive her to the Larkspur Underpass?'

'Yes, sir — But I didn't do it.'

'Didn't do . . . what?'

'The rest of it. I'm not guilty.'

'You sayin' she led you on? 'Cause if she led you on — '

'I'm sayin' I didn't do it.'

'You didn't do it.'

'Not . . . really.'

'Not really?'

'I . . . witnessed it.'

'You witnessed it.'

'Bein' done — yes, sir.'

'Bein' done — by who?'

'I don't like to name names, Judge. I just — '

'Bein' done by *who*, damn it?'

Billy Ray closed his eyes.

'By . . . Sam.'

'Sam?'

'Sam Johnson, Your Honor.'

'Sam Johnson?' Judge Hobbs picked up the brief. 'I don't see any Sam Johnson listed in this — '

'Sam Johnson,' said Billy Ray. 'My . . . thing.'

'Your . . . thing?'

Buddy Linz stood up.

'My client is referring to his . . . member, Your Honor, his . . . sexual member, his — '

'I can see what he's referring to,' said Judge Hobbs. 'He's clutchin' the damn thing.'

Judge Hobbs leaned forward.

'Billy Ray — you're sayin' that *that* is Sam Johnson?'

'Yes, sir.'

'You've givin' him a . . . name?'

'That's his name, Judge. *Sam*.'

'A first name too.'

'Well, sir, there's a lot of Johnsons out there.'

'Hopefully not related to this case,' said Judge Hobbs, picking up his pen and beginning to write. 'Mister Johnson? *J-O-H-N-S-O-N*? He's the guilty party?'

'I call him Sam,' said Billy Ray. 'It's not so formal.'

'Well, I want to keep things formal as possible,' said Judge Hobbs. 'Samuel Johnson. No middle initial?'

'No, sir.'

'Just first and last name — you didn't make a little checkered coat for the sonofabitch, did you? With a little straw hat and a cane?'

'No, sir.'

'And you say that this 'Samuel Johnson' on the night of April seventeenth, and against the person of Eunice Tillman, did willfully and forcibly, without your aid, cooperation, or collaboration — '

'He's got a mind of his own, Judge,' said Billy Ray. 'There's no reasoning with him — he just gets a notion and does . . . anything that comes into his head.'

'I know, son,' sighed Judge Hobbs, 'but as an innocent observer and witness to the alleged attack, did you do anything to restrain the aforementioned Samuel Johnson from — '

'There's no holding him, Your Honor,' said Billy Ray. 'He's . . . unrestrainable — I tried — he just . . . shook me off.'

Lew Porter was on his feet.

'And what the hell were *you* doing, while Sam Johnson was forcing Eunice Tillman into the backseat? What were you doing when your buddy Sam was forcing Eunice Tillman to perform a — '

'I couldn't have gone against him,' Billy Ray pleaded. 'I was afraid.'

'Afraid?' asked Judge Hobbs. 'Afraid of what?'

'Of what he might . . . do . . . to me.'

'To *you*?' Judge Hobbs was wide awake now. 'What could he have done to you?'

'You don't know him, Your Honor. The bastard's got no conscience — he might do . . . anything. He's got a . . . power, Judge. He just . . . takes over. You don't know Sam Johnson.'

Lew Porter was up and screaming now — the veins in his neck about to bust. His face was right in Billy Ray's.

'And I imagine it was the same Sam Johnson who drove your Thunderbird to the Larkspur Underpass. I wanna see it, Your Honor, I want a demonstration of Sam Johnson drivin' a stick shift, I wanna see Sam Johnson holdin' a knife to somebody's throat — this knife, Your Honor — I'm introducin' this barlow as Exhibit A. And I wanna see — '

'You don't have to introduce that knife to me,' said Judge Hobbs, picking up the barlow and turning it over slowly. 'This was your daddy's fishin' knife, wasn't it, Billy? I believe if he knew you were leavin' it layin' around within easy reach of such unsavory characters as this Sam Johnson, he'd be spinnin' in his grave.' He turned to Buddy Linz.

'Buddy, this defense that you've cooked up is highly unique and creative, I must say. You realize if I allow it and it becomes a precedent, any forger can claim that it was his hands that did it, and not him. Anybody can kick somebody to death and claim it was his feet.'

'Next thing you know,' chimed in Lew Porter, picking up the line of reasoning, 'next thing you know the arsonist is blaming the match, the sniper is blamin' the bullet, the ax murderer — '

'That's our defense,' said Buddy Linz, 'and I've got a trunkload of psychiatric books and psychological studies and psychiatrists' opinions that'll back me up.'

'Sam Johnson did it,' said Billy Ray. 'I'll swear to it.'

Lew Porter was sweating now. That

three-piece suit was beginning to look like wet cardboard.

'Your Honor,' he said, 'this . . . this incredible 'my-pee-pee-did-it-not-me plea' is so outrageous — so desperate — so without any legal foundation, that no one can possibly — '

'I'm going to allow it,' said Judge Hobbs, 'and if it brings down upon my head a torrent of legal criticism and controversy, well, then, they'll just have to put me on the same bench with boys like John Marshall, Louis Brandeis, and Oliver Wendell Holmes — in presenting a ruling that will forever influence future jurisprudence.

'Because, gentlemen, I find this theory of a . . . member . . . having a will of its own to be reasonable and within the scope of human experience.

'Have we all not at some time or other been led down pathways dark and devious? By something stronger than our hearts or heads? And is justice not to be tempered with mercy? And who indeed can stop the sap from rising in the young sapling?'

Lew Porter groaned and held his head in his hands.

'Billy Ray, I find you innocent of all charges specified here. I do find you guilty of witnessing a felony and not immediately reporting it, but in light of your coming forth now and identifying the guilty party, I'm suspending sentence. I don't suppose Sam Johnson has any money.'

'Not a cent, Your Honor,' said a cheerful Billy Ray.

'Well, then, seein' as how he's a friend of yours — '

'Former friend,' said Billy Ray.

'Whatever — I'm ordering you to pay whatever medical costs Eunice Tillman may run up due to the actions of your former friend Sam Johnson. And I hope this serves as a lesson to you to refrain from any associations with violent, abusive members.'

'Thank you, Judge,' said Billy Ray, getting up with a grin. 'And I'm sure gonna be more selective in the future about hangin' out with bad company.'

Judge Hobbs sat there. Billy Ray was hugging Buddy Linz. Lew Porter was putting his papers together. Clarence was fiddling with the horizontal. Billy Ray started toward the door. Judge Hobbs picked up his gavel.

'Where you goin', son?' asked Judge Hobbs.

'Home . . . to dinner . . . like you said. I think my momma is makin' a meat loaf.'

'Well, good,' said Judge Hobbs, 'but who you takin' with you?'

'Buddy . . . if he wants to come — hell, all of you, if you like meat loaf. There'll be plenty.'

'Well, you ain't takin' no convicted felon home to your momma's table, are you?' asked Judge Hobbs.

Billy Ray looked confused.

'I mean, son, you're innocent and free to go — free as a bird.'

Billy Ray sighed.

'But that heartless cold-blooded sex fiend, Sam Johnson, I'm findin' him *guilty*' — Judge Hobbs banged his gavel — 'of aggravated sexual assault and kidnapping, I'm sentencing the ruthless sonofabitch to twelve years' confinement in the state correctional facility at Joliet.'

'Judge — ' said Billy Ray.

'Son,' said Judge Hobbs, raising a restraining finger, 'I know how hard it is to take leave of a loved one for an extended period of time, so as a special consideration, I'm gonna give you the opportunity to accompany your friend, your former friend, to Joliet, or you can stay behind and let him go on alone . . . You look pale, son . . . Mr. Linz, why don't you escort your client to the men's room. I think he needs a glass of water . . . Oh, and Clarence — give Billy Ray his daddy's barlow — he's innocent and it's his property. Take all the time you need, son,' he said softly to Billy Ray, 'but when you come out of there, Sam Johnson *is* goin' to prison . . . Next case — '

'There ain't no next case, Judge,' said Clarence.

'Well, then, turn up the sound,' said Judge Hobbs, 'and let's find out whether or not that Lewis kid can hold a six-run lead for five damn innings.'